I0762095

Immortal Coil

James McNally

First edition Hardcover

This book is dedicated to Beatrice Moffat who said it was not a book she would normally read but she would read my book. I would have held her to it, too.
We miss you Bea.

Prologue

The blind woman with the wavy gray hair turned to the shadowy figure walking beside her and blinked milky-white eyes. "The boy approaches in a car from the west. Turn here."

The shadowed man and the woman walked side by side through the darkened streets of Philadelphia without regard to anyone around them. The occasional pedestrians also walking the streets gave the couple a wide berth, mostly without realizing they were doing it. Some people quietly stepped aside as they approached, and still, others crossed the street to avoid the pair. Perhaps, it was because when this woman looked at you with those white, damaged eyes, you knew she was seeing you—really seeing you. And it was an unnerving feeling, to be looked upon by this woman.

The moon was the only light visible in the night sky; the stars were drowned out by the street lamps and the glare of headlights on passing cars. But these city people in the 21st century didn't appear to notice the lack of starlight and were as oblivious to the lackluster sky as they were to the danger that stalked the streets that night.

As the pair soon reached Lansdowne Drive, which was almost completely deserted except for the man who came upon the two, thought better of his course and found a more suitable street elsewhere.

A RAV4 sped by them and drove up the slope. The vehicle stopped on the street in front of a Victorian mansion near the crest. The travelers stayed at the bottom of the hill and looked up at the RAV4 sitting in the light of a streetlamp. The young man in the driver's seat climbed out of the car and headed toward the house. He suddenly changed direction and returned to the car, grabbed something from the front seat, tucked it under his arm, and started back toward the house. Once he was safely in the house and out of sight, the couple climbed the hill and stopped when they reached the house, standing just out of the lamplight.

They stared at the house.

"I believe we've found him," the woman said. She turned to her companion and studied his expression with her second sight.

"It's been a long time. I wonder if he'll remember me." The shadowy man laughed.

The woman did not laugh. "Though we have found him, this is not the time to make our presence known."

The old woman turned and walked back down the hill. After a moment the shadowy man followed her.

Part One: Antony

Chapter One

The sun had set, and darkness shrouded the neighborhood on Lansdowne Drive. The only light came from the streetlamp at the top of the hill. Whistling, the blonde young man climbed out of the RAV 4 parked on the opposite side of the street. As he reached the sidewalk on the border of the property surrounding the large Victorian mansion, he stopped.

He pounded a fist into his forehead. "Damn."

He twisted on his heels and returned to the car. He opened the driver's side door and reached in for the newspaper rolled up in the console between the seats. Closing the door, he used the key fob and locked the car with a quick beep. Tucking the paper under his arm, he resumed whistling and strode up the walkway to the house.

More out of habit than security, the young man peered down the street then turned and looked toward the top of the hill. He saw no one. Satisfied, he used his key to enter the house.

The porch's floorboards creaked slightly under his feet, but as he stepped through the door into the dark interior, a change occurred. He stopped whistling and closed the door behind him without a sound. Without turning on any lights, he moved soundlessly through the house and, exhibiting a talent generally associated with the blind, he avoided creaking floorboards with long strides. He required no light as he spun to avoid a chair and then hopped over something low, landing toe to heel without even so much as a squeak of rubber on the hardwood floor. Spinning and gliding as though possessed by Fred Astaire's ghost, the young man danced his way through the house. After seven years of practice creeping through this house in complete darkness, he was exceptionally good at it.

He ignored the unconscious man tied with plastic zip ties lying on the ten-foot-long dining table in the room beyond the stairs. He ascended the stairs two at a time, sneakered feet as silent as silk slippers. Sprinting lithely to the room at the end of the hall, he stopped and opened the door. He entered the room and closed the door behind him making no sound, not even a click of the latch falling into place.

Lit only by his imagination, he looked around the room. Memory told him that two paces forward and two to the left put him at the foot of the oak bed. From there, it was another four paces to the wall at the far end of the room. To the left, set into the wall, was a window with the glass removed and replaced by bricks, preventing any light from passing through. To the right of the window was the only other piece of furniture in the room: an antique roll-top desk made from the same oak as the bed. Moving seven steps from the edge of the desk put him in front of the bathroom door. Side-stepping to the right two paces was the closet, and its French-style double doors, which were also made of oak. Stepping back two paces and again to the right another two put him back where he started. Of course, he had never really moved, except in his head. The only other object was the Persian rug, placed perfectly centered in the middle of the room.

The blonde guy stood still, listening. When he heard the rustle of bedding sliding over bare skin and the muffled yawn, he made his first sound and exhaled.

From the bed came a sleep-trained, cracking whisper. "David, please turn on the light."

David reached out and hit the switch next to his shoulder, dousing the room in a dull yellow glow. It was weak light, forty watts or so, but after the utter darkness, even this seemed blinding.

The man in the bed pushed back the sheets and threw his bare legs over the side until his feet touched the floor.

"Antony, I was declared legally dead today." David held his head high, and a broad smile stretched his face. "It's in this paper if you want to read it." He walked across the room and set the paper down on the desk.

"I do, but maybe later." Antony's voice still held a slight Scottish lilt. He smiled, showing fangs, and his eyes flashed red. "I'm hungry."

The vampire ran fingers through his ruffled brown hair, pulled on a pair of jeans, then slipped into a tartan chambray shirt. Without missing a beat, he glided his feet into a pair of loafers and exited the room.

"I figured you wouldn't want to travel tonight, so I've brought the meals to you. The rapist is on the dining room table. The other two are in the panic room."

Antony and David descended the stairs to the first floor. They moved down the hall, past the dining room to the stairs leading into the basement.

The panic room, a stainless-steel box that had been built to be a safe haven for the homeowners during a home invasion, had been altered to fit Antony's needs.

He had no need of any such protection, so he had the room made to lock from the outside. The only panicking going on in this room came from the people kept inside.

David waited at the foot of the stairs as Antony approached the room.

Antony opened the thick steel door and peered in. Two men—bound and gagged—stared at him, shivering and bleary-eyed. Stepping into the room, which looked like a giant hot tub from the inside, Antony sat down next to one of the men. He pulled off the man's gag and let it dangle around his neck.

"Please, mister." The man's lips quivered. "Please don't…"

"Do what? Hurt you?" Antony's eyes had gone crimson with blood hunger.

The man moaned.

Antony used his preternaturally sharp fingernails to cut the zip ties binding the man's hands and feet. The man hesitated, then took off running.

Antony looked at the remaining captive. He smiled, showing fangs, then vanished in a crackling gush of wind. He reappeared seconds later, the escaped man in a chokehold. While the other man watched, Antony tore into his prey's neck, drank the body dry, and tossed the corpse out the door. He wiped an arm over his mouth and turned to the remaining man.

The condemned man's eyes seemed to go out of focus. He showed no sign that he could see Antony. He did not react when Antony removed the gag. He did not plead, or scream, or cry. The man shivered at Antony's touch as the binding was cut. As Antony leaned forward, the man turned away as if purposely exposing his neck. The vampire's fangs touched the neck, and the doomed man urinated on himself.

As Antony finished the man off, he brushed the corpse from the bench. The body folded over on itself in a crumpled heap.

Once Antony was finished, David stepped into action. He decapitated both bodies and tossed the headless bodies, as well as the heads, into the incinerator in the adjacent room under the stairs.

David turned on the hose and washed any remaining traces of blood down the drain in the center of the cement floor then rinsed his hands. Once the basement had been cleaned, Antony and David walked, single file, up the stairs to the ground floor.

Antony moved to the dining room and sat at the table near the head of the man lying there. "You have done well, as always." He climbed up onto the table and straddled the man.

"Thank you." David beamed.

"Wake him, I am still hungry." Antony's eyes had again clouded over with the red haze of hunger.

David woke the man with ammonia under the nose. The rapist opened his eyes in a confused state of shock.

"What…?" The man started to speak, but Antony shushed him.

"You are a serial rapist."

"No…"

"Do not deny it. I can see who and what you are."

"Who are you?" The man narrowed his and lifted his chin.

Antony glanced over at David with the hint of a smile. He turned back to the man under him.

"I ask the questions here."" He studied the man beneath him more closely. "Your clothing is expensive, and your beard is trimmed with precision. You are extremely well groomed for a rapist."

"I told you, I'm not—"

"Do not deny it. I've looked into your eyes and seen into your soul." Antony barely finished speaking before ripping open the man's carotid and gulping down the hot fluid gushing from the wound. As Antony finished draining the body of blood, he sat up with a sigh. "His blood is exquisite, and I taste all the vile acts this man has committed. David, I can hear the screams of his victims. In the blood is the sweet taste of vindication. I cannot fully express just how intoxicating this experience is."

"If you make me into a vampire you wouldn't have to. I'd know." David raised an eyebrow.

Antony flung a leg over the bloodless body and dropped into a chair. "Do not start with that tired argument."

David shrugged. "Oh, I almost forgot." He ran up to the second floor and returned with the paper. "I wanted you to read the article. It's not long, but it's sweet. Dear old mother remarried."

David handed the paper to Antony and let him read the article.

"Very interesting." Antony set the paper aside.

"I think we should revisit that old argument." David took a seat opposite Antony and looked at him across the body still lying on the table. "When are you going to give me the gift?"

Antony glared at him. "Why would you want it?"

"I want to live forever, too." David laughed. "Why should you be the only one?"

Antony pushed his shoulders back. "Perhaps it is time I told you why I will not turn you—why I will never turn you. Maybe once you have heard my full story, you will stop asking."

"I doubt that but go ahead."

Antony's Story

"Early in my life as a vampire—this was many centuries ago, but never mind how long I will not say—I took the innocent and the vile in equal measure. When it was time to take my victims, I simply plucked them off the street like ripe fruit from the vine. However, I soon started to feel the weight of the memories in the blood. Taking the murderous did not seem to bother me, as I relished in their destruction, but innocent blood was a different story.

When I started feeling haunted by the memories of my victims, I knew I was not going to last if I didn't stop killing innocents. There were too many memories of people making plans for a future that I had ended. I began to wonder if I was the only vampire who felt this high amount of grief over their own actions, or if this was my own personal curse for being what I was. When I chose to stop killing innocent victims, my mind cleared of the grief I felt. I started to feel the power that comes with the vindication of killing people with evil hearts and bloody souls.

In the year 1350, I was passing through a small English town known as Huntsworth. It seemed like a ghost town. Many houses were sealed up with boards nailed across their windows and doors. One door had a fading sign which read: Quarantined.

At this house, a curtain shifted in the window, and I stepped closer to see who, if anyone, was there. An old woman, barefoot, wearing only a nightgown, staggered from her house. She dropped at my feet, tired and weak. I could see something was seriously wrong with her; she had black sores on her lips and fingers.

I tried to push her away as gently as I could, but she clung to my legs. There were tears of desperation glistening in her eyes as she begged for help. Her fever was so hot, I could see the heat rising off her in waves, and the great lumps on her body stuck out at odd angles, swollen with illness. She was in pain and saw me as a savior.

"I cannot help you. I have no cure." I shook her off my leg and continued on my way.

"It ain't no cure ah seeks. It's death."

"Kill yourself then."

"Ah can't. Don't 'ave the strength. But you do, kind sir. You can drain ma blood. You won't get sick an' you will end ma pain."

I stopped and turned back to face her.

In a cold voice, she said, "Ah knows what ya're."

I walked back a couple of paces to stand in front of her. "What do you know, old woman?" When I get upset, my Scottish accent gets very thick.

As I stood over her, she bared her neck to me. "Ah sees ya comin' in ma dreams, ah 'ave. An ah knows wha'chu can do. Please help a dying lady with her last request. Ah'm a beggin' ya." She threw herself into the dirt at my feet and cried.

I didn't deny her claim. What would be the point? "I took an oath not to harm the innocent," I said. "I'm sorry for your suffering, but to take your life would put me on a path I am not willing to travel. You must understand the consequences taking your life will have."

"Harm? It's not harming me to end ma sufferin'."

She didn't have the strength to pull herself out of the dirt. She just laid there crying and waiting to die. I sighed and lifted her into my arms. She weighed nothing. She felt like sticks wrapped in rags. I carried her back into her house and laid her on the bed. She looked up at me with tears glistening in her eyes. I drained her and, in her blood, I tasted her relief; there was no misery for me in the flavor of her blood. I knew I had done a good thing. I decapitated her with a knife from the kitchen and left her wrapped in a sheet on the front porch. The corpse collectors would carry her remains to the mass gravesite just outside of town. I know that sounds harsh, but it was the time.

As I stepped away from her house, and once again headed down the road, more people stepped out of their homes and watched me walk by. In their faces, I could see they knew what I had done for the old woman, and they wanted the same release for themselves. I did not deny them their request. It took me a month to clean out the town of the sick. When I left, I walked to the next town. I sought out the seriously ill and offered my services. I had a very steady food source for the next decade.

When the plague ended, I had to seek out a new source of food. With the population so severely depleted, thieves and cutthroats were rampant. I merely had to present myself as a vulnerable wanderer, and my new victims came to me. From that point on, my food source has never wavered; only my hunting styles have changed over the years. At first, I would just wander the streets looking for crimes taking place. But as methods of policing these criminals became more sophisticated, my hunting methods needed to be… revamped.

But there were always other ways around an obstacle. I would read wanted posters and hunt the criminals the police could not seem to catch. Where there was one criminal, you could usually find two or three more. I thought that I would run out of food and have to resort to feeding off the innocent again as I bled one criminal after another. Of course, that is not the case. It amazed me the violence and hate man could show toward one another.

It was about five hundred years ago the first time loneliness hit me. The vampire inevitably feels isolated as they roam the centuries alone. I wanted companionship, craved it as hungrily as I craved blood. One night while feeding, I noticed a man who had seen me.

For several nights I allowed this man to watch me feed. It is in the vampire's best interest to be invisible, but I felt no ill will from him; only a desire to know who and what I was. He was apparently afraid, but still, he watched. He kept his distance and did not approach me, but he was ever in my presence. I decided the only way to resolve this dilemma was to contact him.

One night I used my vampire speed and pinned him to the wall he had been crouching behind to watch me feed. I moved his head to the side and placed my fangs delicately close to his neck. I could feel excitement coursing through him.

"You know what I am," I whispered into his ear. He shuttered in my grasp, but he did not struggle.

"Yes, he said.

"Are you afraid?" I asked.

"No," he said, and I saw the lie in his eyes. Although he was apparently afraid, he was not scared. I believe he was worried that I would not pass on my gift to him.

"You should be," I said.

It is essential to understand that vampires do not feel lust as humans do. A vampire having sexual urges is the stuff of movies, a myth. We are quite literally dead down there. My only interest was in his blood. I wanted companionship so I would give him the gift. I was going to take his blood and allow him to rise, but I also needed to know he was worthy of the gift. I pulled away. His initiation into my world would not be as easy as that. He had a lot to prove before I would do this thing.

"If you had approached another vampire," I said. "He would have taken your blood, decapitated you to prevent you from rising and have been done with you. It is only coincidence that you stumbled onto me. I am not like the others. Vampires can be sadistic and cruel to their prey, like when a cat plays with a mouse. That activity holds no interest for me. I merely wish to feed, so I choose to feed on killers who have no remorse for their acts. I wish to be left alone, so I do not make a spectacle of myself. My prey will not be missed. I will not take your blood this night."

I pushed him away. As he started to protest, I sped away so fast he had no idea how to find me.

He did not need to find me; however, because I sought him out the following night. He was there every night waiting for me. He was persistent. After a month of waiting for me to convert him, I decided to give him what he wanted. If I was going to spend an eternity with someone, he was as good a choice as any. Also, my resistance was crumbling.

"What is your name?" I asked.

"Bane Haywood," he replied. "When will you change me?"

"When and if I deem you are worthy," I said.

"You are a liar then." He pointed an accusatory finger at me.

"What?" I asked, perplexed.

"You said you don't toy with your prey, but you're toying with me. You're torturing me." He screamed at the sky in frustration.

I laughed. I took his face in my hands and pulled him closer to me.

"Bane, what you are asking for is very gruesome. You have to be sure it is what you want. There is no going back once the process has begun."

"I never want to go back to this weak, pointless life." He staggered back as I released his face.

"It is a painful thing, to have your blood drained. For the vampire, it is an ecstasy like no other, but for the victim, it is pure misery."

"I don't care. Whatever it takes I am willing to endure it," he said.

"I will drain you, and you will die. By not beheading you, your body will rise at dusk of the following night. You are willing to go through with this?"

"I am," he said with a tiresome lilt. "I know this; you've told me before," Then, more seriously, he added, "I mean it. Whatever it takes I will do it."

"You must promise me you will adhere to my code of taking the truly unrepentant. Never drain an innocent. Innocent blood corrupts the vampire, makes him turn insane. Promise me you will only take the vilest of victims."

"I promise," he said. His impatience was palpable.

He offered his neck to me, and I bit down. His blood tasted exquisite, and I regretted that I would only be allowed to take his blood this once. I could have drunk from him forever.

I drained him, took him to my lair and slept through the daylight hours. We woke together, and he was very excited. He was like a child with a new toy. It pleased me to see his excitement.

"But where are my fangs?" Bane asked as he examined himself in the mirror. I explained it took several months for his fangs to mature. "Damn, that long?" He turned away from his own reflection. "Then again, I have an eternity; what are a few months?"

We hunted. I would procure his prey, open a wound and he would feed. He wanted more, however.

"Let me kill my own prey?" he asked.

He acquired a razor and I no longer needed to kill for him. He lavished in the kill more than I found comfortable. His fangs were fully developed seven months later, and for the next twenty years, we were unstoppable and inseparable. Then the question I had most feared finally passed through his bloody lips.

"Why must we only drink from the wicked? I fancy taking a defenseless young lassie; wouldn't that taste mighty refreshing right about now?"

"That lassie would quench your desire to taste innocent blood but think of all the evil killers you have tasted over the years. How do you think it would feel to have the memories of an innocent girl trapped in your head? You will wonder what she would have been able to accomplish had you not ended her life."

"I don't think I would be bothered by that. Only you worry at such trivialities. You are a coward."

My anger was quick to come, but I suppressed it.

I needed to find a new tact to postpone his inevitable decision. "You made an oath. You promised not to take an innocent life if I agreed to turn you. Would you abandon your promise to me?" I asked.

"A human made that promise, not me. I am a vampire. No vampire in their right mind would have made such a promise. Your trickery makes that promise null."

I looked at him like a child lost; for that was what he was. I knew it was only a matter of time that I would lose him to the desire for innocent blood. "Taking guiltless blood will wear on your sanity. I have seen it before… felt it myself, in fact."

"I think I can handle it," he said.

I think Bane did not wish to openly disobey my wishes. He continued to choose rapists and cutthroats for several more years. When he did take his first innocent, there had been no discussion on the subject. When I saw the young lady he had made, I knew that the curtain had been lowered on our time together.

"There is no guilt," he said with her blood still on his lips. "And you did not tell me the power her innocent life would fill me with."

"That power you feel will fade fast, and you will crave more. Soon you will be seeking more and more innocent lives to take. There is no end to the craving. It will control you, this power you wish to feel. It is a disease."

"So you say." He was unconvinced. He was lost to the desire to feel that power.

I tolerated his indulgences because I still longed for his company. But I soon realized he was no longer the friend I had created. He was now a beast of immense cruelty, torturing and terrorizing his victims before doing them in.

Our lair was an abandoned building on the fringes of London. We had reinforced it so that no light could penetrate its walls. We avoided staying in the city for fear that our lair would be inadvertently discovered. We pulled up the floorboards and hid in the ground beneath the building so that even if some unsuspecting wanderer stumbled onto our hideout, they would not know we were there beneath their feet. On a few occasions, we woke to the pleasant surprise of having a band of thieves taking refuge in our building, counting and dividing their loot. Imagine their surprise when two men popped out of the floor right in front of them.

"There is nothing tastier than taking back the shock and horror of our prey's victims," I said as we finished off the last of the gang members.

"I disagree," Bane said, and I had no trouble taking his meaning.

"You risk insanity if you continue to indulge," I admonished.

Bane laughed off my warning. "You fret like an old woman."

My companionship alone did not amuse Bane anymore. He took his first inferior one night while I was prowling, and I returned to find him burying the young woman in the floor of our abandoned building. The female was the first of five underlings Bane took for his own pleasure as four male underlings came soon after. The original lair had become too small, so I set out to find us a new den that would accommodate the extra bodies. I located an abandoned coal mine not far from our original lair that suited our purposes. When everyone agreed it was satisfactory, we settled in.

Months went by, and the group began to get restless. Bane was unable to control his underlings, but when I pointed this out to him, he overlooked their troublesome behavior.

"You are too much of a worrier, my oldest and dearest friend," he said. "I'm sure your worrying will give even you wrinkles." He laughed.

We invaded a pub one evening when the female of the group decided it was time they learned to hunt in a pack instead of individually. I went along because I did not want any surprises.

The pub was full of regulars, so they were immediately suspicious when seven strangers walked through the door. Our female was very outspoken and garnered the attention of the men in the room. There were twenty-five people in the bar so I would have to take my share. A vampire might be able to take the blood of five victims if he must, but the extra weight slowed them down. Made them vulnerable and lazy. Too much blood led to a vampire's death. I would have to help kill.

The room consisted mostly of men, but there were three serving wenches and the bar owner's wife. In the back of the bar were several tables set up for card games. Closer to us in the entrance was a table set up for Shove Board. This is basically where shuffleboard originated, but in this early stage of its evolution, the players shoved coins across a table. No one in the pub was interested in what they had been doing before we walked in, as now all eyes were on us.

Behind me, I heard the click as one of the vampires bolted the door.

"My, my." Our female companion giggled as she walked up to the bar. "So many serious faces I see around me."

"We don't want any trouble miss,' said the man sitting at the bar near where she stood. 'This is a respectable establishment, and we don't take kindly to wanderers like you. If you be looking for trouble, you best be moving on."

"We're not going anywhere," she said.

Her eyes must have turned red because the man's mouth dropped and his face turned pale. He didn't even have enough time to scream before she was on him.

The room came alive. People scrambled to get out, but at every turn, there was a vampire to prevent their escape. Shadows passed through the room with the crackling of our kind moving at the speed of sound. The prey must have believed there were more than just seven of us because they would no sooner avoid capture when another vampire seemed to materialize out of nowhere to prevent their escape. People were dropping exponentially as one after another was drained.

The female drained her third victim then turned to me. "You must help us, old man. We cannot handle them all alone, and you know as well as I that no one can live to tell of what happened here."

I grabbed a man who tried to bust a chair through the window near where I stood. I pulled him into my embrace.

"Please help us…" The man amended his plea. "Help me."

"I have only one kind of assistance I can offer," I said. "I will end your suffering." I drained the man quickly, and in his blood learned that he was going to be a father in a few months. He had recently helped his neighbor build a barn. In the blood, I learned that there had been so much potential for good dwelling inside this man that I had just killed against my will.

I killed three more, including the bar owner's wife. She had been saving up to take a trip to Paris; it was her life's dream.

Her dream would go unfulfilled due to my actions.

Another of my victims, I would learn to my distaste, was a man with an engagement ring in his pocket. He was merely at the bar to tip back a few pints of ale and muster the courage to ask for his girl's hand. He already had permission from her father.

When the bar was emptied of all living humans, one of the male members of our group retrieved a cleaver from the kitchen and started the task of beheading the dead. When he was finished with all but my four victims, I took the knife from him. I insisted that I take care of my own dead. When I completed the task, as the others were looting and reveling in their deeds, I hid the blade in the waistband of my pants.

We burned the bar to the ground and retreated to the lair.

The next night I announced that I would be hunting on my own. Only Bane seemed to care.

"I think you should stay with us," he said when he knew the others could not hear.

"Do you worry about my safety?" I asked.

"I do; as much—or more—as you worry about my sanity, my friend." He grinned at me, and I saw a shadow of the Bane I had known when I first turned him. Then his cheerful demeanor faded and the blue eyes clouded over with the dark anger I associated with so many vampires before him; they were the eyes of the insane.

"I will not do this again. I will not take any more innocent lives. I do not understand how you can. You are as moral a creature as I, and still, you cavort with these heathens you brought into being. Let us destroy them then, and be done with this mummer's farce."

He touched my cheek gently. "Perhaps you were right," he said sadly. "My sanity must have abandoned me because I cannot destroy my children. I need them as much as you needed me. I wanted our future to be as you wished: just you and me. But I could not shake the desire for more. I am sorry that you alone were not enough for me. I need them as well."

"They will turn on you," I warned.

"I'm sure one day they will," he said. "And when that time comes I will deserve what I get. But I will not turn on them. If you must move on, it is with great sadness that I let you go. If you wish to stay, you will have to abide by my rules. What will you decide?"

I chose to linger, and he was relieved. But I would never live by his rules. I had another reason for staying.

And so it was, one hundred and twenty-seven years after creating Bane, I made the decision to destroy him. The only question left was how?

The underlings would be first. I still had the cleaver and could dispatch the group one by one, but Bane would not be so easy. Once he had learned of my actions, he would hunt me down. I decided I would use his anger against him.

On the night that I had chosen for our final night as a group, I waited until the others had gone and approached the female. She was the strongest of the group, besides Bane and me.

"Your hold on Bane will not last forever," I said.

She laughed. "You have that backward, old one," she said. "We have nearly convinced him that you have outlived your usefulness and should be destroyed. Soon, you will be no more. Just as soon as I have worked the last few desperately clutching fingers from him, he will agree to let us rip you apart where you stand."

"I believe you are too late," I said.

"What are you saying?" she asked.

In reply, I reached out and snapped her neck. She dropped to the ground. This alone, however, will not kill a vampire. Given time, she could regenerate. She would revive and warn the others of my attack, but I had effectively incapacitated her long enough for me to sever her head with the cleaver. I stored her body in the old lair.

I took out the second vampire by merely approaching him from behind and severing his head. He was stored alongside the female. The third was not as easy as the first two. I managed to get him alone, but he was a suspicious lad, had been even in his human form. I did not get the right hold on his head I needed to break his neck as I had with the female. She had been easy because she felt herself to be superior to me. She had forgotten that I may have been old, but in vampire lives older means stronger, faster. This distrustful dolt feared me and was ready when I tried to make my move.

He screamed and attempted to flee. Holding onto him was like trying to catch a slippery fish in a rocking boat. When I finally pinned him down to where I could finish what I had started, it took several tries with the cleaver to sever his head. At one point, I had to saw through his neck to break the tendons. As his vocal cords were severed, he managed an eerie garbled cry that sounded like someone gargling acid. When I finally finished with this one he, too, was taken to the abandoned lair.

I killed the third male as quickly as the first two attacks; as he, like the female, was a conceited fool. He did not think I had the strength, speed, or the stones, to defeat him.

For my final victim, I would need to be very fast. I planned to kill him in front of Bane, invoking his anger. If my plan failed, the two of them would have no trouble taking me down. As I approached the last of the underlings, I saw that Bane, too, was there. I walked up to the vampire and bowed slightly. He nodded a greeting back.

"It is close to sunrise," I said.

"So," the vampire said.

"Bane," I called out. When he looked at me, I said, "This is your last underling."

"What?" the inferior said.

I grabbed the buffoon by the shirt and watched as his eyes widened at the sight of the cleaver. I took off his head in one clean swipe. His head fell back, bursting into ash. The husk of his dead body drifted to the dirt below my feet.

"He was the last," I said. "Now there are no more of your bastard underlings, and it is just us once again."

Bane stared at me for a minute or two. His eyes narrowed into angry slits. Then the chase was on. I moved through trees over grass, stone and dirt paths alike. Bane followed at almost the same speed. He showed no trouble keeping up with me. If I started to pull too far ahead of him, I would slow just enough to keep him in sight.

At one point, I was almost caught because Bane realized what I was doing and adjusted his speed to make me think he was falling behind, but when I slowed, he sped up. He reached out, and I felt his fingertips graze the back of my neck. I leaned forward to prevent him from grasping my shirt collar, forcing more speed into my legs.

The near miss must have motivated him because suddenly I was racing at my top speed and he was still at my heels. When I reached my destination, I leaped to the side and decelerated. When Bane realized I was no longer in front of him, he stopped and turned back. He saw me standing at the opening of a crenellation in the ruins of a castle. Earlier I had positioned a stone slab to serve as my barricade, and now I pushed it into place. It effectively blocked out all light. I could hear Bane hammering at the outer surface of the massive stone. I had known Bane long enough to judge his strength accurately, and I didn't misjudge him. This slab was too cumbersome for him, and the sun was about to rise.

There was nothing nearby to use as protection from the sun. When he stopped assaulting the barrier, I knew he was heading back to the coal mine lair. The sun rose, and I fell into death sleep.

The following night I woke and pushed the barrier aside. I climbed out into the fresh night air and waited for Bane. He did not come. I raced back to the mine shaft lair. I had used dynamite to destroy this entrance to the retreat, preventing entry. The rubble had not been touched. Next, I returned to the original lair Bane and I had shared for so long. But this, too, was not a viable shelter any longer. I had burnt the building to the ground, the floorboards were torn up. The charred remains of the five vampires I had killed still rested where I had placed them. Not far from the remains I found something else.

I stood over the bubbling puddle of oozing, putrefying flesh, and shards of bone. "Goodbye my friend," I said and turned away from the remains.

After Bane, I vowed to never turn another vampire, and I must continue my restraint or risk losing another friend to the madness."

"I would never do that," David said and leaned back in his chair. "I think Bane had always had it in him to kill and torture, but that's not me. I care about life, and I would continue to care, even as a vampire."

"I believe you," Antony laced his fingers together thoughtfully. "But I will not change you. Now be a peach, will you, and dispose of this body?"

Chapter Two

"I have a surprise for you tonight," David said as he followed Antony out of the dark bedroom the following night.

Antony turned to face David and waited patiently for the surprise.

"I found a baby killer."

Antony's eyes furrowed. "Who else?"

"A couple of killers, but those we'll have to collect in the wild. I didn't have a chance to nab them."

"A hunt?" Antony turned and continued down the hall. "I am up for that."

David drove him to hobo row, where a homeless guy had been nabbed for killing two tourists but released due to a mix up at the evidence locker. The killer was dumped right back onto the street. Antony strolled up behind the man and spun him like a ballerina, dipped him in a dance of death, and then sunk his teeth deep into his unshaven neck. The head and the decapitated body were tied down with bricks and dumped into the canal where they descended into the muck, never to be found.

Next, David drove Antony to the other side of town where the second target's apartment complex was located.

The target wasn't home. In a panic, David searched through his notes until he found another suitable blood bag for Antony. The next man lived alone. Antony entered his house and took him as he slept. When the man was dead, Antony opened the front door and allowed David entry to dispose of the body.

The extra time put Antony in a hard spot. He needed his third transfusion quickly, or risk letting the blood sickness make him go insane with bloodlust. If that happened, even David wasn't safe.

In the passenger side of the Toyota RAV4, Antony said, "What are the details for this…baby killer?"

David glared at his companion for several seconds before turning back to the road. "Her name is Maggie Owens. Her daughter was murdered. This isn't crib death or an outraged community. The baby died by being shaken. The mother went on trial but was acquitted due to lack of evidence."

"But are we sure she is the killer?"

David, mouth agape, turned to Antony. "You would question my investigation skills?"

Antony had to point to the road and remind David to turn his attention back to the task of driving.

"The baby is dead because of injury, and she was the only person in the house. She was suffering from postpartum depression."

"Why was she not found guilty?"

"She claimed the baby's daddy killed the girl, but although Daddy couldn't be found—and even though there was no proof he'd been in the picture since the birth—the jury sided with her. Reasonable doubt. She killed that baby and got away with it. I'm sick of these baby killers getting away with their vile crimes. It's time for a little payback, right?"

Antony ignored the diatribe.

David pulled up to the curb outside Ms. Owens's apartment building. He told Antony the apartment number and floor.

"Baby killers are difficult to confirm," Antony said before getting out of the car. "So many are accused but are not guilty of the crime, but merely accessories after the fact. That is not good enough. I could wipe out the entire human race if I fed on every person who knew about a crime. I need the person whose heart had been muddied by the deed."

David gripped the steering wheel with white-knuckled strength but didn't turn to look at Antony. "She's guilty."

Antony entered the home without effort: locked doors were no match for him. He slipped silently through the rooms barely even touching the floor. He left behind no fingerprints, dead skin, or hair. There was no way to trace his DNA from any dead skin or hair that dropped off his person instantly turned to ash and disintegrated. He found the woman asleep in her bed.

A crib sat empty nearby.

Antony paused. That was not a sign of a guilty mother. She was a grieving mother. Her loneliness and pain were palpable in the room.

They had made a mistake.

But Antony's bloodlust began to take over, and there wasn't time to start again. This had to be the right person. His stony gray eyes filmed over with a blood-red tint. He needed to feed soon. Once the madness took over, there was no stopping the hunger. He either fed now, or no one was safe; not this grieving woman, or David, or any innocent bystander on the street. This woman would have to die. If nothing else, Antony could at least relieve her of the pain of grief.

Antony moved closer to the bed and woke her with a hand over her mouth. She looked up at him as he stepped into position; she was already awake. In fact, she had been waiting for him. He removed his hand.

"I knew you would come," she said.

Antony was startled. Did she know who he was—or more to the point—what he was?

He peered into her eyes, into her soul. What he found there confirmed his suspicions. This woman did not kill her child. "I am sorry. I know you are innocent of the crime of killing your baby, but I must feed." He closed his eyes. His head dropped toward her neck, and he prepared to take her.

She didn't scream as he had expected her to. "Please wait."

"I must." He opened his eyes, and she saw that they were red.

She gasped. Antony had hoped to save her the added fear of seeing the bloodlust in his eyes, but she had seen anyway. Now she knew he was more than just a killer.

"Please," she said again. Sobbing overtook her, and she couldn't speak.

When Antony saw the terror in her eyes, his sanity momentarily flooded back to him. He could control it, but only in short bursts. Whatever she had to say would need to be fast, and there was no guarantee it would do her any good.

Antony stood abruptly. This movement was so fast, she flinched. Maggie opened her mouth as if to scream but managed to keep her wits long enough to realize that his action was away from her, not nearer to her. She closed her mouth and sat up.

Antony paced. It took all his strength to control the hunger. He turned toward her again. "I must do this." He jumped on her, moving so fast she didn't see him until he was straddling her, his mouth moving toward her neck, toward the throbbing vein there. The instant he was about to penetrate her skin, the door to the bedroom burst open. Antony froze, his fangs touching the flesh of her slender neck.

"What the hell? Bitch, what are you doing now?" said the man at the door.

Maggie whispered the words that would save her life. "It was him."

Antony understood, and He flew at the man in an instant, landing on him like a leopard taking down a gazelle. His teeth ripped into the man's neck, and he sucked up the pulsing fluid. His sanity slowly returned, but his ability to taste his victim's memories did not. He was feeding on this man without knowing for sure he was the killer. It didn't matter.

No, it did matter. To Antony, it did. Antony stopped feeding long enough to peer into the man's eyes. What he saw there satisfied his need, and he continued feeding. His victim lost only enough blood to pump out in a single beat of the heart, but it was the first time he had wasted even a drop of blood.

David entered the room moments later with a black body bag draped loosely over one shoulder. The drained man had been decapitated. Antony stood at the window. Maggie sat huddled on the bed, staring at the corpse. She looked up at the David, her questioning glare shaded with confusion and awe. She shivered and began to hyperventilate. Antony glanced at her, concerned. He moved toward her, but she motioned for him to stay back. He obeyed, not wanting to aggravate her condition.

Maggie reached into the drawer of her bedside table and pulled out a small, crumpled paper bag. She started breathing into it. After a moment, she was able to talk.

"I'm okay." She panted but her breathing steadied, and she continued. "I have panic attacks. They came on after Molly died, but I've learned to control them without medication."

David stared at her. "Aren't you afraid?"

"Who's going to take care of that?" Maggie used a flippant wave of her hand to indicate the body of her ex-lover; her baby's killer.

Antony gave the briefest look then turned to David. The anger in his voice caused even David to shiver. "Take care of this."

The vampire stormed toward the door but turned before leaving. "And bring her. She will have to come with us until I can figure out what to do with her."

Chapter Three

David laid the body bag out on the floor as if he was about to pack a suit. Once it was flat, he unzipped it. He dragged the headless body to the opening and tucked it in, then tossed the head in by the hair. He zipped up the bag and draped it over his shoulder once again. With his free hand, he offered to help Maggie stand. She ignored him and got up without help. From her closet, Maggie pulled out mounds of clothes and tossed them on the bed. David turned away as she pulled off her night clothes and dressed in a blouse and slacks. She threw the rest of the clothes, along with a few other items, into a duffel bag. She grabbed a jacket off the hook at the front door and slipped into it.

She motioned for David to lead the way.

Antony stood at the car, waiting. After David flopped the corpse into the trunk, Antony took the driver's seat. Maggie sat down in the back. They rode back to Antony's house in silence. Although it was not a cold night, the woman pulled her jacket tighter around her shoulders and shivered. David observed her as she stared out at the dirty and empty streets.

When they reached the house, David led her inside and guided her to the sofa. Antony fixed her a cup of hot tea. He handed her the drink, and she accepted it without gratitude. She didn't drink it right away. She sniffed it first and held its warmth close to her body. After recovering from a bout of silent crying, Maggie took a sip of the tea. Perhaps she thought being poisoned was better than sitting in the awkward silence, or maybe she was finally starting to trust that the two strangers were not out to harm her.

Antony broke the silence. "I am a vampire."

Maggie stared at him through the steam rising off her cup.

He continued. "I hunt killers, and we believed you to be the killer of your child, so you were chosen for extermination." He spoke with such cold efficiency.

"Ex... extermination?" Maggie shivered again, despite the hot tea.

"I don't think we should be telling her all this," David said.

Antony lifted a hand, quieting him. "We must."

"She won't believe it, or she will run screaming from here even if she does. She will have the police at our door before we can say 'twenty-five to life.'"

Ignoring him, Antony continued. "I trust you understand how close to death you came tonight; I am hoping you will believe what I am saying. We have brought you here in the hopes that we can convince you not to involve the authorities."

"I already knew who you were."

David glared at her.

"I mean I knew you were coming. I didn't know what you were, not until you got there."

David had been pacing, and he stopped to look down at her "What?"

Maggie sighed and tried again. "I didn't have all the details, but I knew someone was coming for me. I also knew that Grover was coming. I had the vision of him showing up when you did. When I realized you were there to kill me, I figured I had to stall until Grover arrived."

David chuffed.

She ignored him. "I have visions. I see things in dreams and sometimes even when I'm awake. They aren't always totally accurate, but they always serve their purpose. I can also teleport."

"Teleport?" David made that chuffing sound again.

Maggie stood, no longer wishing to have David looking down at her. "You believe in vampires, but not in witches?" She growled at his narrowmindedness. Then, softening, she continued. "Okay, it's not exactly teleportation. I think it's technically called astral projection. I send my consciousness to another place. I can be seen in this other location, but I can't move or interact with the surroundings. I am like a ghost or a hologram. I don't know how else to explain it."

David said, "Regardless of what you may, or may not, have seen in your visions, you saw us in your apartment tonight, killing your boyfriend. That is what concerns me."

"Grover killed Molly." She spoke with the voice of a woman who knows how to demand attention. "I would have decapitated him myself if I could. He killed her on one of his drunken rampages. I might have been able to prevent her death if I had just gone to the cops and turned him in, but I was afraid of him. One thing I didn't see coming was her death. Nor, subsequently, did I see myself being accused of her death. My visions don't work like that." Her eyes filled with tears. She sobbed and turned away from them.

"Explain your visions to me, please?" Antony asked when she had control of herself again.

"I can see events from the past, and I can see what will happen in the future. I can also see events happening at the moment, even far from me. I just have to relax and concentrate, and I can see what I need to see. I can also see the auras."

Antony stopped her. "What is an aura?"

"Auras are a glow that surrounds a person. They tell me if people are in danger, or if they are a danger to me. You have an unusual aura. I think that's on account of what you are."

"What is unusual about my aura?"

"It's... black. Normal auras are white—for innocent people anyway. The more a person commits evil acts, the redder it turns. Red auras are bad. That's how I can help you, even without my visions."

Antony contemplated this silently.

"If your aura is black because you are a vampire, it would explain why David's aura is white since he's not. David's is glowing so white that I would have thought he was very young. The only auras I've seen that white is on babies."

"I'm not a baby." Though he sounded like one at the moment. "Auras? This sounds like nonsense."

"I can also dream of events to come, although what I see isn't always what actually occurs. I must admit there is some interpretation involved in my visions."

"So, you're a witch." David said this with apparent disdain.

"I'm expected to believe he's a vampire, but you can't believe I have visions?" Maggie was ready for a fight.

"He can prove his claim," David said. "Go ahead, prove it to her."

"David, please. You are not helping," Antony said.

"Listen." Maggie walked around and examined her surroundings. "I haven't felt this alive in years. I'm totally open to what you are telling me, and I am happy to stay and assist you in any way I can. I'm sure my visions will be of great service to your cause." Maggie turned to Antony, not wanting to deal with the human any longer.

"Our cause? We're not a cult or a non-profit organization. We don't take in members." David snorted. "I'd say tell people she's crazy, but people probably already know."

Ignoring David, Maggie stopped looking at the objects in the room and turned around. "Where is Grover… his body, anyway?"

"Burning in the incinerator downstairs," Antony said.

"Tone," David shouted. "We can't tell her…"

"We have must now take her in."

"We can't 'take her in.'"

Antony did not react to David's mocking tone.

He continued. "…and we shouldn't be telling her our trade secrets." David glared at her as he spoke.

"Jealous much?" she said.

David jumped out of the recliner where he had been sitting, but once he was up, he had nowhere else to take the threat, so he sat back down.

Antony growled. "David, enough."

David rolled his eyes and turned away.

To Maggie, Antony said, "You are telling us that you are psychic. That could come in handy. How can you assist? And can you demonstrate this gift for us?"

"Is this like a job interview or something? I'm not doing parlor tricks here. I don't have visions on demand. I can see what people are going to do and what they have done. I'll be a much more efficient handler than your current one. With me, you will never have to ever worry about a sloppy night again." She glared at David as she said this.

"I do just fine," David stated flatly.

Maggie dropped the six-inch pewter statue she had been examining back onto the mantle. She turned on him. "Not tonight you didn't. I almost died because of it."

"I've been doing this for seven years. This was the first time I ever…" He stormed out of the room.

Antony said, "We will just have to see how things play out. I am keeping you here until I can get a sense of how well I can trust you. Betray me, and you will be back on the menu."

Maggie shivered again.

"The boy wants to be what you are," she said. "You don't have to be psychic to get that. You can give him what he wants. I will gladly repay your generosity for ridding the world of that killer by taking over David's job. My abilities are much more efficient than his sleuthing techniques, anyway."

"An intriguing boast, and it remains to be seen. But you should know I will never give him what he wants. I will not ever make that mistake again, not with him or with anyone. You will be free to do as you wish once I know you will not be of any trouble to us. I cannot ask you to stay and be our prisoner, either."

"It wouldn't be like that. I would be happy to stay. I don't think you understand. I've been just going through the motions since Molly's death." Tears formed in Maggie's eyes at saying her daughter's name, but she didn't let them fall. She gritted her teeth and continued. "I need this in my life."

"We will see." It was the end of that discussion.

Maggie fell silent. Then another thought occurred to her. "How did you enter my room without my permission? I thought vampires had to be invited in."

Antony laughed noiselessly.

"Years ago, we had a member of our kind who was obsessive compulsive and could not enter a home without first asking permission. I believe he was the start of that myth."

"Where is he now?"

"He was eventually killed by sunlight, or so I heard."

"So sunlight does kill you?"

"Yes, but little else, so do not get any ideas."

Now Maggie laughed.

"He loves you, you know," she said, changing the subject. When Antony's right eyebrow rose inquisitively, she explained. "David—he loves you deeply. He wants to live forever, so you'll never have to be alone."

"I love him, too. That is why I will never turn him."

The room grew quiet.

David returned to the living room. He held out the newspaper article. "I meant to discuss this with you until…" He glanced at Maggie.

"You are still free to discuss anything you wish," Antony said.

David averted his eyes from Maggie. "It'll keep for another time." He walked away.

Antony turned back to give Maggie his attention. "As I said, you are free to go. But if you wish to stay, I will show you to a room."

Maggie's mind was made up. "I want to stay."

Antony stood. "Before we go to your room, I will show you the basement. The incinerator and panic room are down there. I will show you how they work."

"Great, lead the way."

###

Maggie had not been asleep when she heard David checking on her. Earlier, she found a dresser full of clothes and dressed in a black turtleneck sweater and black sweat pants. She had been ready to go for an hour. He had been slow to leave, and she wondered how he could manage to get anything done. Maggie could have been finished by now if she didn't have to wait for that slowpoke to go before she put her own plan into action. When she heard David leave, Maggie climbed out of bed fully dressed.

She would show him how a real hunter worked.

The time was a little past five in the morning when she followed David to the industrial-sized garage at the bottom of the hill. She waited until he drove away, then picked out the vehicle she wanted. Plucking the keys labeled van from the pegboard in a small room that served as an office, Maggie trotted through the darkened building to the white, windowless van in the back. She referred to these vehicles as "rape vans." Now that name was going to take on a whole new meaning.

Last night, she'd had a vision of a woman getting attacked. She suspected the rapist would be in an alley between the First National Bank and the government building and could stop the vile act before it happened. She didn't have to worry about getting the wrong man because he'd done this before, and his aura would be red.

"How many times have men used just this type of van to abduct their victims?" She whispered to herself. "Now, they're going to get a taste of what it's like to be thrown into the back of one."

She drove to the alley where she knew the first of her three targets would be loitering. She parked the van midway between the alley entrances and then waited until she spotted him coming from the south. His aura was the right amount of red to tell her she had the right guy. She always imagined that their auras were filling up with their victims' blood.

She slipped out of the driver's seat and hid until her target walked by. He shuffled through the alley on the other side of the van. Her heart raced as she realized she would have to act or lose the opportunity do what she planned. She released her held breath and stepped away from the van. He didn't see her, so she scuffed her feet to attract his attention.

When he turned, he locked eyes with her. She acted scared but, in truth, it wasn't an act. She started to have second thoughts about her plan. But it was too late to turn back now. She could sense him approaching her from behind just as she reached the back door of the van. When he attempted to grab her, Maggie swiveled on her heel and hit him with the stun gun she had purchased off the internet, initially to use on Grover. As the 1200 volts hit the man, he toppled. She quickly tied his wrists together with a length of nylon rope using a square knot.

First, she wrapped the rope around and then between his wrists. The more her victim struggled, the tighter the knot would bind. She used nylon because it was soft but sturdy. As long as he didn't fight too much, he would be fine. She tied his legs the same way. She bound his mouth with duct tape to avoid anyone hearing him scream. She lifted him into the van. In his stunned state, he could do little to resist. She returned to the house using the back door that opened directly into the cellar. She walked him to the panic room, and at the sight of the stun gun, he gladly obeyed. She locked him in using the keypad on the wall.

Her second target was taken down the same way. She delivered him to the panic room as well and saw she was still doing fine. David had yet to return.

Her third target was not alone, which complicated things. She made sure the man caught sight of her and then smiled inwardly when he dismissed himself from his group to seek her out. She led him back to the van. She needed privacy, so she would have to lure him into the truck before she made her move. She was nervous being so close to such a dangerous predator in the confines of the van's interior, but she had no choice.

"Hey there, doll," he said as he climbed into the van.

What a dumbass, she thought. She pulled the stun gun and hit him in the chest. The man instinctively protected himself and knocked it out of her hand before it could incapacitate him. He recovered quickly and struggled to get out of the van. She scrambled for the stun gun and went at him again.

"What the hell, stupid bitch." Spittle flew from his mouth.

He knocked the gun from her grasp again. He drooled; enough of the volts had hit him to make his mouth go numb, as well as his hands. He fumbled with the latch on the sliding door. She didn't have time to retrieve the stunner again, so instead, she picked up the tire iron that had been lying on a grease-stained blanket and hit him as hard as she could in the back of the head, low and near the neck. She didn't want to kill him; merely prevent him from moving for a few seconds. Her plan was effective. He dropped to the floor of the van just as he had managed to get the door open.

As he fell away from the door, she peered out to see if anyone had heard the struggle. No one was approaching, so she closed the door and positioned him where she could tie him up comfortably. She allowed herself a moment to catch her breath and stop shaking before placing him in the panic room with the others. David had still not returned by the time she finished her task.

She released a devilish giggle and waited for David to see what she had done.

Chapter Four

Using a GPS and the target's Facebook status, David located the first man on his list. This man had killed his girlfriend and gotten off due to no physical evidence. The man, twenty-seven-year-old Hugh Winters, actually bragged to friends how he had gotten away with murder. If the code had allowed, David would have also snatched the friends who had high-fived him for his success, but Antony would not accept that. Only the offender could be taken; it mattered little to Antony what the others may or may not have done to encourage or entice him.

So instead, David followed the mark, staying well out of sight until the killer was alone. The mark stumbled with his keys, trying to open the door to his apartment. The man was drunk at noon. "What a loser," David whispered as he took aim with the tranq gun. The tranquilizer was strong enough to take down a small bear. With Antony's endless bank accounts and the internet, there was no end to the number of toys David could buy for a successful hunt.

The dart hit precisely where David wanted, and after a three-second delay, the mark dropped. David collected his prize, throwing the man's arm over his shoulder and dragging him back to the car as though he was the sober buddy taking care of an unconscious drunk friend. Anyone who knew this scumbag would no doubt believe this ruse. When no one was looking, David tossed the lump into the back seat.

David's second victim had a pedophile conviction. These were David's favorite marks, and they always brought him back to his time as a sixteen-year-old runaway. Although this target had been released on good behavior, and most pedophiles never killed anyone, the damage done to a child's psyche placed them on Antony's kill list. Antony agreed that these vile creatures could not be redeemed. Taking them off the street was a necessity. David bagged the pedophile without incident.

The third member of David's daily roundup was a suspected rapist the police had been trying to track down without success. The police were looking for Andrew Gregory for questioning in connection with the rapes but were unable to find him. They knew he was the son of a wealthy businessman, and no one was willing to give Andy up.

But David knew something the police apparently didn't: according to Facebook, Andy frequented the White Dog Café. Andy was crafty. The police were looking for him in the posh part of town, but ole Andy wasn't there. He was slumming; hiding in plain sight, on the shadier side of town. And this was where David found him.

But Andy was not an easy takedown. The first tranq did not put him out right away, and like the pig that he was, Andy squealed. Worried that Andy would draw attention, David used a second dart. If the second dart killed him, David would need a fourth mark, someone Antony could track down himself. This was not a big deal; it happened all the time.

With Hugh and the pedophile in the back seat, Andy got to ride shotgun as David drove home. He pulled up to the back, opened the outer door leading to the basement and started unloading bodies. Using zip ties, David bound his quarry's arms and legs. As he was working, Maggie strolled into the basement through the inner entrance stairway.

"Need any help?" she asked, smiling.

David was suspicious. "No."

He dragged his first victim to the panic room and stopped when he came face to face with three gagged and bound men who were already in there. He stared at them with the same shocked and confused expression he could see mirrored on their faces. David looked at Maggie. "You?" He mouthed this with a nearly inaudible whisper.

She nodded vigorously, still smiling.

"How?" he asked, louder this time.

She relished the surprise on his face. "I told you. I have mad skills." She helped him pull the other two into the panic room and locked them in.

"You tell me your tricks, and I'll tell you mine."

"I'm a psychic; I already know your tricks."

"You're lying."

She smiled ruefully then relented. She told him, only leaving out the part where her last target had almost escaped. "Sounds dangerous. Antony would kill me if anything happened to you. But the stun gun is sheer genius. I want one."

"I lived with a man who beat me on a regular basis. Trust me when I say I can handle myself."

David grinned. "I think I finally understand." He bowed to her. But then a thought occurred to him. "If you knew Antony was coming for you, why didn't you use that thing on him? I'm sure it would have worked."

"I didn't use it in my vision," she said as if this explained it all.

He supposed it did.

Later, when Antony rose, they discovered that poor Andy did not revive. Antony looked into the panic room at the five scared and sweating faces. Poor Andy still breathed and his heart still pumped, but he was slumped over in an irreversible coma. And thanks to Maggie, there was no need to hunt again for another night.

Andy, who had an uncertain shelf life, was first. Maggie's three had to watch this, knowing the same fate awaited them. Antony studied these three men carefully. Their eyes confirmed that they were what Maggie suspected them to be: rapists. She waited at the doorway to the panic room for his approval.

"Well done," Antony said to her.

"Yes." Maggie cheered. Then to the three men, she said, "How does it feel to be the victim for a change?"

She watched as Antony drained the first one.

"Don't worry," she said, mocking sorrow. "You only have to wait one more night, and this will be your fate as well."

Maggie's smile faded, however; when her eyes met that of her first victim's, and his pain and fear took away her desire to celebrate. They were being taken off the street, and that was good, but lavishing in their agony caused her to cringe. She exited the basement and let Antony do his thing privately.

Later that night David, Antony, and Maggie converged in the living room, and Antony remembered something from the previous night. "Last night you were talking about something you thought could be important but did not say due to Maggie's presence. Please, now, speak freely and explain what you meant to say."

David thought a moment and remembered.

"Yes, I came across this one article. A possible future victim, but the M.O. was so close to home it was eerie. The FBI is investigating a serial killer that invades houses with at least three family members. All three victims are drained of blood and decapitated—"

"Let me see that."

This was the first time David had seen the worry on Antony's smooth, ageless face, and it scared him.

"What is it?" Maggie asked.

"It's another vampire."

"Are you sure?" David asked. "This could be a human—or humans—who just happen to have an M.O. that mimics a vampire."

"No, it is a vampire."

Maggie closed her eyes and after a few seconds opened them again. "He's right, and I can help you track him."

"How?" David asked.

"He will have the same black aura as Antony. If we get close enough for me to see the aura, I'll know."

"We will need to be very careful with this one. He has been feeding on the innocent for a very long time. He is not trying to hide his presence. These are all signs that he may be well beyond any kind of rational thinking. He is…"

"Insane." Maggie finished Antony's sentence, and he nodded agreement.

"About this aura stuff," David said. "I'm still not happy that you said my aura is as clean as a baby's."

"What?" Maggie blinked, bewildered.

"I'm no angel. I've committed crimes."

She laughed. "Well, your aura is clean, so you must be doing something right."

David returned to the original topic. "This... insane... vampire, if he is one, has caught the attention of the FBI. They have been tracking his movements. I have much of their information through newspaper clippings and internet details. With this information and your abilities, we should be able to do what the FBI can't."

"Where is he now?" Antony asked.

"The FBI last placed him somewhere in Pennsylvania. His last victims were in the suburbs. They believe he has moved on from there though, and do not have any idea where he will strike next. Maggie, does your sixth sense tell you anything?"

"I'll need time. But yes, I believe I can. Unfortunately, it will be much easier after he takes his next victims. Their pain and suffering will be like a beacon leading us directly to him."

David grimaced. "That's gruesome."

"But we will be able to stop him," Antony said.

"Hey, you know what this means, don't you?" David squirmed with excitement that caused the other two in the room to look at him. "It means a road trip is in order."

Maggie tilted her head slightly. She glanced at him, confused. "So."

David pretended to be shot with an arrow. He dropped dead to the floor. "Didn't you see it in the garage?" He stood back up.

"See what?"

"The Zephyr." He used his hands to mock an explosion and made the noise with his mouth.

Chapter Five

He called himself the Dark One. He supposed he had once used a given name, but so many years had passed without hearing it spoken that he had long since forgotten it.

He glanced down at the paper on the newsstand and read the headline: The Houseguest Killer Strikes Again.

He chuckled. "I can call myself the Unwanted Houseguest." He looked up when he heard a forced cough.

The attendant scowled at him. "This isn't a library, mister. Buy it or get outta here." The attendant stood in front of the rack and crossed his arms over his chest.

The Dark One raised his chin and smiled, letting his fangs show. The attendant peering at him took an involuntary step back, bumping the metal rack and causing some of the papers to fall. He unfolded his arms and stooped down to pick them up.

The Dark One lifted his wooden staff with the ivory tip and considered hitting the attendant, knocking him unconscious. Instead, he turned with a flourish of his dusty old trench coat and walked away.

He strode through the parking lot of a shopping mall and looked at the decals on the back windows of the vehicles he passed. This almost always told him how many members were in the household. He preferred three, but no less than that. To date, he had never picked a house with more than five family members and probably never would. He wasn't a glutton, after all.

He was a vampire.

He only required three blood-filled humans to satiate the need. Everyone beyond that was just wasteful, really. But it was just too much fun watching them bleed out.

Tonight's meal consisted of a man, the man's wife, and the wife's elderly mother. He spotted them returning home from some day-long outing and thought, why not?

The Houseguest Killer kept a lair in the Poconos, in a mansion that had once been an expensive bed and breakfast during the sixties but was now just a rundown and abandoned haunted house with graffiti decorating its facade. He tried to stick close to home and mostly hunted in the city of Allentown, or the surrounding area therein. His latest family lived in the town of Cherryville. They owned a quaint little house in the suburbs.

He meandered around the house peering into windows. He assessed that the man and woman were in the downstairs sitting room, drinking tea and reading. The man flipped through the local paper, and she read a hardcover book, maybe a novel. The old woman slept in an upstairs bedroom. He would take her first, quietly and without too much fuss; he derived no thrill from torturing the elderly, who were probably not even aware what was happening to them.

The vampire's dusty brown trench coat flapped like batwings as he moved through the yard to the next window. His aging black slacks and the loose, dingy yellow shirt presented no resistance to his movements as he hopped up into a tree and climbed over to the window to the old woman's bedroom. The window opened without difficulty and jumped in. He straightened out his clothes and stepped up to the bed where the elderly woman lay. He laid next to her and put his arm around her. This woke the woman and she gasped. She tried to sit up.

When she couldn't, she merely asked, "Who are you?"

"I'm your husband, don't you recognize me?" he said.

"Larry?" she asked in a sleep-raspy voice.

"Yes, it's Larry."

She rolled over and planned to go back to sleep.

"Wake up, stupid old hag. Have a little respect for the one who's going to kill you." The vampire rolled over onto her and sank his teeth into her neck. The teeth bit precisely into the soft, loose flesh of her neck, penetrating the slightly tougher skin of the carotid artery with a soft pop. The blood began to fill his mouth immediately.

He sucked at the wound, not wanting to wait for her old heart to pump the blood into his mouth. He felt the old woman's heartbeat flutter as he drained the last bit of blood from her body. In a matter of minutes, the old woman laid still and cold… and dead. He slipped a knife out of a sheath on his belt and cut off her head.

The decapitation was an essential ritual unless he wanted the old woman to return as another living dead like him. She would not become miraculously young and vibrant; if she turned she would be the same as she was in life—old and senile… but eternal.

He left the old woman's room and listened at the top of the stairs for any commotion from below. Apparently, he had not attracted the attention of the couple down there. The only conversation he heard from them was regarding the tea they were drinking.

Time to interrupt this heartwarming moment, he decided. He stomped down the stairs, making more noise than was necessary and invading their peaceful existence. The couple looked up at the man standing on the stairs, confused but not yet alarmed.

He leaped and took the man first, landing on him and driving him into the back of the sofa. He tore the man's throat out, sloppy and quick. The man's fear made his blood pump quickly. When he'd had enough from the man, he left him to bleed out and turned on the woman.

The woman began screaming as soon as the vampire had made his move. She continued yelling the entire time drained her husband was being consumed, but she hadn't tried to fight, or run away

"Shut up," the vampire shouted, trying to make himself heard over her screams. The blood on his lips splattered across the woman's face.

She just kept screaming, clutching her book like a talisman. He'd had enough, and leaped forward and attacked, knocking into her like a linebacker. The book flew from her hand and hit the floor with a muffled thump. He silenced her only when he tore out her throat. He drained her, then decapitated her and the husband before leaving, without bothering to clean up after himself.

He glanced down at his blood-covered clothes. He pulled his trench coat over the blood spatters and buttoned it up. Although he always left behind a mess, he was careful not to attract attention to himself. Though it was fall, the night was warm, and there was a comfortable breeze. On the wind, he smelled the familiar scents of popcorn, cotton candy and funnel cakes. He was in the presence of a carnival and headed in the direction from which the aromas were calling him.

He walked casually around the park, paid for a ticket, and went for a ride on the Ferris wheel. When he was up at the very top, before the carriage started down the other side, the vampire spotted something he very much wanted for his own.

It was a boy. He was a scruffy, black-haired boy with freckles across the bridge of his nose and on his cheeks. He was asking his mother for money—had to be his mother, she looked just like him—then ran off to join his friends.

The vampire kept the boy in his sights, and once the ride stopped he followed this boy and his friends for most of the night. He thought he might take the boy now, here, at the park, and then kill his friends. They were a group of troublemakers, picking on little girls and trying to break things. The black-haired boy laughed and carried on with the troublemakers; but he, himself, didn't partake in the troublemaking.

As the night wore on, he thought it best if he didn't take the boy here, after all. He regretted that he wouldn't be snapping the necks of those other boys, but there was just too much lighting. There was a possibility that someone would see what he had done, and he couldn't risk getting caught. He wasn't afraid of being taken down by the authorities; he could easily break out of every jail, but it would mean moving, and he didn't want to leave. He liked his newest home.

So instead, he waited and followed the family home. He knew where they lived. There were four in the group: Mom and Dad, sis and the black-haired boy. He would not take them tonight, but he would go to them soon. Maybe tomorrow night, perhaps not; but soon the little black-haired boy would be his.

Part Two: David

Chapter Six

Tearfully, Maggie explained the scene she had envisioned of the Houseguest Killer taking the elderly woman and her family. "It happened in the Pocono region," she said. "There was a green highway sign in the background as the killer approached the house." The exact location was still out of her reach, however. "I didn't get a street address."

"At least we have a direction to point to," David said, turning the RV toward the turnpike and the Pocono Mountains.

David didn't have a license. In fact, he had no identification at all. At least, none that genuinely identified him. He did have state-of-the-art fake IDs that Antony's shadier human assistants created for him. But David continued to fly below the radar. He didn't need to earn a living since Antony had acquired a fortune over the last several centuries and David could access these funds any time he wished.

Antony also owned property all over the world under different names, and there were safeguards in place to be sure that the homes could be accessed whenever the need for them arose. David's favorite was not a house, but the Zephyr, an RV, but it was also so much more than that; it was a mansion on wheels. It sported a faux fireplace and a plush, eggshell white sofa and loveseat combo. There was a bed, but David rarely used it. David hardly slept at all. With the help of energy drinks and his own adrenaline, David slept a total of five hours in a forty-eight-hour period. Maggie was welcome to the queen-sized bed if she wished, he had told her.

Beneath it was a reinforced titanium compartment that was airtight and free of sunlight for Antony to retreat to during the day.

David had been a natural at driving since he had learned years ago. He could drive the Zephyr or a tricycle with the same ease. Still, if David were to be pulled over, there was an army of lawyers that would swoop in and protect his identity with just a touch of a button on the key fob. David didn't want to test the system, however, so he drove only at legal limits and never got crazy behind the wheel.

Maggie watched him drive with a look of fascination on her face. He caught her looking and took his eyes off the road for several seconds to see what she was staring at, and then finally looked back at the scene outside the large windshield.

"I'm sorry for staring," she said at last. "But when you're really happy, like now, when you're driving, or when you're with Antony, you light up with this beautiful aura that makes you almost angelic."

David raised an eyebrow. "How do you like having visions? Do they make life easier, or harder?"

"Most times it makes life easier, but sometimes it's a cross I have to bear."

David let the silence stretch out between them.

She sighed and turned to look out her window at the tree-lined highway roaring by to her right. There were a couple more miles of silence before she decided she could take it no more, and she finally spoke up.

"You don't like me much," she said.

He glanced at her briefly. "I'm just watchful. I will protect Antony with my life if I must. What he's done for me…" He trailed off because there were no words to explain it.

"I totally understand. And I hold no ill will toward you."

"Ill will?" David looked at her again. "For what?"

"You singled me out as prey."

"Oh." David squirmed uncomfortably. "Thank you."

"I want you to like me, David. I like you." She tilted her head down and smiled.

David hadn't seen her look so innocent and so devilish at the same time. He squirmed again.

The sun, high in the sky, beat down on them in the cockpit of the massive house on wheels, drawing perspiration on their brow despite the air conditioning. Antony was safely tucked away in the steel compartment under the dining table. They were still about an hour away from their destination. After another mile of uncomfortable silence, David conceded that like it or not, Maggie was now a part of the group and he would have to "share" Antony with her. He sighed; a defeated little sound, and turned to face her.

"I like you just fine," he said at last. Maggie laughed, leaned over, and kissed him on the cheek. David blushed.

"I'd really like to know you better," Maggie said. "What can you tell me about yourself?"

"What do you want to hear?"

"Everything," she said.

He hesitated for a minute and then decided he would tell her what happened in his life to bring him into Antony's orbit. He kind of wanted to say it—

needed to, really—so he could cleanse his mind of that dark past and be done with it once and for all. Not to mention it would also help pass the time.

"My father died—my real father—when I was three, so I never really knew him. I have vague memories, but that's about it. My mother didn't like to be alone, and her remedy for loneliness was an armada of "uncles" she would bring home. After I turned seven, she married one of these uncles, a man named Ralph. At first, he was no different from the myriad other men that passed through the door, except this one never left. He also had something else none of the others had. He owned two purebred blue pit bulls, Ghost and Frankenstein. Ghost was almost entirely that bluish-gray color that makes the breed so beautiful, and Frankie was a splotchy gray and brown with a white belly. They were brothers.

"Our house was a two-bedroom shack on the north end of Philly. Mobile Street, but it was more like a back alley than a street. The house was drafty in the winter and stifling in the summer, but it was home, and I was used to it.

"I learned from the age of ten that I was attractive, at least the girls at school seemed to think so. I was always surrounded by girls, and although I never officially agreed to be exclusive with any of them, Darlene Clawson considered me her property sometime during middle school. She would get extremely jealous if the other girls showed me any attention. She especially didn't like Rachael McFadden because I showed the most interest in her. But Rachael wasn't one of the girls who hung around me so I couldn't get to know her as I would have liked. But then, if she had been like all the other girls that scuttled around me, I probably would have ignored her like I did them. But she was unattainable, so I was into her.

"I was ashamed of my home life, so I never invited people over, and I would tell them lies about how great my life was just to sound cool. I used my meager allowance and the money I made doing other people's homework at the Goodwill and bought designer clothes that I wouldn't have been able to afford otherwise. No one knew I couldn't afford new American Eagle or Hollister jeans. Sometimes the clothes were too small, but I was thin and muscular, so it just made me look like a trendsetter.

"I was twelve the first time Ralph took me hunting. The dogs were with us, but no one else came. It wasn't what I call exciting, but I did enjoy being outside. Learning to shoot was fun, too, but little else about hunting with Ralph could be described that way.

"Ralph was a serious hunter. He wore camouflage greens with a hunting cap and combat boots. His favorite hunting knife was a sharp Bowie with a green camouflage handle. It was the knife I would eventually use on him, but it was his turn to do the damage then. And on this hunting trip, I would soon learn the true meaning of fear.

David's Story

The dogs moved ahead, sniffing the ground and marking trees. When we located a flock of pheasant, the dogs rooted them out, and Ralph took aim. He took down two of the birds. He was a good shot.

"Why didn't you shoot, boy?" he asked and cuffed the back of my head.

"Cut it out," I griped.

"Don't talk back you little wimp, or I'll give you worse than that." He walked ahead, and I raced to keep up. "Next flock, I expect you to take a bird of your own, hear what I'm saying?"

I said I did.

And I did get a bird, but Ralph complained about my form. He criticized how I held my gun and even how slow I was retrieving the kill. I was a little annoyed that he sent the dogs in to collect his kills, but I had to get my own. Not a big deal, though since I only had one bird.

Toward the end of the day, when it was just about time for us to head back, things took a strange turn. Suddenly Ralph was aloof, distracted. He walked behind me most of the time. When I stopped, he would stop, too.

"Go on up ahead," he said.

I stared for a long time before moving. I was looking behind me every couple of steps just to make sure he was still there. I suddenly had a feeling that I was Hansel about to be left in the woods. But what was going on was even more sinister than that.

When I was about five hundred yards away, I heard the click as he cocked his rifle. I stopped moving, afraid to look back. Was he pointing the gun at me? Somehow, I knew he was. My blood ran through me like ice. I suddenly wanted to hug my mother really bad. I would miss her. She was never really that good to me, but she was the only mother I had. Would she cry when I didn't return? I would like to believe she would, but I didn't know. I squeezed my eyes as tight as I could and waited for the rifle shot.

"It's a dangerous world out there, you should be careful," Ralph said then pulled the trigger.

The gunshot echoed through the trees stirring up all kinds of wildlife around us. I dropped to my knees, felt at my back for the hole that wasn't there. About twenty yards to my left a wild turkey lay headless and bleeding, its body still twitching. Behind me, Ralph was laughing. Did he know I had wet myself at the moment the gun went off? Probably not, but would soon figure it out, though. He had the nerve to be angry at what I had done.

This wouldn't be the last time Ralph would play this game, but future episodes would not be as fun for him, because I never wet my pants again, and I wasn't half as scared. Yes, there was always the possibility he would go through with the real thing, but by then I just didn't care anymore.

When we got home, he said, "Go clean yourself up; you're disgusting." As if I had done this out of stupidity or something.

I showered and dressed for dinner, and in the kitchen, my mother was preparing the birds, so I watched.

As she plucked the feathers from my pheasant, I asked if she needed any help.

"I got this," she said.

My mother was seventeen when she had me. She was young now. She married a man twice her age just so she wouldn't feel alone, or so I believed. She was convinced this was her last chance at happiness. I was a distraction from her true happiness, and a threat to it as well, I think. At least, that's how I felt.

"That's my bird," I said.

"Tough bird," she complained. "And probably not even worth cooking. I'm tempted to throw it to the dogs."

My good mood faded. "I'll eat it."

"It's full of buckshot. You should have used the Remington 7600 and saved some of the meat."

That's the gun your husband intended to shoot me with, I wanted to say. But she would have hit me for being a liar and threatening to destroy her marriage.

"That's not the gun Ralph let me use," I said instead.

I helped her when I could, but mostly I just sat there staring at her wondering how she could be so blind to Ralph's evil. Eventually, I would give up trying to figure her out. But back then I still held out for her love and attention.

I ate some of the turkey that Ralph shot instead of shooting me, and it tasted good. But I credit that to my mother being such a good cook. My bird was tough like she said. It ended up in the dog dish. They seemed to like it, anyway.

The dogs slept with me most nights, and I enjoyed their company. That night they were belching up my bird and reminding me of my colossal failure. Ghost slept at the foot of my bed and Frankenstein slept on the rug next to my bed. They were my protectors, and I slept better knowing they were there with me.

When I turned thirteen, Ralph started with the physical attacks, no longer satisfied with the verbal and mental abuse, I guessed.

My first encounter with his wrath was brutal. I had been out late after school with some friends, and because I didn't want them seeing where I lived, I walked the long way home. I arrived back around 10:00 p.m. I was quiet, hoping maybe no one would know. The house was dark as I headed for my room.

I don't know where he had been, but suddenly, Ralph was behind me. He had taken off his belt and was holding it with the buckle dangling to the floor. I didn't even know he was there until I heard the whistle of the leather cutting through the air. By then it was too late. The buckle caught me in the back about mid-way up on the left side. I fell to the floor gasping for breath. He took the buckle into his palm and commenced slapping the strap across my back and legs. I still hadn't recovered from the buckle when the barrage began. When I gained my breath, I started screaming.

"If your curfew is nine p.m. then you should be stepping through that door at nine p.m.; not nine fifteen, and definitely not ten. Do I"—another slap of the belt— "make myself"—another— "clear, boy?"

I was crying, and tears streamed down my face, but I could see my mother cringing in the doorway to their bedroom. Outside, the dogs barked and yelped, trying to get in and see what was happening.

"Do I?" he asked, huffing and red-faced.

I couldn't speak, so I just nodded. This seemed to be enough because he walked away without further "behavior modification." He brushed past my mother and went into the bedroom. My mother stared for a moment longer with a half sad, half angry look on her face as if this was my fault.

When my tear-filled, puffy eyes didn't turn away from her, she walked away. I staggered to my feet and walked to the back door where the dogs were still trying to get in. They knew I was upset and were visibly concerned about me. Ghost was at my side like a four-legged bodyguard, and Frankie was whining and sniffing my leg, looking for the source of my distress.

The next day, I checked my back in the bathroom mirror. There was a grapefruit-sized red mark on my back and in the center of that was a black bruise shaped like a square belt buckle. There were some welts on my arms and a few scratches here and there, but almost everything could be covered up.

I was a natural at math and science and English, and I made lots of money doing homework for other kids. As I made my transactions in the hall, I wondered if any of them were aware of my stiffness and pain. No one suspected anything, but then why would they? When my friend Tim Warner sneaked up behind me and poked me in the ribs, I gasped in fear and pain.

"What's up with that?" he said and tried to poke me again. I instinctively protected my back, but he could tell there was something I was hiding. "What did you do?" he asked, trying to lift my shirt.

"Cut it out, fag," I said, and he backed off.

"What's up with you and Darlene?" he asked, changing the subject. I would almost prefer to talk about my abuse.

"What do you mean?" I asked.

"She said you were dissing her all night."

"I wasn't dissing her," I said defensively. "Not on purpose."

"Anyway, I was going to ask you if you wanted to go to a Phillies game with my dad and me in a few weeks. We have an extra ticket..." He caught sight of Rachael at the other end of the hall and watched her as she came toward us. "Hi, Rachael," he said when she walked by.

She looked up and said "hi" to him, but she was looking at me when she spoke, and I got the distinct feeling she was really talking to me. He smiled, oblivious to the misdirection.

After she was gone, he turned back to me and said: "So how about it? You want to go?"

"I'll have to ask my folks," I said. I really did want to go, but I wasn't going to get my hopes up that Ralph would allow that. "I'll let you know."

The next day I told Tim I would go, even though I hadn't asked Ralph. I figured I had two weeks to come up with an excuse if I couldn't go.

At home, I wasn't planning to ever let my guard down again, so I never entered or left the house without the dogs at my side. I tried to work up the courage to ask Ralph if I could go to the game with the Warners, but honestly, I was more worried about him saying no to the request than any punishment he might inflict.

I didn't ask. I couldn't bear the rejection, and I knew Ralph would never have allowed it. And my mother was useless. She wouldn't have stood up for me. Maybe I was making unfair assumptions, but I don't think so. I knew their history too well to believe anything else was possible. Instead, I worked out a different plan. The game was on Friday night. I was instructed to be at their place by 7:00 p.m., so we could head out and be there by eight. The game started at nine. On the day of the game, I went to my room early, faking illness. The dogs, tied up out back, barked constantly. I fixed my bed to look like I was sleeping in it, then climbed out my window. I made it to the Tim's house ten minutes early. We went to the game, and it was as nice as I had hoped. I thought Tim's dad was the greatest guy on the planet. I wished he could have been my dad. I was jealous of Tim's family—his life, for that matter. During the game, I didn't have a care in the world.

On the way home was another matter, though. Had Ralph figured out I wasn't in my room? What kind of hell was I in for? So many terrible scenarios raced through my head. Tim was oblivious to my distraction, but I think Mr. Warner knew something was up with me. I caught him glancing into the rearview mirror at me several times. But if he was suspicious of my behavior, he didn't say anything about it.

"We arrived back at their house around two thirty. Tim's dad offered to drive me home, but I told him it would be okay with my folks if I spent the night. When Tim was asleep, I slipped out of the house and walked back to my place. The window I had escaped through was still unlocked, and I climbed back into my room. I removed my bed camouflage and jumped in for real. I guessed I had pulled it off.

I was wrong.

I woke with a gasp. Ralph was at the foot of my bed. He had my foot pinned down and was holding a lit cigar to the bottom of it. I kicked and screamed, but he wouldn't let go until he was finished. As soon as he released my foot, I curled into a ball.

His eyes were sinister slits as he glared at me. “Maybe you'll think twice about running off without telling me now,” he said.

With tears of pain, fear, and frustration in my eyes, I spat at him. Or maybe I just wanted to, I'm not sure at this point.

He puffed at the cigar. “Your mother doesn't like me smoking in the house, but hell with her. She doesn't make the rules around here.” He said this as if it was just another conversation. He turned to leave. “Remember what I said; it's a dangerous world out there.” He blew smoke at me. “You should be careful.”

I put aloe on my burned foot when I thought he was through with me. Later that morning, when my mother asked me why I was limping I could have sworn she was smirking. Did she know? I just glared at her and didn't answer.

There were more moments of abuse through that year, but mostly just the typical hitting; sometimes a punch or two. Ralph started to notice that when the dogs were around, and he hit me, they'd growl and even snap at him.

At school, I started avoiding Darlene when I realized Rachael would visit me more often if Darlene weren't around. Tim still liked Rachael and encouraged her company whenever he could. Suddenly, the group went from Darlene and her posse to just Tim, Rachael, and me. That was just fine with me. And it was okay with Tim, too.

During the summer break, the three of us would head down to the Jersey shore and swim in the ocean. We hung out on the boardwalk, and ate funnel cakes and cotton candy. I started asking Ralph for permission to spend time with my friends and, oddly, it was granted.

I was eating curly fries with vinegar, a boardwalk staple, and Rachael shared them with me. Tim was ripping off chunks of his funnel cake and threatening to wipe his sticky fingers on us when it dawned on me that I was actually acting like a typical teenager. I wasn't afraid for my life or in pain of any kind. I wanted to stay there forever, and never return home. I suddenly looked very sad, and when Tim left to throw his trash away, Rachael asked why.

Could I tell her? I wanted to, but I didn't think I could. Not now, and not there. "I just wish this day could last forever," I said.

"We'll have more days like this," she assured me with a grin.

Tim returned and announced he was heading to "the dunny, the can, the loo."

"To do number two?" I asked, purposely rhyming with him. He flipped me off.

When we were alone again, Rachael asked: "Will you tell me what's really bothering you? Most times you're this sweet and happy-go-lucky guy, and you look so handsome when you're smiling. But then I see you when you think no one is looking and you're so sad. I can't help but think you're hiding something bad, and it scares me."

When I looked at her, tears brimmed in her eyes.

I tried to speak and instead made this strange stuttering sigh, and then my eyes were filled with tears. "I don't have a good home life," I admitted in a whisper. It was the hardest sentence I ever had to utter. I didn't want her to know this, but I had to say something. "Besides my dogs, you and Tim are the best things in my life right now, and I never want to—"

Before I knew what was happening, Rachel leaned in and kissed me. When she pulled away, there was a line of spit connecting our lips. When it broke, so did the spell.

Tim returned and sat down between us. Had he seen? I didn't think so; he didn't act as though he had. He placed an arm around each of us. "Who's up for some games?" he asked.

We went off in search of fun and laughter in the hot Jersey sun.

After that, I made it a point to bottle up my unhappiness when I was with them.

We three were together for most of that summer, and although Rachael tried to get more information out of me about just how bad my home life was, I was tight-lipped on the subject. We spent a lot of time in Tim's backyard. He had some cool games like ladder ball and yard darts.

When the summer was over, and we went back to school something seemed to change between Tim and me. He was not as outgoing as I usually knew him to be. We still hung out together, but Tim suddenly seemed more depressed than me. This worried me, and it also kind of angered me. What did he have to be so sad about? He had the life I wanted. I thought it was odd that Rachael noticed my depression but Tim didn't, and I noticed Tim's depression but Rachael didn't. We were a bizarre triangle.

It was a subtle transition, but our trio was now more of a duo as Tim slowly stopped hanging around with Rachael and me. It started with him skipping lunch and then finding other stuff to do during study hall. Eventually, we didn't see him after school either. Rachael was okay with this, but I wasn't. Tim was my "brother from another mother" (his saying, not mine) and I missed him.

Rachael and I had been hanging out at the park after school, but she could tell my thoughts were elsewhere. After about an hour of my moping and she was unable to get me to talk, she gave up and went home. I walked the seven blocks to Tim's house and stood across the street until I could muster up the nerve to confront him and get him to tell me what was going on. When I did, he answered the door on the first knock.

"What are you doing here?" he asked.

"I came to find out why you're avoiding us. Avoiding me," I answered.

"I'm not," he said.

"Bull," I snapped. "You've been avoiding me, and I want to know why. Is it because of the kiss? It didn't mean anything—"

"What kiss?" he asked. The alarm faded from his face when he realized it didn't really matter anyway. "I knew she liked you better, anyway." He sounded defeated and hurt. "You should have told me, though."

"If it's not that, then why have you been dissing me?"

I was desperate to know now. He still hadn't let me in yet, and I was beginning to think he wasn't going to. Had things between us gotten that bad? "What did I do that made you hate me so much?"

"I don't hate you," he said.

He seemed to realize then that whatever he was keeping from me couldn't be kept a secret anymore. He moved aside and let me in. I followed him to his room passing the living room where his parents said hello. I returned the greeting but didn't stop. We entered his bedroom, and he closed the door. I sat on his bed while he pawed aimlessly through his CDs. There was nothing he wanted to hear, he just needed something to do with his hands while he tried to come up with the words.

With a sigh, he turned to me and said: "In a month or so my parents and I are going to be moving to California. My dad's got a new job out there, and we have to..."

I didn't hear anything else he had to say, couldn't listen to it. My head was pounding, and one word was echoing over and over again in my ears: moving. He was walking away and leaving me to face the hell that was my life alone. Tim was the only one that could keep me feeling unbroken and grounded in reality. When I was with him and his family, I felt normal. I felt wanted. I felt safe.

"Dave, are you hearing me?" he was asking when I was able to focus again.

I looked up at him, and with tears rimming my eyes, threatening to spill over, I said, "Take me with you."

He stared at me for a minute, not sure how to respond.

I knew this wasn't a possibility, but still, I had to do something. I could no longer carry this burden alone. The tears flowed, and so did my story. "If you don't take me with you, he's going to kill me. My stepfather is crazy. He beats me and terrorizes me. I have burns and cuts; I have scars from his abuse and torture." His expression turned from confusion to outright horror. "I'm afraid," I admitted with a shuddering breath.

Tim went to his bedroom door and flung it open. For a second, I thought he was going to demand that I leave, but instead, he shouted, "Mom, Dad. Come in here, quick."

They were in the doorway in seconds. I had broken down sobbing uncontrollably when they appeared, and I couldn't speak anymore. Mrs. Warner was at my side right away, holding me and trying to calm me down. "David, what's wrong?" She turned to Tim. "What happened?"

"I don't know. I told him we were moving and he… he wants to go with us. He said he's being abused by his stepdad."

When I had calmed down, I told them what I had already said to Tim. I told them about the hunting trips. I showed them the marks on my back, the cigar burns—there were more than just the one on my foot by then—and I told them how Ralph had threatened to cut off my penis if I had sex with "that floozy" I was hanging around with. He was referring to Rachael, of course.

By the time I was done, Mrs. Warner was crying, and her husband just looked outraged.

"David, come with me," he said.

He drove me home and confronted my stepfather in the doorway. He pushed his way into the house and demanded to know what was happening to me. He accused my mother and Ralph of being horrible parents.

My mother was afraid, and she started crying; but Ralph was just looking at Tim's dad with contempt in his eyes and a half smirk, half snarl on his lips.

"You have a lot of nerve coming in here and accusing us good people of such atrocities," Ralph said.

"Good people," Mr. Warner spat. "I've seen the bruises and the scars. I know abuse when I see it."

"He's a clumsy kid, what can I say?"

"He has stories. He told me about the hunting trips where you threaten to kill him. What is it you say? "It's a dangerous world out there, you should be careful?"

At this, my mother looked at Ralph with alarm. He glanced at her only briefly then back at Mr. Warner.

"Lies," he said. "Stories, just like you said. He tries to get attention by making up stuff."

"He wants to come and stay with us." When Tim's dad said this, I cringed inside. "I think you should let us take him until we can get this straightened out."

"Is that what this is all about? You want to take our kid away from us? There's no way that is going to happen."

"Maybe the police should have a say in this," he said.

"How dare you barge into my home and tell me I'm unfit to raise my own son," my mother charged, suddenly finding a backbone. "This is an outrage, and I won't stand for it."

It had happened so fast that even I didn't see it coming. While my mother was expressing her outrage, Ralph had dipped out of the room and returned with a pistol in his hand. He pointed it at the intruding man. Mr. Warner put an arm out to me protectively and moved me behind him. I loved him for that.

"I suggest you walk out that door and not look back," Ralph warned.

"Not without David," Tim's dad spoke with a particular inflection, as if to a child who had just done something naughty.

My mother had been slowly inching her way toward us, and with the gun pointed at us, we hadn't noticed until she had snatched my arm and pulled me away from the other man. Ralph stepped up and planted the gun to his forehead.

"I don't recall inviting you in here," Ralph said. "You just barged in here and tried to steal my son away from me. That's the story the cops are going to get as they're cleaning your brains up off my floor."

Tim's dad put his hands up in front of him. He backed up slowly and left the house without turning his back on the gun. He walked backward to his car, careful not to take his eyes off the weapon, climbed in and drove away. I never saw him again.

A few minutes passed before Ralph stepped over and closed the door. He then turned on me with a rage like no other. He charged at me with the gun raised like a club.

At some point during the confrontation, the dogs had entered the room. Now, as Ralph ran at me, the dogs charged Ralph. They were snarling, and saliva dripped from their mouths. Ralph backed off. He left the room muttering about ungrateful dogs not knowing who their rightful owner was.

If the Warners ever called the cops, or social services—which I do think they did—nothing came of it. No one came to get me out of there.

There were no other repercussions from that night, but in school the next day I learned that Tim had been pulled from all his classes. I never saw him again, either.

I didn't blame the Warners for leaving the way they did. I'm sure they worried about me, but in the end, they had each other to worry about as well. If anything had happened to Tim or his parents, I would never have forgiven myself for getting them involved.

My relationship with Rachael tapered off after that as well. I just couldn't risk putting her in danger the way I had with the Warners. I would prefer she hated me for being a jerk than allow her to stay in the line of fire.

Strangely, though, Ralph seemed reluctant to touch me after the incident with Mr. Warner. If it was the dogs standing up for me or just the mere fact that his hateful ways were no longer just something he and I knew about, I couldn't tell. He stopped hitting me and torturing me.

Instead, he started going after my mother.

When I got home, she was sprawled out on the floor, blood running from her nose and a bruise on her cheek. Ralph was standing over her with his hands still clenched into fists. When I saw, her I ran to her. He backed off, and I heard the back door slam as he left the house.

"What's going on?" I asked. I helped her to her feet.

"You don't concern yourself with what goes on between a woman and her man," she said. "It's private business."

"We can't keep letting him treat us like this," I said. "He's going to end up killing one of us."

"I shouldn't have made him angry. He really does love us you know. He doesn't know how to show it, that's all."

"That's bullshit, and you know it. He's crazy." I helped clean her bloody nose. She seemed more concerned about the blood on her blouse than what was coming out of her.

"This shirt is ruined. It was my best one, too." She fussed at the stain.

"Why are you ignoring me when you know I'm right?" I asked, but she kept wiping at the shirt. "I think we should go."

"What?" she said shaking her head. "We aren't going anywhere."

"It's We should leave him. Go away and never look back."

She slapped my face then. I stared at her, stunned. It was the first time she had ever struck me. She understood the significance of that slap and turned away from me.

"He's a good man," she said as if she was trying to convince herself of this. "He takes care of us. Without him, we would have nothing. Is that how you want to live?"

"Anything is better than this," I said defiantly.

"I can't listen to this." She left me standing in the bathroom holding the rag with her blood on it. I wasn't aware of this fact yet, but this would be my last night under that roof.

After dinner, I went to my room to digest my venison in private. In the living room, I could hear my mother talking. I went to the door and opened it a crack.

"Something's got to be done," she was saying. "He's talking about leaving again, and I just don't know what to do about it."

I closed the door feeling as though I had been punched. My own mother turned me in. My head swam. It didn't take long to get over the shock, however. Ralph stormed down the hall and kicked my door in. I flew back from the force and landed half on my bed. Ralph grabbed me by my leg and dragged me out into the living room.

My mother pretended not to see what was happening.

Ralph hit me repeatedly in the face. One eye swelled shut. My lip split. When I couldn't take any more hits to the face, he moved to my stomach. The pain was so severe I thought something inside me had exploded. I writhed and groaned, barely able to stay conscious. And just when I was sure I could take no more, salvation came in the form of two pit bulls.

The back door burst in, and the dogs charged into the house. Frankenstein was the first to get his teeth into Ralph. Ghost wasn't far behind. As Frankie bit down on Ralph's wrist, pulling him off me, Ghost bit into his leg. When I was free, I scrambled out of the way.

Ralph used his free hand to pull out the gun in his waistband and shot Frankenstein in the head. The dog flew back and landed on the floor with a final thud. I stared with my one good eye, dumbfounded as his brains leaked out onto the dirty hardwood floor. Even before I had time to register what was happening, Ralph turned the gun on Ghost and shot him in the side. Ghost yelped and released Ralph's leg. Ralph leveled the weapon at Ghost's head.

I charged. I hit him in the midsection, but not before the gun went off, killing Ghost. After the bullet left the chamber, the gun went flying as Ralph went down under my weight. His hit head the floor with a satisfying crack. I scrambled off him and reached for the gun, so did he. I got to it first and leveled it on him. He froze.

Tears poured from my eyes as I glanced around at the two dead dogs. My finger itched to pull the trigger. Instead, I backed out of the living room, went into my mother's bedroom and located something I thought might be expensive. I grabbed up a jewelry box and walked back into the living room, stuffing the prize into a pillowcase. I said nothing as I pointed the gun at Ralph. I walked around him and out the front door. As I was leaving, I heard him say no matter where I went he would hunt me down. I didn't care. When I was out of sight of the house, I threw the gun into the sewer.

I ran. As I was running, I pulled the box out and emptied the contents into my pockets. I tossed the box and the pillowcase away. I ran until I thought my legs would just break off, and I would go rolling down the street, nothing but a torso and a head.

I wasn't sure where I was running to, but I was no longer in my own neighborhood. I couldn't believe there were neighborhoods worse than mine until I found myself in one. I walked between thick pillars holding up the train rails above my head. I managed to get a couple hours of sleep sitting there, but when people started showing up around me, I stood and walked on.

I was either walking in the wrong direction or the right one depending on how you looked at it because the longer I walked, the more decrepit the streets became. There was colorful and expressive graffiti on the rundown buildings. There were many empty buildings with boards covering broken out windows. Everywhere I looked were obscene words and pictures spray painted on walls. I stopped when I saw a restaurant with people inside eating.

I felt the lump in my pockets, wondering if—in all that costume jewelry—there was something worth enough money to buy a hot meal.

"You hungry, kid?" A voice behind me asked. I turned around and confronted a man wearing a dirty wife-beater and grease stains all up and down his pants. "Wow, that's some shiner you got there," he said when he saw my face.

"I am hungry," I admitted.

He took my face gently in his hands and examined me. "I'm gonna get you cleaned up," he said. "I think I could use a kid like you in my organization."

He took me into the restaurant bathroom and cleaned my face. He was careful not to touch my bruises or open any cuts that had already scabbed over. When I was somewhat presentable, he took me back to the restaurant and ordered me bacon and eggs with toast and orange juice. I gobbled up the meal like a man who'd never seen food before.

"So," he said as I ate. "I will help you out, but do you have anything to trade?"

Stopping only briefly from shoving food into my mouth, I pulled the mounds of trinkets and jewelry out of my pockets and placed them on the table. I resumed cramming the food into my open maw.

The man, Michael, glanced over the items placed in front of him. "Junk," he said, "garbage. No good; junk; junk."

"Well, what's this?" he said and pulled out an engagement ring from the strings of fake pearls and cheap bracelets. He scratched it across the window next to him, and it left a mark in the glass. "This is actually worth something."

"It's yours," I said. "Could I have some more?" I held up my plate.

He stopped admiring the ring and looked at me. He ordered more food, and when that was gone, we left the restaurant. In about six months, I would be back at that same restaurant eating a burger and fries and trying to talk a vampire into letting me join him, but I'll get to that.

Michael took me back to the motel he worked out of and introduced me to the other boys. They were all about my age, and they were all handsome and thin… and hungry. They were all runaways like me. They were trapped in a world I was about to get ensnared in as well. At that particular moment, I didn't care what I was in for as long as I was away from Ralph and his murderous tirades. Michael informed me of the rules.

"I set you up with clients. I tell you which room the client will be waiting in and you will go to that room and do whatever the client asks of you. Wake up at six thirty. Breakfast at seven. Lunch is at 1:00 p.m. and dinner, is at 6:00 p.m. You're free to roam during the day, but you will want to rest as much as you can. Some clients can be quite tiring." He grinned knowingly at the other boys, and they nodded agreement.

After Michael left the room, I turned to the other boys. "What is it these clients want us to do, exactly?" I asked.

One boy stared at me for a long time, sizing me up, and then said: "Use your imagination, newbie."

I was not in a good place, no one could ever deny that—me especially—but I was off the Ralph Radar and that was a good thing. It was about a month into my new purpose when I asked Michael if it was possible for me to sit out one night. I wasn't feeling up to entertaining that night. He gave me a look of pity mixed with disgust, and then he slapped me with the back of his hand. I was grateful it didn't leave a mark. But then that was the plan, wasn't it? I had just healed from my beating at home, and I was one of the more attractive boys; so, messing up my face was not good business. He only meant to get his point across.

"Do not presume to tell me how to run my business," he said.

I ran off to join the others.

But do you want to know something? That old softy did precisely what I asked and gave me the night off.

The only adult supervision I had was Michael. The pimp's breath smelled of stale beer and rotten meat. When he smiled the skin on his wrinkled, unshaven face stretched over his rotted teeth in a purely repulsive mask. His beady black eyes seemed to be looking in two different directions but never directed at you. His stained and dingy wife-beater rode up over his fat, hairy belly, and he rubbed a hand over the exposed flesh. "Got a special client lined up for you: asked for you personally," he said to me one day.

I walked past the nauseating pimp, without looking at him, to the motel room Michael indicated. The room was dark as I entered. I could hear heavy breathing and could see a dark form in the recliner at the back of the room, past the bed.

"Turn on the light," the figure said. I thought I recognized the voice. My heart raced, and all I could hear in the dark and quiet room was the blood pounding in my ears.

"Turn on the light," the shadowy figure said again. I reached out and put my hand on the light switch, but I didn't flick it just yet. Something was telling me not to; something told me to run out the door and keep running. But that was a bad idea, too. Michael would catch me, and the punishment would be severe. Against all reason, I clicked on the light.

The shadowy figure came into view. Stunned, I fell back against the door, dropped into a crouch on the floor. I started to cry, turning from a streetwise youth into a helpless child in an instant.

"I told you I'd find you, boy." It was Ralph.

I reached back and tried desperately to locate the doorknob. My stepfather stood and came toward me. I worked to get my fear under control. My only concern now was getting the door open and getting away from the murderous man coming at me. Nothing Michael did could match the brutality Ralph would show me.

"You're coming home," he said, almost sounding sincerely concerned. "Your mother is worried sick." Then he finished with a snake's venom: "You selfish little bastard."

I saw the steel-toed boot bearing down at my head. In the next few seconds either the door would open, or the foot would connect with my head, and it would all be over anyway. But the door did open, and I rolled through the gap just as the boot came down.

I rose to my feet and ran, but even before I could get out of the circle of light cast by the overhead streetlamp, Michael grabbed me by the back of the shirt. I flew backward and crashed into the fat belly. I looked around for help, but all the other boys were in their assigned motel rooms. There was no help. I fell to my knees in front of Michael. I winced when Michael's meaty palm flew up over his head. I prepared for a beating the likes of which neither my jaw nor the hand, had ever felt. I turned my head, not wanting to see it coming.

When the strike didn't come, I looked up at Michael. I saw the glint of silver seconds before Michael gasped in pain. His hand dropped to his side, and he tried to turn, but he couldn't. He was only able to turn around after Ralph pulled the eight-inch hunting knife out of his back. Michael stared in shock and horror as the blade arced down and plunged into his heaving chest. He gaped at the green and black hilt. I watched as the knife moved with Michael's still beating heart.

Then Ralph yanked the serrated blade from the pimp's chest with a grunt. An atrial spurt splattered his evil face. Michael's heart must have stopped then because he dropped to the ground like a stone. His killer reached down and grabbed me by the hair, dragging me back to the motel room.

"I'm going to kill you, boy, but not before I have my fun with you first." I don't know if he meant to torture me or something even more sinister.

The door to the motel stood ajar, but he picked me up by the back of the shirt and the seat of my pants and threw me through the closed window to the left of the door. Glass and wood splinters blew inward as my head crashed through the window's grid. I could feel small slivers of glass piercing the palms of my hands as I tried to protect my face. I landed on the floor in a bloody heap. The maniac passed through the doorway and picked me up off the floor. He heaved me onto the bed. My head slammed into the wooden post. As the room began to spin and go dark, I saw him advancing on the bed, shedding his pants as he approached.

"You'll scream with what I plan to do to you before I kill you—"

What he said beyond that I don't know because I passed out.

Sometime later, I woke to semi-darkness. I still lay on the bed where Ralph had thrown me. My head throbbed and my palms hurt where the glass was still embedded in them. My stepfather lay on the bed next to me. His face was inches from mine, blocking most of my view. Ralph had an odd look in his eyes; was he using his eyes to plead with me, begging for my help?

I ignored my throbbing head and bleeding palms and sat up.

I dove off the bed then and stumbled backward against the wall. I would have clawed through the plaster if I could.

I saw a man sitting on Ralph's chest. The man's head was down, so all I could really see was the hump of his back. After my thudding heart slowed, I could hear something else in the room: a moist sucking sound. Then the sucking stopped, and the man straddling Ralph sat up. He turned toward me. The man's eyes glowed red as if a film of blood covered them. His lips were smeared with red, and it dripped from his teeth. With a hysterical laugh, I realized it was Ralph's blood.

"Vampire," I said in a whisper that was more awe than fear.

The stranger climbed off the bed and licked his bloody lips. He straightened his clothes. He wore a light blue button-up shirt, relax-fit jeans and a pair of Italian loafers. I was only dimly aware that the man's blood-soaked eyes had cleared, and piercing light gray eyes appeared. I approached cautiously, studying the eyes that had changed so drastically. It was as if they had been filled with blood, and then were suddenly drained.

The stranger studied me for a moment and then stepped forward. He took my bleeding hands into his own. Abruptly, the stranger placed his mouth over the wounds on my palms, and sucked at the cuts, spitting out shards of glass. When he was sure I was free of all the glass slivers, he pulled me to the bathroom, located a first aid kit and wrapped the cuts.

"Is there somewhere for you to go?"

At first, I found it hard to speak, but after catching my breath, I managed to croak out a reply. "Take me with you."

He told me "no" once again.

"I have nowhere to go. Take me with you. I will die if you don't."

He said, "You will die if I do."

At first, I didn't understand. Then he turned toward Ralph.

"You won't kill me. Else, you'd have done it already."

"Your stepfather was my third infusion," he said. "I do not need any more blood tonight. If that were not the case, I could very well have fed on you next."

"I don't believe that," I said defiantly.

He had a charming smile. "Believe what you wish."

"I believe you will take me with you." I laughed. How could he continue to say no to me? I'm adorable—or so I've been told—and it's hard to say no to me.

He said, "You should go back to your mother."

"She brought that into my life." I pointed to the open bathroom door at Ralph. I saw something that shocked me. I stood, headed into the bedroom again. Ralph was sitting up, looking at me. "He's not dead," I said.

His neck had been torn open and didn't look like any vampire bite I'd ever seen in the movies. A trickle of blood oozed from the ripped skin, but it didn't seem life-threatening.

"I didn't completely drain him, and he has a strong will to live," the vampire said. "But he does not have enough blood to sustain his life. I must decapitate him to keep him from coming back. It's the only way."

I climbed onto the bed. I looked over at the hunting knife lying in the folds of sheets. Ralph stared at me with glossy eyes—begging eyes. Please save me, those eyes said. I leaned down closer to him.

I whispered softly, thinking of the years of torture, pain, and fear I endured at his hands. "What is it you always said? It's a dangerous world out there, you should have been careful."

I picked up the hunting knife. His eyes filled with tears. I dropped the knife away from his neck. When he saw me backing down, a steely resolve replaced the tears. He whispered to me then. Coward. He glared at me with the hate he had always shown toward me.

He wanted me to do it.

And so I did; I sliced through his neck, hesitantly at first. But soon the knife hit bone, and I made the final push to the spine. I felt a sick sense of dread and couldn't cut any further. But I had done it and had shown Antony I could be his assistant. Antony had to finish the job. I turned away, but when I hear the spine crack, I retched and ran to the bathroom to throw up. He didn't show me any judgment for that, though.

He didn't bother looking at Ralph's body. "You cannot come with me," he said.

My shoulders slumped, defeated. My stomach must have growled then; because the vampire gave me an inquisitive look.

"You are hungry," he said. "Let me buy you something to eat. We will talk."

He took me to the corner restaurant and bought me a burger and fries. We sat in a corner booth and talked in hushed tones. He told me his name and explained the details of his existence. He required at least eighteen quarts of blood every night upon waking at sundown. If this quantity was not reached, he entered a state of confusion and could attack anything—or anyone—in the vicinity. At that point, a choice was off the table for any vampire.

"You're really a vampire." I couldn't stop looking at his protruding fangs. "How can no one see what you are?" I looked around. No one even seemed to know we existed. No one cared who we were, or what we were doing there.

"Yes, I am a vampire. I will never get sick, I will never grow old, and I will never die; assuming I keep my head, that is."

I chuckled at this, but I could tell he hadn't meant what he said as a joke. My laugh turned into a nervous cough. "Can the sun kill you?" I asked. "Like in the movies?"

He said it could. I asked him how many vampires were in the world.

"Very few," he said. "We are territorial, and if another vampire invades your territory, the turf war is usually bloody and costly—to both vampire and prey."

I asked: "Do vampires ever work together?"

"Yes," he said. "We team up all the time. We take mates, as well; although not for the same reasons humans do. Vampires take a mate for the comfort of having someone lying next to them during the death sleep."

"What's death sleep?" I asked.

"It is what vampires refer to when they sleep during the daylight hours."

"Oh." I was too fascinated to say much more.

He continued. "We also join alliances and can work together for a common cause. A colony of ten or twelve vampires can take out an entire army."

"Are you...?" I took a moment before asking the next question.

"Go on." Antony urged me on with that handsome face.

"Are you evil?" I said.

Antony smiled; it was precisely the question he was expecting, I could tell. He explained that evil was in the act, not the individual. He believed religious fanatics came up with the notion of good and evil to justify their own actions.

"Let me hunt for you," I said it with such conviction, I practically growled it.

Antony cocked an eyebrow.

I went on while I had his attention. "I can be your daytime lookout; I can scour the streets for just the right victims, read newspapers, and search the internet. By the time you wake at dusk, we can have your night planned out. It can't be easy looking for prey all the time. You need me."

Antony seemed to think about this. Then he said no.

"Yes, please let me do this. I know it could work. I want—I need to be in your life. Please, I'm begging you. Take me in... or..."

"What I said next almost ruined my chances with Antony.

"Make me like you. Make me a vampire. We can hunt together, as equals."

Antony flinched. Or perhaps he had jumped to his feet but sat back down again so fast that he only seemed to.

Despite his refusals, he did take me in. He was lonely and looking for company. He wanted me to join him. It was why he let me see him in the first place.

Ralph found me when the diamond ring showed up in a police raid on a pawn shop in the neighborhood where I was working for Michael. It didn't take him long to track me down after that. Years after Ralph's death, my mother remarried, I had learned. I found that out in the same article I discovered my mother had declared me dead in absentia. She took out an insurance policy on me when I was young, and the only way she could collect is if I was legally dead.

I think about her sometimes, but I don't miss her. She hadn't been a perfect mother, and I can't seem to bring myself to really care what she's doing with her life. Someday I might forgive her for what she has done to me, but right now I'm better off without her, and she's better off without me. I'll leave it at that."

Maggie stared at David for a long time. Tears glistened in her eyes. She reached out, and he thought she was going to hug him, but she turned away instead. She turned back, blinking away her tears.

"Thank you for sharing your story with me." She placed a hand on the lump caught in her throat.

Chapter Seven

Sarah Winston drove home from work around 5:15 p.m., stopping once to gas up her Jeep Cherokee. She pulled into her driveway and casually locked her vehicle using the key fob. She used her house key to unlock the front door and stepped inside. She looked around the living room, admiring and cherishing its cleanliness and beauty before the rush. Soon, her husband or her kids would burst through the door, destroying everything in their path.

She rushed to the kitchen and started pulling ingredients out to make dinner. As she kneaded the eggs, panko breadcrumbs, and raw hamburger into meatloaf, she thought of how she might approach the subject to her husband that her boss planned on giving her a promotion. Should have been good news, except the new job was in Texas, and they would have to move. She was sure her husband would be okay with this news, but the kids would be furious. She was elbow deep in the raw ground beef when she heard the door swing abruptly open then closed again. She listened to the book-laden knapsack hit the floor, and then the Converse high-tops being kicked off and crashing into the wall. Moments later, her boy scurried into the kitchen.

Randal Winston scuffed along the floor in stocking feet to the fridge and opened the door. He stared into the cold interior of the appliance for several seconds before deciding to ask, "What do we have to snack on?"

"Apples, carrots, kiwi..."

Randal slammed the refrigerator door. "Mom."

"Okay, there are Hot Pockets in the freezer."

"Make them for me?"

Sarah showed him her meat covered hands, but he had already hurried away. She listened as the boy stomped his way up the stairs. Sarah shook her head. As if whispering a secret to the meatloaf, Sarah said ""He's only one child, and yet he's like a herd of Clydesdales thundering through my house."

She sighed; of course, she would cook Hot Pockets for him.

Randal was thirteen with his mother's jet-black hair and blue eyes. He had a peppering of small brown freckles across his cheeks and his nose. As his mother entered his room with two Hot Pockets on a paper plate, she wrinkled up her own freckled nose.

"Smells like a locker room in here. Put those dirty socks in the laundry chute. Don't fill up on this junk. Dinner will be ready at seven."

It was fall, and the sun was due to set at 6:43 p.m.

Cindy, Randal's sister, came home next. She breezed into the house, ran up the stairs, and closed the door to her room down the hall. Randal barely registered her presence as he continued dodging zombies on the Xbox 360, waving the controller to force it to his will. Sarah's husband, Thomas, walked into the house not long after Cindy. Sarah called her children down to dinner.

Randal pressed "pause" on the game controller and rushed down the stairs. He was the first one at the dinner table. After a bit of coaxing from Sarah, and much protesting from Cindy, the seventeen-year-old staggered from her room, stomped down the stairs, and plopped down at the dining table in a boneless heap.

She huffed.

"I'm not even hungry," she said.

Her father glared at her from the head of the table.

As Sarah made the first cut into the steaming meatloaf, the front door burst open with a crash. Sarah screamed, and Thomas popped up from his chair. He turned toward the intrusion. Sarah dropped the knife she was holding and pulled Randal closer to her in a protective stance. Everyone stared dumbly at the stranger standing in their doorway.

The man standing there was six and a half feet tall, wearing a ratty old gray trench coat, black trousers, and black cowboy boots. In his fist, he held a cane—no, not a cane—a staff: a wooden rod almost as tall as the man with a knob of ivory at its top as big as a baseball. The intruder entered the house and closed the door behind him.

"What the hell." Thomas Winston rushed to confront the intruder. He reached for the trench coat's collar.

Faster than the human eye could see, the ivory head of the staff sent Thomas to the floor, unconscious and bleeding.

The House filled with screams.

###

Randal's heart pounded painfully in his chest as he watched the intruder step over his father's limp form. He blinked, and the man was no longer standing near his dad. He turned and watched as this stranger tied his mom's arms to the chair. Randal stood, and took a step toward his mother, but the stranger used his staff to shove Randal back down in the chair. Randal stared at his shaking hands when this man tied Cindy to the chair around her waist.

The stranger then tied a rope around Randal's neck at one end, and to his belt at the other. The man dragged Randal, choking and crying, through the room to where Thomas lay. Randal, driven to the floor face first, could not see what was going on. A framed family portrait fell from a stand and smashed to the floor. He reached out and crammed the picture into his pocket.

The intruder glanced up at Randal's sister and mother. They cried, screamed, and struggled against their bindings.

When Randal was able to move, he turned to face his dad.

"You will taste so good," the intruder moaned, then dropped down to straddle dad.

Thomas opened his eyes and looked around as if trying to figure out where he was. He seemed to become aware of the stranger hovering over him and struggled against the attacker. Dad's blows were as useless as wind. He stiffened when the stranger bit into his neck. Randal watched as his father went limp. He stared numbly at the floor where his father's blood seeped into the carpet.

The intruder stood, lifted Randal's dead father into his arms and sucked feverishly at the wound. With an exhalation of satisfaction, he released the body to the floor and used the back of his hand and wiped the blood from his mouth. "Good stuff."

Randal, unable to run away, watched as the intruder turned to mom and Cindy.

The man dragged Randal to where his mother and sister were bound. From his kneeling position, he stared through the legs of the table at what had become of his father. Pulling his eyes away from his father, Randal watched as Cindy became the next target.

Cindy's cries stopped as the monster dragged a sharpened fingernail across her throat. Holding her head up by her hair, he leaned over and commenced lapping up blood from the wound as if drinking from a fountain. He caught as much of the flowing blood as he could, but much of it spilled down his face.

As the blood slowed to a trickle, Cindy's eyes lost any sign of life. The intruder released the hair, and she dropped to the table. Her head rolled to the side and landed on her arm, making her seem as if she had merely laid her head down to rest. The only thing disrupting that illusion was the blood puddling onto the table around her head and dripping to the floor.

The intruder straightened, pulling Randal onto his feet. Hefting Randal under his arm like a football, the stranger moved on his mother. Randal barely registered the movement, but the intruder now straddled mother, the man's knees pointing behind her as he faced her. She screamed out in pain. The intruder dropped Randal on the floor next to him and lifted his mother's chin, looking into her eyes.

The stranger slowly dropped his gaze to Randal. Sarah's terror-filled eyes followed the attacker's gaze to him. She struggled to cry out, to defend him, but the man's powerful grip squeezed her jaw shut and she couldn't move her mouth.

The stranger looked back at her. He smiled weakly, with mock sympathy. She panted frantically, tears streamed down her cheeks.

"I'm going to keep him," he said. "It makes me happy to look at him, so I think I'm going to make him a pet. I'm going to give him the gift."

Her face grew crimson, and she struggled violently against her ropes. "He's only a child." She spoke with her jaw clenched shut. She struggled against the intruder on her lap with a fierceness that made the man laugh. She had almost managed to throw him off. Spittle flew from her lips as she struggled. "Hurt him over my dead body."

"That's the plan." The stranger's eyes sparkled with glee. He leaned down, and his fangs slipped into her neck. She struggled, valiantly at first, but her struggles soon weakened, and then ended altogether as she gave her final breath.

The man sat back. "I didn't waste a drop of her blood." He turned his attention to Randal once again. "Now it's your turn."

But Randal wasn't listening. He couldn't stop looking at his mother. Her head hung limply to the side. Her dead eyes were still open, staring at him. His shock was so great that when the man began speaking, he barely understood the words.

"I don't want them to come back, so I'm going to destroy them. I'm going to cut off their heads and then burn the house to the ground—but you I will not destroy. I'm going to keep you. I will drain you, and you will die, but then you will turn. We will roam the night looking for fresh blood, you and me. We will live together forever… or until I grow bored of you. Would you like that?"

Randal didn't react. He stared at his mother, concentrating on her face, unwilling to forget what she looked like. He remembered the picture in his pocket and hoped his captor didn't find it and take it away.

The man gave Randal a loving smile, exposing his fangs and, with a large rough hand, caressed Randal's cheek. He reached up to where the stranger had touched him. His hand came down, red with his mother's blood. Randal closed his eyes when the attacker leaned over and bit into the tender flesh of Randal's neck.

Chapter Eight

Maggie sat up in bed, gasping. She struggled to catch her breath after seeing the attack in her vision, she felt as though she'd been the woman who was killed.

As Maggie stepped through the bedroom door, she drew David and Antony's attention. They had been gathered around the table, going over their plan, but turned in her direction when she approached. Maggie had been sleeping for about two hours but was now wide awake. She joined them at the table.

"He's close," she said. "He's killed another family. Only this time he has a… a hostage."

"A hostage?" David asked.

"Well, not a hostage. His exact words were 'a pet.' He drained a small boy with the intentions of turning him into a vampire. He tied a rope around the child's neck like a leash."

Antony closed his eyes. "The child will have to be euthanized." He opened his eyes and focused on Maggie. "By the time this beast is stopped, the boy will have gone mad and will be extremely dangerous."

Maggie, saddened by this news, but unclear how else to proceed, said nothing.

Antony saw the anguish in Maggie's eyes, so he continued. "Please understand, even if he is not insane, he will not have the strength or the ability to hunt. Child vampires do not have the same abilities and advantages as an adult vampire, and his canines will not grow in for a long time."

"What do you mean?" Maggie asked.

"Vampire canines do not just magically appear, nor can they be summoned at will. They grow in after the change—sometimes within a few months, but typically it takes up to a year. Until then, vampires use razors or needles to extract their blood meal. Biting through flesh with flat teeth just makes a mess."

Maggie nodded as if she had made up her mind about something.

"I'm going to save him," she said.

Antony looked at Maggie curiously, wondering if she had heard anything he had just said. She clarified.

"I understand that he will be dangerous, but until we know that he's beyond hope, I want to try and save him. Promise me you won't destroy him unless there's no other choice."

"He may not survive the encounter, anyway," David said. "When we go after the vampire, we may not survive the encounter."

"Promise me," she said again, and this time she was talking to both of them.

They promised.

Antony said, "Do you know when he attacked this latest family? And can you pinpoint where?"

"It just happened," she said. She pulled a map out of a drawer and circled the vicinity where the attack occurred.

Antony studied the circle she had drawn on the map. It was quite a big area. "Can you narrow it down more?" he asked.

"Yes," she said. "Just follow the fire trucks."

Chapter Nine

There was barely a charred shell left of the house by the time they arrived. Blackened, windowless panes dripped with moisture from the fire hoses. Small tendrils of smoke reached up to the night sky where the burning remains still held just that little bit of heat. The trio moved closer to the wrecked building. All bodies had been removed from the premises, and the rescue vehicles were mostly gone. Only a few onlookers remained in the vicinity, with only one or two police officers around to finish the investigation. If anyone noticed the Zephyr's approach, they were not concerned.

Maggie stared intently at the house, trying to get some kind of reading from it on the vampire, or the child. She turned away, distraught and overwhelmed. She sagged against David, exhausted from the emotional toll the images of the house hammered at her. David held her. She turned to him and hugged him, burrowing her head into his neck. She began to cry.

"I can't do it." She groaned, defeated. "I can't stay here. It's too much. We have to go."

After a minute, her sobbing subsided, and David led her back to the Zephyr. She lay down on the bed to rest, and David drove back to their campsite. She cried, disappointed with herself for not obtaining the information they needed.

With the Zephyr parked for the night, David and Antony sat at the table and talked.

David said, "What should we do if we can't locate the vampire?"

"We will not give up. We will be there to stop him when he makes a mistake."

"How many more people will have to die before we finally catch him?" David didn't expect an answer, and he got none.

Toward the end of the night, just as Antony was about to retire to his steel box under the table, Maggie woke and joined them in the small kitchen of the mobile home. She seemed rested and energetic, and ready to fight.

"I can't track him," she said. "Maybe because of his age or maybe because he feels no emotion; I don't know. But..." She paused and smiled. "I can track the boy."

Chapter Ten

Jake Shields was a lonely kid, and school was not easy for him. He was fourteen and pimple-faced. He was tall and skinny—lanky, his grandfather called him—and he wore glasses. Kids at school bullied him, calling him names with fierce intensity. They called him the usual names such as four-eyes and queer, but there were crueler names as well. Once, in English class, he had written a paper where the words "does not" had been separated improperly to read "doe snot." The teacher corrected this in red ink. Another student saw this correction and started calling him Doe Snot. The name stuck.

But probably the one name that bothered him the most was Bird Boy. The other boys chose this name for him because of his long thin nose, and because a boy in the gym locker room commented that his flat white chest and stomach looked just like a bird's. Suddenly the name Bird Boy had replaced Doe Snot. Kids in the hallway would see him coming and squawk, "Bird Boy is coming."

He loathed the name, not because of this negative attention, but because it was a slight on his personal imperfections. These were physical traits about which he was very self-conscious. He wanted to be strong and physically fit but just hadn't been blessed with those specific traits.

But as Jake stood in his room looking at himself in the full-length mirror, none of that mattered. Jake did have one trait that made him proud. Although his hair was always greasy no matter how much he washed it, and his pimply face oozed, he at least knew how to dress. He pressed all wrinkles from his clothes. He tucked his shirt in and admired his perfect gig line. A gig line was the invisible line the clothes made when the tie, shirt buttons, and fly all lined up seamlessly. Though he may have been ugly, he was a snappy dresser.

Jake also kept his room as clean and orderly as his wardrobe. This pleased his mother.

And although no school kids called him a friend, to say Jake had no friends was not entirely accurate. He had no friends at school, but once he sat in his computer chair and turned on the computer, he had many friends. In fact, he had three hundred and forty-six to be exact. Jake was the guild master of a very popular and productive guild in an online game. Tonight, he and his online friends were about to lead a raid on the enemy stronghold. Jake was now a level eighty-five undead hunter named Toade.

The hunter and his pet tarantula, Leggs, as well as twenty-five others, were about to go after the enemy faction's king. As Jake donned his headset to talk with the other players via a Ventrilo server, he decided it was going to be an excellent night. What Jake didn't know was that he was about to have visitors, and before he could make it through the enemy's castle, he and his family would be dead.

Chapter Eleven

He woke to darkness. And hunger. The hunger burned like hot ash in his guts, but it didn't seem to stop there. The heat seemed to rip through his veins. He could smell the food he needed to quench this all-consuming, fiery hunger somewhere in the air, but it was far away. It was out there somewhere waiting for him. The food he craved with such ferocity smelled like coppery soup. The rich, thick broth called to him like a dinner bell ringing inside his head.

Something stirred beside him, and he realized for the first time that he was not alone in the darkness. There was movement, and a latch clicked. Momentarily, another lock was thrown, and then a creaking of old hinges as the lid above him rose. He was inside a coffin, and the light that flooded over him felt like hot lava burning his eyes. He squirmed away from it.

"It's only lamplight and cannot hurt you, boy." The speaker's whispered breath brushed at his ear, and the voice was unfamiliar.

After realizing he was not harmed by the light, the boy climbed out of the coffin. He still craved the source of that enchanting scent, but he was also confused by the unfamiliar surroundings. He looked around the room and spotted the door a few yards away. Beyond the door, he saw stairs leading up, perhaps to safety. He rushed for the door and managed to come within a few inches of the steps beyond the threshold, but then was tugged back. He landed in a sprawling heap at the feet of the one who had shared the coffin with him. The man laughed. Confused and embarrassed, the boy reached up and touched the rope around his neck.

The rope was tight, but there was no feeling of strangulation. The stranger had given him the gift, and now he no longer needed air. The line was merely to keep him from wandering off. The other end was attached to the stranger's waist. The man looked down at him with a smile that had no humor in it. The boy turned away to escape his captor's piercing eyes and that twisted snarl.

"You will call me Dark Father." The stranger scowled. "I have rules. You must obey them without fault, or I will destroy you. Rule number one is don't talk back. If you talk back when I give an order, I'll destroy you. Number two: don't look directly at me. Look away whenever speaking to me. If I catch you looking at me, I'll destroy you. Rule number three is to speak only to me. If I catch you speaking to our victims—or any strangers for that matter—I'll destroy you."

The vampire boy averted his eyes from the Dark Father. "I'm hungry."

The man ignored the complaint and continued. "This last is not so much a rule as information you need to know. I have an aversion to dots. They irk me and make me dizzy. Do not draw dots or make dot-like patterns of any kind. Do you understand these rules?"

When he nodded, the Dark Father dragged him up to the main floor of the house.

The boy looked around at the cathedral ceilings and the lavish artwork hanging from the walls. The house was a mansion, but it was in terrible disrepair. The old wallpaper was peeling, revealing the plaster underneath, and in many places, large chunks of plaster had crumbled away, leaving black cavities where anything could be lurking, watching, waiting.

He wasn't afraid, though. He remembered that in this new world he was the monster. There was nothing left for him to fear; even in this dark and dingy place where shadows lurked like living things and sounds echoed like lost souls calling out their woeful songs. The boy tried to get used to his new surroundings, but every time he tried to examine the furniture or the ornate paintings on the walls, the Dark Father pulled him away by the rope.

Father spoke to him, but the boy barely understood the words. He remembered that this strange man had promised the hunger would go away and he grew excited with the prospect of finally getting to eat. He was dragged by his rope through the streets at a speed that caused the scenery around them to blur into light and dark streaks, and there was sound; a harsh crackling sound like rocks being struck together. When Father halted, he would sniff the air. If nothing interested him, he would move on. They stopped at several houses before the man smelled something that pleased him enough to enter the house. He showed no fear of capture as he dragged the boy into the house behind him.

He looked around the living room. It was an ordinary room. It reminded the boy of the house he had once lived in, but that was before the Dark Father had entered his life. There were two large, fluffy brown recliners and a matching sofa. The walls were covered with large framed pictures of family members. One wall had a red brick fireplace built into it. On the mantle were trophies for bowling, hockey, baseball and other sports. On the other side of the room was an opening that led elsewhere. Beyond that was a stairway leading up.

From down the stairs, a young girl approached. She stopped and stared at him. She stared at the thick rope around his neck with a confused expression on her face. She glanced over at the strange man in the beat-up trench coat and understood she was in danger. She let out a short, frightened little gasp.

"Cindy?" The word was a mere whisper on his lips, but then the rope around his neck pulled him nearly off his feet, as the man took flight after the escaping girl that might have been Cindy but wasn't.

He tried to tell himself he didn't know anyone named Cindy. That the name held no meaning for him anymore.

Cindy was his sister, and he was Randal.

He felt himself gliding across the smooth, perfectly polished hardwood floor. The strange man had cornered the girl in the brightly lit, clean kitchen. He stood over the girl as she cowered, her opportunity to escape lost. The boy wanted to say, Run Cindy, run. But by the time she could get her frightened legs to move, it was already too late. The strange man reached out and pulled the girl to him. He ripped out her throat and drank the blood as it poured out of her. Randal no longer thought of the girl as Cindy. Now she was food.

"No." The Dark Father pulled the dying girl out of the boy's reach. Blood splashed across the floor from her wound like cheap wine. "She is not for you. You must wait until I allow you to feed."

The Dark Father removed a hand ax from his belt and decapitated the dead girl.

The sound of movement upstairs drew the man's attention away from the body. He dropped her to the floor and climbed the stairs, dragging the Randal behind him. The upstairs landing was carpeted, and Randal liked the feel of the plush carpeting under his bare feet. He looked down and saw with some distaste that he was leaving red smears on the tan carpet. He was tracking Cindy's blood through the house.

No, it wasn't Cindy.

A woman wearing an evening gown and fixing a shiny silver earring in her left ear stepped out of one of the rooms and screamed at the stranger coming down the hallway. The vampire was on her at once, and her scream died as quickly as it had begun. The Dark Father didn't share any of this delicious nectar, either. The vampire dropped the empty body on the floor, and Randal licked his lips when he saw that the neck wound was still oozing blood. He wasn't allowed even a taste, as the Father decapitated her and was moving again, dragging him like a tail.

The hallway turned at a forty-five-degree angle with the banister over the stairs, leading to another hall and a single door at the end. The man and his appendage walked down this hallway and pushed the door open to reveal a man sitting on the toilet in this room. His boxers were gathered around his feet. The startled man didn't know if he should stand or cover himself. He attempted to rise and at the same time lift his shorts. Randal caught a brief glimpse the man's genitals swinging between his legs before turning away. Daddy wouldn't want him to see that.

No, that was not Daddy. He had no Daddy, not anymore. Now he only had the Dark Father.

The startled man cursed and pulled his boxers up to his waist, but the vampire took him without even so much as a defensive blow. His struggles were useless anyway. When the man was drained, he fell back onto the toilet at an awkward angle where he hovered there for a moment, and then slipped to the floor in a heap.

The dead man was decapitated with the ax.

The Dark Father dragged the boy from the bathroom before he had a chance to reach the food. They moved as one back down the hallway to the top of the stairs. There was a door here the boy had not seen initially, but it was now being presented to him by the Dark Father, like a game show host revealing the grand prize.

The boy inched toward the door, and then a little more. He was suspicious because his every attempt to quench the burning hunger had been thwarted. He was afraid this was just another cruel joke being played on him.

The vampire pushed the door open, but before he had time to enter the room, he hissed and backed away from the door. The boy watched as the Dark Father fell backward and crab-crawled away from the doorway. He stopped when he saw how the boy was looking at him. The vampire stood and collected himself but didn't go near the room again.

"Dots," the vampire said in explanation. "I hate dots."

The boy merely stared dumbly at him.

The boy turned and looked into the room, at the black dots covering the wallpaper.

To the Dark Father, they were swirling and expanding, threatening to swallow him up. He turned his back on the room.

"Go ahead" Father urged the boy in a soft whisper. "I'll wait out here. The dots hurt my eyes."

The boy did not enter the room right away. He looked in and studied the surroundings. He spotted the boy sitting in front of a computer on the other side of the room, and finally, he understood. This other boy was about fourteen years old. He was tall and skinny and wore glasses. His head was turned away from the door and had not yet realized he was no longer alone in the room. The other boy had some kind of headset on.

The vampire boy studied the kid in the room for a long time. He turned and sought direction from the Dark Father.

Without looking into the room, the vampire said, "He's for you, my pet. Now you may feed."

###

Randal entered the room, and his vision turned blood red. The boy sitting in the room turned around now. He saw the strangers and stood. The headgear snapped back and landed on the floor. This caused a distraction that Randal used to act.

The vampire boy leaped, and with hunger driving him like fuel, he pulled the prey toward his open mouth, biting at the skin on the neck. Randal did not have fangs, and his flat teeth were useless. Although the taller boy was weaker and did not have the speed of a vampire, he did have something more potent going for him… adrenaline. He pushed Randal away. He stumbled backward and landed hard on his backside. He jumped back up and came at the boy again but could not get close enough to bite into the prey's neck. His teeth clicked together harmlessly out of reach.

His preternatural speed did not seem to be enough. He could snap the bones in his prey's arms if he could pin the wiry boy down. Just as he bit down on flesh, the weasel screamed in pain and shoved one last time, sending Randal sprawling.

He skittered across the floor. Behind him, he heard the familiar mocking laughter of the Dark Father. The prey had crawled into a space between his bed and the dresser. Randal let out a cry of frustration and fury that only fueled the mocking laughter from the Father. The boy turned to the man in the hallway. The Dark Father's trypophobia kept his eyes averted.

With a sudden and blinding joy, the Randal realized that, although the rope was still around his neck, it was no longer attached to the vampire's waist. Had he been released to hunt, or had the cord come loose by accident? It didn't matter. His missed prize was curled up on the floor, crying. Though the hateful hunger still burned like white fire in his belly, Randal ignored the prey, finding the thought of freedom much more alluring.

Without realizing what he was going to do until he did it, Randal bolted out the bedroom window. There hadn't been any movement the human eye could have detected. There was just the crackling sound—like a paper bag being crumpled—a warm breeze blew, and then the crash as the window smashed outward.

Randal flew through the night seeing everything in the reddish glow of his vampire haze. The people he passed were sometimes shocked, sometimes saddened (who would let such a small child wander the streets at night alone, they would think), but all who saw his blood-tinged red eyes were afraid. These people saw him gnashing his teeth and snapping at them like a wild dog. He tried to bite the people who reached out to help him, and the good deed was quickly forgotten. They pulled away before he could make contact. He scampered off, searching for the ever-elusive food source that seemed to be everywhere, but always out of his reach.

Randal came across a bum sprawled out on the dirty sidewalk, with empty soda cans and discarded fast food wrappers lying all around him like strange trophies. In one dirty hand, the bum held a bottle wrapped in a brown paper bag. Randal turned the hand over and, ignoring the grit, attempted to bite into the soft flesh of the man's dirty wrist. Fluid poured out of the bottle, which woke the man.

"Hey." The bum growled and pushed Randal away. "This is my Hazlitt. Go find your own."

Randal crawled away from the bum. The hunger throbbed in his veins like poison. He continued his search for relief from the powerful thirst, but no one seemed to be offering up their blood to him. After moving down several streets that held nothing but empty cars, Randal was finally rewarded with the bright lights of a shopping center, and he headed in the direction of the store full of hope, full of promise, full of people who were full of blood.

Chapter Twelve

Maggie screamed as she came out of the vision. After recovering from her fugue state, she blurted orders. "David, drive. I'll explain as we go, but we have to go now. Drive."

David didn't hesitate. He jumped into the driver's seat and started the Zephyr, pulled out onto the road and headed in the direction Maggie directed him. Maggie led him through the streets, using her intuition to guide them. When he was directed to a highway, David opened up the throttle and drove with reckless abandon. She pointed at the twenty-four-hour superstore on the left, and he pulled into the parking lot. The three jumped out and ran toward the entrance with Maggie in the lead. They passed through the sliding automatic glass doors, past the row of checkout lines, and stopped at the back of the store where the meat section was located. A group of people had gathered there, gaping at the boy Maggie had seen in her vision.

Antony was the first to react. He raced past the onlookers to the boy standing on top of the packages of raw steak in the meat cooler. The red-eyed boy was ripping into the containers of raw meat and drinking the liquid pooling in the plastic.

David pointed at the wild boy. "He's drinking the blood from the packages of meat."

Maggie shook her head. "That's not blood. It's myoglobin from the muscles."

Antony stepped forward. "It does not matter. Cow blood—or any animal blood, for that matter—won't satiate the hunger. He must drink directly from a living human source." He reached out, and the boy growled. He gripped the boy by the arm. The child bit down into the hand, but his flat teeth were no match for Antony's vampiric flesh.

"You're gonna need a rabies shot, mister," said a male voice in the crowd.

Antony reached out with his other hand and pulled the hemp rope up and over the boy's head. He tossed the line aside and lifted the boy into his arms. As the boy bit the hand holding him, Antony carried him out of the store and back to the Zephyr. Inside the Zephyr and away from the eyes of onlookers, Antony had a better time controlling the wild boy. He pulled his gnawed palm out of his mouth and held the squirming boy with his gnashing teeth out at arm's length until the need to thrash and fight subsided. The boy then lay still and lifeless, a grimy form sleeping soundly on the pristinely white sofa cushions.

Antony reached for the knife in its sheath on his belt.

"No." Maggie's voice was a mere whisper. "Please, you can't do that while he sleeps. We must give him a chance."

"We have to get him blood if we are not going to euthanize." Antony reluctantly replaced the knife back in the sheath.

They returned home, and Antony carried the unconscious vampire boy to the basement. There were three men locked away in the panic room, which had been Antony's nightly feeding regimen. He could hunt later. Antony opened the panic room and chose the nearest, wide-eyed and terrified form to the door. He pulled the squirming man—a serial rapist and a murderer—into the open area of the basement. The man's hands and feet were securely bound, and there was no danger of him escaping.

Antony stimulated the unconscious vampire by opening a wound in the prey's throat. Blood pumped out, and at the scent, the vampire boy's red-tinged eyes popped open. He saw Maggie first and flew at her with supersonic speed. Maggie cried out, and her hands flew up, but even before the sound left her lips, Antony had caught the boy and pulled him back to the bound man.

"No." Antony forced the boy to look at him as he spoke. "You must not harm anyone in this house unless they are dedicated to feeding us. You may feed on this man here." Antony directed the boy to look down at the prey. The boy salivated like a wild dog and moved closer to the wild-eyed man.

"Look into his eyes; can you see his deeds? This is how we choose our prey. They are the vile humans, the killers, and rapists."

The wild boy looked at Antony and then at the fearful man. The boy peered eye to eye with the prey. Unsure if any of his words were having an impact on the little vampire, Antony opened the man's throat with his own teeth and moved back. The boy latched onto the wound instantly. He sucked much too quickly at first, choking on the blood, and started over. This time, drank without difficulty. The boy finished the man off and looked around for more. Antony led the wild boy to the panic room and set him loose on the others stored there.

With a growl, using his bare, flat teeth without difficulty now, he tore open the throat of the first man in line.

"He loses more blood on the floor than he drinks."

Maggie stepped forward, peering in. She couldn't tell if Antony was disgusted by the act or amused by the boy's antics.

The child finished with the third victim and curled up in a corner. When Antony approached, the wild boy kicked and squirmed, struggling to get away from him. Antony backed off. He pulled the corpses out of the room.

Antony closed the steel door, and she heard the slurping sound of blood being licked off the floor.

Chapter Thirteen

The boy had gone out the window—right out the window—and into the big, dangerous world. His roped boy was out there somewhere. In his hands, he had another boy. During his flight back to the lair, he had crushed the boy's chest, effectively stopping the boy's heart. As he stared down at the still, limp form, he realized his error.

He dropped the dead boy on the floor and went out in search of his lost boy. He scoured the streets and abandoned buildings, but he did not find his little boy. He returned to his lair, dejected and irate. How had he been so stupid? And to make matters worse, he had killed the boy who could have been his pet's replacement. He growled.

Then another thought occurred to him: could he make a new pet from this dead boy? Would he drink from a corpse and revive it? He had never taken blood from a corpse, but what could it hurt to try? And what would the blood do to him? He decided to try. Anticipation raced through him as he leaned over the dead boy and bit into his neck. The blood was thick, clotted and cold. He spat the first two attempts onto the floor. Dead blood was not to his liking, but this wasn't about feeding. He was making history here.

So, he tried again. He had to suck hard, really hard, to make anything come out. He ripped the neck open wider to get the remaining blood to come out. The blood was foul, and he had to stop several times to keep from gagging. He smacked his lips and grimaced at the fullness. He pumped the chest to get the coagulating blood to flow out of the wound. He squeezed on the boy to get all the blood from the body.

He bit into each wrist, squeezing blood down from the shoulder. Then he bit into the inner thighs and drained the legs. When he was sure he had gotten all the blood possible, he tossed the corpse over his shoulder and carried it into the basement.

His lair was a large, four-story mansion in the Pocono Mountains at the end of a dirt road high atop a hillside looking down on the small valley town of Bear Creek Village to the east. To the west was a scenic view of the Lackawanna State forest. He only saw it at night, however, and he wasn't that impressed. He didn't care about the scenery. He merely wanted it for its seclusion. He treasured his privacy. And the occasional trespassing hooligan would soon learn the error of their ways when he caught them.

He married the old bitch who owned the land, drank from her, and brought her back. When he had sufficiently staked his claim to her money and her estate, he destroyed her. He never wanted her companionship, only her property.

The sun was coming up soon. He carried his corpse boy gently in his arms into the cold darkness of the coffin. He closed the lid and slept.

The following night when he rose, the boy did not. Feeling anger and disappointment, he left the corpse where it lay and went out to hunt.

He found a sweet little family of three and attacked, releasing all his fury and hate on the woman and her two sons. The boys were too old and not to his liking, so he didn't consider making either of them a new pet.

He returned to his lair and slept, waking the second evening to discover the boy still had not.

On the fourth night sleeping in the coffin with the corpse and having no faith that his new pet would rise with him, he decided he would have to destroy the body.

But this night the boy opened his eyes. His flesh was pale, gray and moldering. The skin puckered around the mouth and eyes. The eyes were milky orbs that held no color or irises. The fingernails were yellowed and chipped.

The boy would need food, he surmised; and when he went out and took his family that night, he brought back a streetwalker for his newest pet.

But the boy would not drink, could not. Even when he had slit the screaming, mad-eyed woman's throat and held the wound to his pet, the boy would not drink.

He decided his latest pet was no good. A rotting corpse boy was not a good pet, after all; so, on the morning of the boy's third day as a living corpse, he decided to put the boy out in the sunlight. He chained the boy to a tree in the backyard and retired to the coffin.

The following night he awoke and strode out to the tree where he expected to find a putrefying mess. Instead, he discovered that the boy was still there. The boy was intact and, although his rotting flesh had been visited by flies and maggots crawled through the skin in several places, he seemed unharmed.

He unchained the boy from the tree and pulled him back into the house. He released the chain around the boy's neck, and he just stood there. He seemed simple, stupid. The boy rubbed absently at the flesh on his cheek when a fly landed there. A glob of maggot-ridden skin peeled away, but moments later new, albeit rotten, tissue regrew.

He thought: I have a rotten corpse boy pet that does not eat but can still regenerate somehow. And he supposed he would have to get used to the smell.

"You will call me Dark Father," the man said to his new pet. He doubted the simpleton even understood him, and the boy didn't talk, so he supposed his pet wouldn't be calling him anything.

The boy was obedient and rarely moved unless directed to do so. The boy looked around but didn't seem to have much interest in what he saw. Only once did the boy react to his surroundings with any kind of sentience. The boy walked past a mirror, turned and looked at his own reflection. The boy reached out and touched the face in the mirror. As he pulled his hand away from the glass, he brought the withered hand back to touch his face and studied it as if looking at ants in an exhibit. Next, the corpse boy examined his ripped and dirty clothes. He brushed a clump of dirt off his pants, straightened a tie that wasn't there, and then dropped his hands and continued on his way as if nothing he saw held any interest for him. The Dark Father watched all this transpire and wondered what it meant. His curiosity was short-lived, however.

He slept with the boy even though his corpse boy did not need sleep. He just wanted his boy near him.

No rope was required for this boy.

The corpse boy earned a lot of freedom from the man. He was allowed the run of the property, which covered a ten-acre patch of land. As long as the corpse boy was in the house when the Dark Father slept, he no longer needed to be kept in the coffin during the day.

The corpse boy occupied his time catching flies, tearing off their wings and eating them. He also picked maggots and beetles off his skin and ate those. The corpse boy craved these bugs as a vampire wanted blood, and it was these bugs that gave his rotting skin the ability to regenerate. He did not tell Dark Father of this discovery, and when the man saw what the boy was doing to the insects, he forced him to stop. When the boy refused to stop eating the insects, the Dark Father used a machete to cut off the boy's hands. The hands dropped to the floor and burst into dust like the ashes flicked off the end of a cigarette.

The following night, the Dark Father woke to learn that the corpse boy's hands had regenerated. Not only had the rotting flesh returned, but also the bone and muscle. The vampire was intrigued; he couldn't do this. If his hands were cut off, they were gone. He could not reconstruct severed limbs. Why was this simple creature able to completely regenerate?

"I wonder what else you will grow back," he said and cut off the boy's legs.

The corpse boy sat in the corner looking at the two piles of ashes that had been his legs and learned he didn't have to actually eat the insects. He still caught and ate flies, spiders and other bugs that passed by him, but he noticed the maggots and beetles boring through his body were being absorbed by his rotting skin. He could forgo eating bugs, and maybe then his evil master would stop cutting off his body parts.

The Dark Father woke to learn the boy's legs had grown back.

Now the Dark Father was angry. He didn't have this ability, so why could this festering pile of pus do this regeneration thing? In a fit of anger, The Dark Father decapitated his corpse boy. He looked down at what he had done in horror. The head turned to ash, but the body was still intact. He placed it on the workbench. He would decide what to do with the rotting flesh another night. He hunted and slaughtered a new family with an anger and fervor that did not abate when he was finished. He didn't have time to kill any more that night, although he wanted to. He decapitated the three members of his latest family and returned to the mansion grumpy and unfulfilled. As he returned to the coffin, he stared at the headless corpse on the workbench. He missed his pet and hated his own impulsiveness.

But to his surprise, he woke the next night to learn the head had grown back.

"I can't seem to destroy you, my precious little thing," the Dark Father said.

He resolved to do one last experiment. On the workbench where the corpse boy sat, the Dark Father decapitated the boy with his machete. He then severed the arms and legs and cut the torso in half. With the boy's body parts in hand, the Dark Father dropped the corpse into a bonfire constructed in the backyard. He burned everything, then departed to hunt bums and streetwalkers. His need for blood satiated, he retired to his coffin. "A pity about the boy though." He pulled the lid closed. "Gone too soon."

###

On the table where the Dark Father had performed his evisceration of the corpse boy, a single scrap of rotten flesh twitched. The bit of flesh expanded and pulsed. Soon the lump of flesh grew from the size of a dime to the size of a quarter, then to the size of an orange. Within hours the corpse boy was back. He climbed off the table, picked up the machete and took it to the garage. This new corpse boy had an awareness of everything that had come to pass and could retrieve all the memories of what the Dark Father had done to him.

When the Father woke, he climbed out of the coffin and froze. The corpse boy sat in the corner of the basement staring at him.

The boy tossed a spider into his mouth as if it was a kernel of popcorn.

The Dark Father roared with laughter.

Part Three: Maggie

Chapter Fourteen

Maggie stood at the bottom of the stairs, and David stood in front of her, blocking her from the entrance to the panic room as Antony opened the door. Maggie waited patiently for Antony to tell her what was happening inside the room, but he only stared into the darkened space, saying nothing. She brushed past David and looked inside for herself. She saw the boy sitting calmly on the seat closest to the opening. David picked up the man lying at his feet, bound and gagged, and pulled him into the room. The boy stared down at the man kneeling before him. Without being told what to do, the vampire boy leaned over and peered into the eyes of his prey. He looked up at Antony and smiled. He nodded his head and then tore into the man's throat with a grinding bite of flat teeth. The man gave out a shuddering scream from behind his gag, but the skin finally broke, and the vampire drank. And drank. Once finished, he wiped the blood off his chin.

The bloodlust left the boy's eyes.

Antony said, "Amazing."

"What is?" Maggie didn't take her eyes off their little guest.

At the sight of her, the vampire boy lowered his gaze.

"It would appear he only requires one transfusion a night to sustain him," Antony said.

The vampire boy glanced over at Maggie again, then down at his hands. "I'm sorry." His voice was hoarse; it was the first time he had spoken aloud with his vampire vocal chords.

"You have nothing to be sorry about." Maggie tilted her head slightly. "What is your name?"

The boy paused. He glanced at Maggie, then away again. "Roped Boy." His words were nearly too inaudible for her to hear them. He tried again, louder this time. "Randal." He stood. "My name is Randal."

"Do you want to come out of there and join us, Randal?" Maggie asked. "And perhaps stay with us? We can take care of you here."

Randal thought a moment and then nodded.

Antony took Maggie by one shoulder so that she turned to him. "I will allow Randal into the group, but we must keep an eye on him for any sign of depravity. You must not be alone with him until I am sure he can be trusted."

He stopped and pulled his hand away from her. He seemed to have something more to say, so she waited.

"I have to be the one to deem him safe, not you."

She giggled. "You know me so well."

Antony went off to hunt, leaving David to watch Randal and Maggie.

Maggie and David took Randal to a room that she thought would be suitable. "The windows in this room have been bricked up, so no sunlight can get in. You can sleep here, in a bed. How does that sound?"

Randal inspected the windows. He nodded then sat on the bed.

"It's hard."

Maggie looked at David. But he only shrugged.

"We can replace it," she said. "Get you a softer one."

"No." He stood up and continued to examine the room. "I like it that way." After a few minutes of silence, he stopped and turned to her. "I like the room. Thank you."

They returned to the living room and sat together on the sofa. David took his place in the recliner.

"Does David's presence trouble you?" Maggie asked.

Randal glanced briefly at David, shook his head. "He's all right."

"You're going to be a handsome young man for eternity," she said. "Do you mind?"

Before he could respond, Maggie reached out and removed a lock of hair from his eyes.

Randal's hand came up with preternatural speed and gripped her wrist. David stood. Maggie motioned for David to stay back.

Randal released her arm and turned his eyes away from her.

David took his seat again when Maggie nodded to him.

She turned to Randal. "Would you mind telling me about your family? I'd like to hear about them. It could also help you to remember them."

Randal shook his head. "I mean, not now. Not yet."

"Okay," she said. "Another time, maybe?"

He paused, then nodded.

"I had a family once, too. I had a daughter named Molly that I lost in an unfortunate way. Do you mind if I tell you about it? I'd very much like to tell someone. I like talking about her whenever I can."

Randal met her eyes again. "Yes, please."

Maggie closed her eyes and recounted the most harrowing moments of her life.

Maggie's Story

Molly's father was a man named Grover Dixon. He was four years older than me. I had known Grover since I was young because he used to help my father. He and my father used to go around to junkyards and lawn sales and collect old metal items like lawn chairs and broken swings and whatnot. There were mounds and mounds of discarded and destroyed metal objects in our backyard, piled as high as our one-story house. Grover and my Dad would take Dads beat up old Ford Ranger out and bring back all these fantastic, useless items to strip them for their aluminum parts. My Dad could make money selling the aluminum and would share his earning with Grover.

When I was fourteen, I had come home from school one day, crying. My Dad was out, and Grover was in the backyard with the junk. I didn't know he was there until I heard him knocking on the screen door leading to the yard.

"I'm sorry little Maggers. I was going to ask for a cup of lemonade and heard you crying. Mind if I ask you what's wrong?"

I hesitated. I didn't know what to say and if I should tell him private stuff about myself. But I was hurting, and I didn't have anyone else to talk to, so I poured us both a glass of lemonade, and I went out to the junkyard with him.

I found a metal chair that had not been stripped yet mixed in with all the rubble and sat on it. After a moment I said, "Some girls at school were calling me Raggie Maggie because of my second-hand clothes. Usually, it doesn't bother me, but today I was just a wreck. Everything was making me cry. I hate to cry."

"I'm sorry," he said.

I watched him as he took a long silver magnet and rolled it over different metal objects. He was looking at me and didn't seem to be paying attention to what he was doing. "Why are you doing that?" I asked.

And just like that, had forgotten all about my problems at school.

"I use the magnet on different objects and see if it sticks." He demonstrated.

"If it sticks you want what is under it?" I asked.

"If it sticks, it's not aluminum, and I don't want it. Aluminum isn't magnetic. So, whatever doesn't stick to the magnet, I throw over in that pile to keep. He pointed to a disjointed skeletal mound of silver behind him. The rest I send to the dump.

"Sounds boring, I said.

"Is boring, but its work," he said.

I stayed with him until my father came home.

The next day after school I poured two glasses of lemonade and headed out to the backyard. As I had hoped, Grover was there combing through the debris. He saw me with the lemonades, and his eyes shone as bright as the sun glinting off the metal objects surrounding him. Sweat was pouring off him in buckets, and his shirt was wet with it and sticking to his muscular frame.

Grover wasn't a handsome man, but he wasn't ugly. Sure, his teeth were yellow, and a bit crooked, but when he smiled his lips pulled back into the brightest, happiest expression. At that moment, his teeth didn't seem all that bad. He had some of the most beautiful almond-shaped brown eyes and long eyelashes I have ever seen on a man, and to me, he was the most beautiful creature I had ever laid eyes on. He took one of the glasses and kissed my forehead. I blushed. He saw my redness but ignored it like a real gentleman and drank his lemonade. He drank the entire glass in one long swig, spilling it over his lips and onto his sweat- and grime-stained tee shirt.

When he finished the drink, he handed the glass back to me. I sat both glasses down on a nearby bench. I hadn't touched my lemonade.

He turned to go back to the task of stripping, hesitated with a knowing smile, turned back to me and said, "I have something for you Maggers."

"You have something for me?" I repeated.

He nodded and, without getting it dirty, reached into a sack and pulled out a thin white carton about ten inches by twelve, and about two inches thick. He set the box down on my lap as carefully as a king setting a crown on his queen's head.

I was excited beyond words to learn what was inside the box, but I only looked at it for a long time. I didn't open the box until he said, "Well, aren't you gonna open it?"

I needed no further encouragement. I pulled off the lid and looked inside at a beautiful black dress. I pulled it out and lifted it to my body. I was in awe. It was so elegant and so undoubtedly my style.

Grover said, "I saw that pretty thing, and I said to myself with that jet-black hair and alabaster skin,

Maggers is gonna look mighty beautiful in that. So, I bought it."

He peered at me through those long eyelashes and said more softly, "I hoped you'd like it."

There weren't words for what I thought of that dress. Tears burned my eyes as I carefully replaced the dress in the box and hugged him, not caring if he got me dirty. "Thank you," I whispered into his ear as he rubbed gently on my back.

As I pulled away, I heard the screen door behind me squeak open then slam shut.

"Is this why I'm losing money?" my father said. "My daughter is pestering the help?" My father was stern and gruff, but he was really just an old softy when it came to me.

"Daddy, look what Grover bought me." I held the open box up for my father to see.

"Bought you?" my father asked and looked questioningly over at Grover. I looked up and saw that Grover's attention had been diverted from me and the dress to something metal that needed his immediate care. "Go inside and try that pretty thing on while I have a chat with Grover, pumpkin," my father said.

The dress had fit perfectly, and when I wore that dress to school, no one called me Raggie Maggie.

More gifts followed. Grover bought me some more clothes, books, and jewelry, expensive necklaces, and bracelets.

I was sixteen when my father said, "You're not really that stupid, are you? He's stealing that stuff. I don't pay him enough to afford all that shit."

"He's not stealing it," I said. "He doesn't have the bills you do so he can afford to buy things he wants. You're just jealous."

My father grabbed me roughly by the arms. "Stop accepting those gifts," he said. "They will only lead to trouble."

I pulled away from him and stormed to my room.

On my seventeenth birthday, Grover had a surprise for me, and I wasn't allowed to see it until it was ready. He blindfolded me and led me over a long path. There were stones under my shoes as we walked, so I knew it wasn't going to be in the backyard. When we reached our destination, he stopped me.

"Are you ready to take the blindfold off?" he asked.

"Yes," I said breathlessly.

I was beyond excited. He removed the blindfold, and I had to re-adjust my eyes to the sudden brightness of my new surroundings. I looked at Grover and was stunned to see how cleanly dressed he was. We were under a cherry tree in the orchard near my house. And under the tree was a red and white checkered blanket and a basket.

"A picnic," I said with tears flooding my eyes.

"Happy Birthday, Maggers," he said, and we sat down on the blanket. He fed me sandwiches and grapes and strawberries from the basket. When strawberry juice ran down my chin, he used a finger to wipe it off, and then he licked the juice off his fingers.

About an hour into our picnic, a light wind started to pick up. Cherry blossoms lifted off the trees and swirled around us making it seem as though it was snowing. It was so beautiful. One flower landed on my eye. I lifted it off my face and blew it from my palm. When I turned to look at Grover, to see if he had witnessed the beautiful thing that had just happened, I saw that he was looking at something in his hands. And he was smiling.

"What is it?" I asked, sensing he had something more to show me.

He didn't speak. He cupped his palms together and peered into the crack, enticing me to see what he had there. When I tried to look, he pulled away. When I worked harder to see, he stretched out and prevented me from seeing what was in his hands. I pinned him down with my body to get a look at what he was holding. It was a small black jewelry box. He handed it to me. With trembling fingers, I opened it. There was a silver ring inside with a small diamond embedded in it.

"Will you marry me?" he asked, and his voice trembled.

Tears flooded my vision. Cherry blossoms floated around me like fairies. The ring was simple, but it was the most beautiful thing I had ever seen. I didn't have to say yes. I jumped at him and started kissing his face. He kissed me back. He kissed away my tears.

He took me into his strong arms, and we made love under that cherry tree. It was my first time. Looking back, I can't say it was my most wonderful memory, but I was in love. His strong arms encircled me, and I felt safer at that moment than I ever have in my whole life. I just knew that these arms would protect me for as long as I lived. His breath was a soft tickle on my neck, and then he whispered: "I love you,

Maggers. I'll love you forever if you will have me for that long."

I knew then that he could steal anything he liked and I wouldn't care. I would help him. I would have become the new Bonnie and Clyde if that was what he wished.

We didn't marry. My father refused to even consider such a thing. And when I graduated from school, I left my father behind and ran away with Grover.

We stopped running in Philadelphia when we ran out of money and couldn't afford a bus ticket to go any further. He got a job cleaning floors, and I took up waitressing. With tips and my regular wages, I was making more money than him.

"You have to quit," he said to me when we were cleaning up after dinner one night.

"I can't quit. We need the money. Besides, I make more than you. So, you quit." I was just joking with him, but he got outraged. He rushed toward me and raised the back of his hand as if to strike me. I flinched and lost the plate I was holding. He glared at me for a second or two and then dropped his hand. He helped me clean up the broken plate. Things got quiet in our house after that. Grover and I barely spoke two words to each other on any given night.

I'm not sure how or when, but Grover suddenly started having all kinds of cash. I asked him what he'd been doing to generate so much money, but all he would say was that it was none of my business. I learned soon enough that he was selling drugs. If that wasn't bad enough, he then broke the cardinal rule of any drug pusher and started using. We had all kinds of looser-types tracking through our house. I guess I just got used to it. I got used to the beatings as well. I think that he hit me the most when he was coming down off the drugs. It's hard to bring home good tips when you're nursing a black eye or swollen jaw. People knew where the bruises were coming from, but most just pretended not to see. It was more comfortable that way for everyone, even me. It was Paula, a fellow waitress, that decided she couldn't keep quiet any longer.

"Why are you still with him if he hits you? You need to leave."

"And go where?" I asked. I didn't want to go anywhere, even if there was a place.

"Here, take this." Paula handed me a card. "This place will help you."

When she walked away, I slipped the card into the trash without even looking at it. I just figured I could handle Grover myself. I would find a way to get back the Grover I fell in love with all those years ago.

I was walking into the house when I heard the scream. I dropped the grocery bag I was holding and ran through the rooms to the source of the cry. It was Grover, and he was in the bathroom throwing up blood.

"Oh my God," I cried out as I dropped down next to him. "I have to get you to the hospital."

"No hospital." He groaned.

"Grover, you're puking up blood. This isn't good."

"It'll stop. It always does," he said.

I stood up. "What? This has happened before?"

Maggers, I'm sorry. I'm going to fix this. I'm going to stop doing drugs, and I'm going to take better care of you, I promise. I can't live like this anymore."

I wanted to believe him, and he was as good as his word. He stopped hitting me, his health seemed to improve, and I got pregnant with Molly.

I was nervous about telling him, but when I did, I got the shock of my life.

"Holy cow. Maggers, I'm going to be a daddy?" He hooted and cheered, and those beautiful eyes were back on his face again, although the drugs had taken its toll on them. Dark circles under them made him look older and more tired.

He took good care of me during the pregnancy. When Molly was born though, he was nowhere to be found.

He had been out getting drunk or celebrating as he told it. He sobered up long enough to bring us home from the hospital. The first few days were okay, but I started to notice something odd: Grover didn't play with Molly or help out in any way with her care. He acted as though she wasn't even there.

Grover had replaced drug abuse with drinking, and if I thought he was a mean drug addict, he was an even meaner drunk. When Molly was two months old, Grover came home at two in the morning wanting to climb into bed with me.

"No, Grover. No." I shoved at him, but he would not go away. I pushed him off me and tried to climb out of bed. He struck me several times in the face then tore my nightgown. He had his way with me as I lay there stunned and crying. He finished, rolled over and passed out. The next morning as he still lay sleeping, I packed some stuff and Molly, and I left.

I knocked at the door of the little yellow house, not sure what kind of reception I might get; but when Paula opened the door and saw my face, she had nothing but sympathy and compassion for us. We drove to the emergency room. I was stitched up and allowed to leave. Paula continued to encourage me to press charges, but I refused.

Paula drove me to the shelter. Maggie and I were shown to a room, and that was where we lived for the next twenty-eight days.

I was out looking for an apartment when Grover finally tracked me down.

"Maggers, baby, listen. I made a mistake. I didn't mean it. I don't even remember it—that's how drunk I was. Please don't leave. Come home to me, and I promise I'll change." His plea sounded heartfelt, and he was even crying.

"I have to be on my own for a while," I said. Let me do this, and we'll see where things go from there.

He agreed to let me have my space. I found an apartment and moved in. Grover would come to visit, and he even played with Molly. I almost believed him this time when he said he had changed.

Almost.

I was playing pat-a-cake with Molly when Grover stormed through the door. He was drunk and his eyes, once so caring and warm and beautiful, were now brown sockets with bloodshot orbs that stared out at us, cold and angry.

"Pack up your crap. You're coming home with me now. I'm tired of this bullshit." He was shouting and slurring his words. I cranked at the wind-up on Molly's swing and left her there while I dealt with her father.

"Grover, you're drunk. You promised me this wouldn't happen again. Get out of here. It's over between us. Do you hear me? Over. Leave."

He raised his hand to strike me, but I swung first. I punched him right in the stomach. He doubled over. Before I could back away, however, he swiped a meaty fist out and plowed it into my cheek so hard I literally saw stars. That is true, you know. If you get hit hard enough, you really do see them.

Molly started crying. It was loud and piercing and wouldn't stop.

I shook off his blow, lowered my head and rushed him. I hit him in the chest like a charging bull and knocked him over. I was about to kick him in the balls and end this when he grabbed my foot and toppled me. I landed on my back, the wind knocked out of me.

Maggie was crying hysterically now.

"Shut that brat up," he screamed.

That pulled me out of my stunned state. I crawled to my feet and went for his eyes with my inch-long nails. I growled like an animal.

He put out a hand and struck me in the chest so hard that I flew backward, landed on my butt and continued sliding until I hit a stand and knocked a lamp to the floor. When I looked up, he was taking Molly out of the swing. I heard a siren and thought: Did the neighbors call the police?

No, the wailing sound was coming from me. I was screaming. Grover was shaking Molly, shaking her so hard her little head was swinging and almost touching her back. By the time I reached them, Molly had stopped crying. I pulled her out of his hands and was trying to see what was wrong with her, but my tears were blurring my vision, and I couldn't see.

Grover stood dumbly at my side. "I'm sorry," he kept saying. "I'm sorry, Maggers I don't know... I don't..."

At some point, he must have left, but I was trying to get Molly to breathe and had no idea when. I stumbled to the phone and called 911.

"It's my baby," I said into the phone. "My baby, Molly. Baby, I'm so sorry. Molly, what have I done? My baby isn't breathing."

The operator asked where I was and I told her. Tears and snot drooled out onto the phone, and there was a tennis ball sized lump lodged in my throat that I couldn't swallow away. I couldn't breathe.

The EMTs seemed to take forever, but the report said they arrived on the scene three minutes after the call was made. I was in shock. People were leading me around telling me what to do and what to say. Before I knew it, I was on trial for killing my baby girl.

I was released on bail, but couldn't go back to my apartment, so I stayed at the shelter. The trial took about as long as Molly had been alive. The prosecution brought in all kinds of experts and psychiatrists to say that I was suffering from post-partum depression and probably didn't know what I had done. I was so numb, I barely knew what they were saying half the time. The other half, I just didn't care. At night, as I lay in bed, I would pretend I was still holding my sweet baby and cried until my throat hurt. The only time I would sleep was when my exhaustion was so overwhelming I had no choice.

One of the times I managed to sleep, I dreamt of her. In the dream, I was sitting naked in a field on my knees, and Molly was lying across my shoulders like a cherub. In her hand, she held a straight razor. Molly dragged the blade across my throat, and as the blood rushed across my breasts, I felt such exquisite love for her. I wanted to join her. Upon waking, however; I was thrust back into the real hell that was my life. I showed up for court day after day looking more and more sallow and unhealthy. My lawyer began to worry.

"You have to show emotion. Let the jury see you cry," my lawyer was saying to me. I turned to him with a look of incredulity on my face.

"You think I did it, too, don't you?" I said, realizing the truth.

"That's not important now."

I flushed hot with rage. "How is it not important? If I can't convince my own lawyer I'm innocent, how can I expect to convince twelve strangers?" I wanted to cry. I wanted to scream. I wanted my life to be over.

"This isn't the time to discuss your guilt or innocence with me. Please, Ms. Owens, sit down."

Before I sat down, I looked around the room at all these faces that saw me as a monster. My life was over, and I didn't even care.

But luckily for me, someone cared. Paula cared, and she testified on my behalf. For all the good it did, though.

"So, it is your testimony to this court," the lead prosecutor was saying during her cross-examination.

"That you know for a fact that Ms. Owens was a victim of domestic abuse?"

"That is correct, I helped her— "

The prosecutor cut her off. "Then I guess we in this courtroom would lead to believe that you witnessed this abuse firsthand. Is that correct?"

"Well, no. But I— "

"You mean to tell me that your testimony is based on what Ms. Owens, herself, told you?"

"I saw the bruises. I helped clean her wounds. I know domestic abuse when I see it."

I remember this next moment with complete clarity, and it pisses me off still today.

The prosecutor turned away from her. He was looking smugly at the jurors as he continued. "And why would that be, Ms. Sanchez? Isn't it true that you, yourself, are a victim of domestic abuse?"

Paula leaned forward and said into the microphone, "Yes, I am." She was defiant and strong when she said it. She didn't divert her eyes or cringe away. I was so proud of her.

The prosecutor looked at her now. "Isn't it true that you would see domestic abuse in every cut on a woman's face, or in every bruise, no matter how the said wounds got there?"

"No, that is just not fair. It's not—"

My lawyer objected.

"This witness is excused, your honor." the prosecutor turned away from Paula, even as she continued to protest.

"You may step down," the judge said calmly.

I testified on my own behalf. I spoke of the love I had for Grover and how he betrayed that love with violence. My tears were raw, and they were real. As I looked out at the stone-faced jury, I spoke of the night that Grover came to see us and how that night ended.

"I was busy getting ready for supper when I passed Molly and noticed she was blowing spit bubbles and making funny faces at me," I testified. "I had to stop. She was so beautiful sitting there in her windup swing, playing. I got down on the floor in front of her and copied the faces she was making. She laughed so loud..." Sobs escaped me. I collected myself and continued. "She laughed so loud she got the hiccups. I was playing with her there on the floor when Grover burst into the house. He was drunk and upset. We fought. When I was down on the floor, it was then that he grabbed her, screaming for her to stop crying." I was inconsolable now, although no one was trying to console me. "That was when he killed her."

The prosecutor handed me a tissue. I thanked him, and I blew my nose.

"That's a touching story," he said. "But it's not what the rest of us heard."

He played the 911 tape. The room was stunned into silence. When the tape ended, the prosecutor began hammering in the final nail. "'I'm so sorry,' you say. These are your words. 'Molly, what have I done? My baby isn't breathing.'"

He turned to me. "What were you sorry for, Ms. Owens? What did you do?"

My tears turned to rage. I seethed. "I let that man into my house—let him kill my baby girl. Yes, I feel guilty. I deserve whatever I get, but not for the reason you want to put on me. I never hurt my baby, except by letting that man get anywhere near her."

"This witness is excused." The prosecutor acted as if he hadn't heard anything I said.

Closing arguments were swift and compelling for both sides. Then the case was in the hands of the jury. They deliberated for a week. Both teams were claiming victory. The outcome was a shock.

The jurors could not come to a verdict. Too many of them wanted me to fry for what happened to Molly, but enough of them—four I believe—chose my side and would not budge. The judge ruled the case a mistrial. When the prosecution couldn't come up with enough evidence to bring me to trial again, the case was thrown out. Everyone at the shelter was so happy for me, but I still could not bring myself to rejoice. My daughter was still dead, and I was alone.

The first time Grover showed up at my door after the trial, I flew into a rage. Eventually, however, I just didn't have the strength to fight anymore.

One day he showed up and found me going through old pictures of Molly. I was crying and didn't know he was standing there until he said, "Look on the bright side, she's in a better place."

I looked up, startled. I crammed the pictures back in the box and hid them behind me. "She's in the ground. How is that a better place?"

"She's not suffering," he said.

"She wasn't suffering before you killed her, either."

I expected a beating for that, but Grover wasn't into the physical abuse after what happened to Molly. He was going for the emotional kind now.

He said, "Now, everyone knows you killed her, and you're trying to blame it on me to ease your guilty conscience."

I started to shake. My vision clouded. Anger was the first emotion besides utter despair I had felt since losing my baby girl. I just started beating on him as hard as I could. "You killed her." I screamed as my fists pummeled him. "You killed her, you bastard. You." During the entire tirade, he was laughing—laughing. The more he giggled, the more I attacked him.

When I'd had enough and was too tired to keep up the attack, I tried to force him to go. He left, eventually. But he came back. He always came back to torture me.

Luckily, his visits were few and far between and in his absence, I managed to get my life into some semblance of order.

It was about a year after Molly's death that the reporter started coming around asking questions. I thought: What fresh hell is this? First, I lose my daughter, and then they try to pin her death on me. Now they want me to relive it?

"When I was a child, I sometimes had dreams that would come true. I also had waking visions that would turn out to be things that were happening at that moment. I had a gift.

When that reporter was snooping around, my gifts came flooding back to me. I started honing my different skills. I wanted to use my ability to see the future. I tried to astral project. I decided to use my gifts to fight back at this mob of sensationalists who wished to do me harm. I started really seeing my dreams again. I was looking to see which were coming true and which were fizzling out.

I wanted to know what the reporter was going to write about me. And as I suspected, it wasn't in my favor. Apparently, someone was out to try and reopen the case and get me back into court. I was ready to jump out a window. I couldn't believe how low my life could sink.

Amazingly, it was Grover that managed to get the reporter out of my life.

The newspaper ran the story Where Is She Now: The baby killer that got away? It rehashed the trial and my subsequent mistrial. It ended with a plea to see justice done for baby Molly. The reporter happened to come around while Grover was in the middle of another of his psychological torture sessions. Grover chased him off and the last thing he said to the reporter—and which I believe killed any future stories calling for my arrest—was: "Leave now, or I'll kill you just like I killed Molly." Then he pretended to shake the reporter until his head exploded. He laughed at his own gruesome pantomime.

I asked Grover to leave after that, and he did without complaint.

The reporter never returned and to my knowledge never penned any other stories about me.

But the one article he did write caught the eye of a certain hunter. I was marked for death. And I knew what was coming. In a way, I was happy about it

In my vision, I saw a stranger straddling me in bed. He had red eyes and fangs. He reached down and bit into my neck. As I lay there listening to him suck out my blood, Grover shows up with a stake and kills the vampire that was attacking me. At first, I didn't understand what this vision meant. I had no idea vampires existed. I thought it was like the dream of Molly cutting my throat. But something of it did ring true. I was attacked in my bed by Antony, and Grover was there to save me, but by becoming Antony's next victim. Turns out, stakes don't even kill a vampire.

###

Maggie giggled, and Randal let his mouth turn up slightly.

"And although the real events were different than in my vision, the dream did come true. And how I cherish the day I was attacked by that vampire in my dream. It was David who tracked me. It was Antony who was about to feed on me when Grover walked in. It was Grover who gave Antony an alternate blood source that allowed me to live. David and Antony took me in, and I have proven my worth to them. I don't know how that moment would have turned out if Grover hadn't shown up when he did. Would Antony have taken my life? I don't know. It doesn't matter. Grover did show up, and I thank him for that. If nothing else, he did that one thing right. He was more useful as a source of blood for Antony that night than he had been in all his thirty-two years on earth."

Randal's mouth lifted slightly at the ends.

Maggie laughed. "If that's a smile, I'll take it."

David leaned forward in his chair. His eyes were shining, and there was moisture in them. "Maggie, I never knew all that."

She touched his hand. "I'm glad you know now." She turned to Randal. "I want you to understand that you can trust David and Antony. They are good men, and I love them both dearly. I am the happiest I've ever been since I've been with them. They love me too, and that above all else is worth staying alive for. Their love and companionship make up for all the horrors I have seen at the hands of an unforgiving and ignorant public, and at the hands of a violent, despicable man who fathered a child then removed her from the world. I hope that one day you, too, will overcome the horrors you've seen, and will feel what it's like to love someone again, like the way I feel for David and Antony."

Randal opened his mouth to say something but then closed it. He tried again. "I can't promise you love, but I won't hurt you. I want you to know that."

"I do," she said. "I trust you. And I'm confident that you will know love again. And I want to be there when you find it."

Randal nodded, and this time, he hugged her. As he pulled away, he glanced over at David.

David showed his hands. "I trust you, too, little guy."

"I'm going to really hate it if you call me that for the next fifty years."

Maggie sat back, shocked. She and David laughed.

"I won't call you that then," David said.

Maggie took Randal's hand. "David, Antony and I will help you through this, do you understand? They will hunt for you and keep you from taking innocent life. Will you accept our help, and abide by our way of life?"

He hesitated, offered that quirky smile again, and nodded.

###

David stood in the hallway. Randal was asleep in his room, as was Antony. Maggie closed the door to Randal's room and turned around.

"I think he'll be okay," she said.

David nodded. "Me, too."

He took her hand and led her to the downstairs office. He scanned through newspapers as she took a seat in the swayback chair and closed her eyes. He stopped what he was doing to watch her. She opened her eyes and looked at him.

"What?"

"Nothing. It's just that I'm toiling away while you nap, is all."

"Toiling?" She scoffed. "You're reading the newspaper."

"I'm searching for…never mind."

She laughed. "I'm not napping. I'm trying to bring on a vision."

"It works like that? You can just will yourself to have them?"

She shrugged. "Sometimes."

He sat down on the sofa and faced her. He looked at her with new eyes, seeing her as more than an annoying troublemaker. Her story had affected him, and he wanted to get to know her even more. She fascinated him, but it was more than that. He—

"Why are you looking at me like that?"

David looked away. "Like what?"

She smiled and took his hand. Her touch was soft. This was not the usual friendly handholding. She was caressing his skin.

He looked into her eyes. She was smiling, and her chin was raised as if daring him to do something. He leaned toward her.

She leaned forward as well then joined him on the sofa. He ran his hand up the length of her arm to touch her face. He pulled her to him, and their lips met. His body shivered as her hands worked at the buttons of his shirt. Still kissing her, he pulled the shirt off himself, causing the remaining buttons to fly around the room.

Maggie sat back and giggled. She touched his bare chest, and he inhaled sharply. She pulled her own blouse over her head and dropped it. She unlatched her bra and that, too, hit the floor. David could stop himself from reaching out and cupping one exposed breast. Their lips met again, and the kissing was more passionate this time, ravenous. They squirmed out of their pants and underpants.

He kissed her erect nipples. She arched her back as he entered her. He pushed against her gently, shuddering at the immense pleasure he felt at being inside her. He kissed her neck, her ear, her mouth. He plunged his tongue into her mouth and felt her lips accept it. He moved slowly and rhythmically against her. Their moans melded together. David found a warm spot inside her. He touched that spot again and again until Maggie started to cry out, as if in pain. When David tried to pull away, Maggie pulled him back. He pressed against her. Maggie gasped and dug her fingers into his back, dragging the nails across the flesh and leaving burning welts. She didn't seem to be aware of what she had done. David cringed, enjoying the pleasure in the pain.

He pushed deeper into the pleasure of her flesh, and his movements began to grow more frantic. She wrapped her legs around him, wanting him to release into her.

It took David an hour to finally reach his climax, and with a final gasping heave, David lay still. Both he and Maggie panted wildly. He rolled to the side, soaked in sweat and exhausted. They lay silently entwined in each other's arms, their glistening bodies wrapped into one form. David drifted into sleep.

When David woke, he slipped away from her quietly, stepped into the shower stall, and let the scalding water wash over him. He didn't leave the shower until he had scrubbed every inch of himself red and raw. As he stepped from the bathroom, a wave of steam escorted him into the colder air of the bedroom. He walked naked to the dresser and retrieved fresh clothes.

David returned to the office. He glanced down at her naked sleeping form and draped a blanket over her. He leaned over and kissed her cheek. She squirmed but didn't wake up.

"Thank you." His voice was a whisper. "I need to tell you I love you, but that wouldn't do either of us any good. I want to be your everything, but there is something else I want even more. I want Antony to give me the gift of being a vampire. I think I almost have him where I want him. He'll give it to me soon. Here's the problem. Vampires can't show their love the way people do. What we did here is not a possibility when I become an immortal. I won't trap you into a relationship that will never offer you anything but disappointment. I hope we can have this talk for real soon."

David walked away and let her sleep.

###

The time had come for them to hunt down the Houseguest.

With Maggie's gift, they began devising a plan to track the murderous vampire. Through his victims, Maggie was able to hone her visions into precise locations, but they always seemed to arrive too late to do any good. The vampire was able to cover his tracks too well. Maggie couldn't get an emotional lock on him. There was a moment when she thought she had sensed fear on a street not far from them— a road in Allentown where ladies of the night frequented, but when they arrived, they found nothing.

They decided it wasn't their killer since that wasn't his modus operandi. He didn't kill single victims, and besides, there was no corpse. When Maggie felt the same woman's fear later that night, she felt a pang of regret that they couldn't help her, but she didn't bother telling the others. The only consolation she had was that eventually the girl's killer would cross their path and Antony would dispatch him. Maggie took comfort in that much at least.

"Do you have any ideas?" David asked Maggie.

Maggie looked up from where she was sitting with Randal and shrugged.

"How about you, little man, do you have any ideas?"

Randal glared at him but didn't respond.

"Astral projection," Maggie said.

"What about it?" David asked.

"I'm not good at it and will need to practice, but if I can astral project to the vampire's next target, I could warn them, and at the same time tell you where he is going to strike." She stopped suddenly as if her idea had blown itself out, like a match's flame, burning bright one second, and smoke the next.

"You look doubtful," Antony said to her.

"That's because I am. The only time I can hone in on the killer is when he is in his full-on frenzy. I can be there in an instant, but I can't tell you where it is until I get there. I'll have to come back into my body and tell you where to go."

David nodded. "And we'll be in the same boat as always. By the time we get there, he will be gone, and we will be too late."

"Not necessarily," Antony said. "You said you could warn the family. You could get them to leave before they are murdered."

Maggie slumped in her chair. "I said I could try. I'll have maybe two or three seconds to get them to leave before he arrives."

"Try is right. Sounds impossible," said David.

"This is better than doing nothing," said Antony. "Practice astral projection and the next time he strikes, send your projected self to the family. Warn them to leave. When he arrives, come back and tell me where he is. I will go there alone and confront him. All this could be over tomorrow night if this plan works."

They spent the rest of the night trying to work out the details of this new plan of attack.

Just before dawn, Antony pulled Randal aside and crouched to face the boy at eye level. With a severe look that made the boy cringe, Antony said: "I was not fair to you."

"What do you mean?" Randal asked.

Antony looked at David, and then to Maggie. He turned back to the boy. "When we first heard of your existence, I immediately feared the worst. I believed you to be an abomination that would have to be destroyed. It was Maggie that forced me to admit my ignorance. I am sorry I did not give you a chance to prove your worth."

"You have given it to me now," Randal said. "The past doesn't matter."

"I agree. Now is all that matters." He ruffed up Randal's already messy hair, and they retired to their sleeping chambers.

Maggie practiced by first projecting herself to the other side of the room. Then she astral projected outside. When she projected herself outward, her eyes closed, her head went back, and her body went limp. David was afraid she would fall out of the chair, so when she returned to her body after being gone for about three minutes, he asked her to move to the sofa.

"It's like you're having a seizure or something. I'm worried about you."

She stretched out on the plush cushions. "Are you trying to have your way with me again?" She smiled at his heated cheeks.

The training went on all day, and when night approached, she felt sufficiently adept enough to send her projection anywhere she wanted to go inside the perimeter of her powers.

When Antony woke, she informed him that she was ready.

The group climbed into the Zephyr and headed out to the Pocono Mountains, the Houseguest Killer's preferred hunting ground. When they reached the area most likely to be the killer's next stop, David slowed the RV to a crawl. They made a sweep of one street, then another. Maggie relaxed on the bed and concentrated. No one disturbed her.

"Did you both feed?" David asked his two vampire companions. Randal nodded.

"I took a victim as well."

David turned to look at Antony. "One? That's not enough. Wake Maggie up and have her find you someone nearby. I don't want you attacking us because you were too busy to eat."

"I will be okay."

"Sure, you will, but will I?"

"I have time. Stop worrying."

David ignored him. He pulled the RV to the side of the road and parked. He strode to the back and opened the door to the bedroom.

Maggie thrashed, bucking wildly, then went limp. When she opened her eyes, he knew his time was up.

Chapter Fifteen

Sheila Beadle walked into the living room carrying a huge bowl of popcorn and frowned when she saw her son and husband sprawled out on the sofa. "You two better be planning to make room for me."

Her husband smiled and moved over, patting the seat next to him. "You can sit here."

"I was saving this spot for you, Mom." Her son patted the other side of the couch.

"You were, huh?" She scowled suspiciously. "I don't buy it."

"Scooch over. I'll sit between you. Anyway, you only want me for my popcorn." She sat down and cuddled up next to her husband.

"What are we watching?" her son asked. He reached into the bowl and came out with a massive handful of the treat.

Dad wiggled his fingers in front of his son's face. "A ghost story." The boy swatted his father's hand away.

As Dad pressed the remote to start the movie, a ghost appeared directly in front of the television.

###

Maggie needed a moment to orient herself to her new surroundings after astral projecting to the family's living room. Her eyes darted wildly around, but a large bowl of popcorn tumbled to the floor and she focused on the family gathered at the sofa.

"Please listen to me. You're in danger. The Houseguest Killer… coming… to kill you." Her warning was pointless by that time. The entire family was already in panic mode and racing for the back door. The man pushed the boy along, lifting him when he nearly fell. The woman cried in terror as she followed her family out of the house. Maggie watched them go, pleased with the result.

The front door burst open, and the Houseguest Killer made his presence known with a flourish of his trench coat and a toss of his staff. He appeared somewhat troubled by the sight of the family fleeing out the back door. He watched them leave, then turned and saw Maggie standing in front of the television.

"And who are you?" He brandished the ivory-headed cane at her.

"I'm someone you're going to wish you had never seen." Maggie crossed her arms over her chest. She could control her projected body, but nothing in her surroundings. She couldn't even move from the spot where she landed.

He used vampire speed and rushed toward her. She gasped at the rate of his approach but remembered he couldn't hurt her and relaxed. He reached out for her neck to snap it, but his hand passed through her. She smiled, waved goodbye, and disappeared.

"He's at 236 Church Street," Maggie said upon returning to her body in the Zephyr. Antony needed no explanation. He burst from the Zephyr in a rush of air. The door banged against the frame. After several seconds, Randal, too, disappeared in a whoosh of crackling air.

"Randal, no." Maggie reached for the child vampire, but it was too late.

###

Antony rushed through the door the Houseguest Killer had not bothered to close. His adversary was still in the house staring dumbly at the spot in front of the television. This other vampire was taller than him and older. Antony sensed an ancient quality about this one. He wondered just how many years the monster had spent terrorizing mortals.

"You are an abomination," Antony said to his dumbfounded foe.

"Who are you and why did you chase away my meal? And who was that girl? She is human, but she disappeared. What kind of sorcery is that?"

Then Randal appeared.

The vampire's amused expression faded as he glanced down at Randal, and then back at Antony. He snarled.

"You stole my pet? He's mine."

"Hello, Dark Father." Randal spat the words out like poisonous seeds.

"You should not have come." Antony shoved the boy behind him but never took his eyes off the killer vampire.

"You lost your rope. I'll get you a new one." The ancient one reached into his coat.

Antony flew at his adversary and drove him into the 60-inch plasma TV, breaking it into pieces. Pushing Antony across the room to the opposite wall, the other vampire glanced over at Randal.

"This will be over soon, and you and I will be once again reunited. I can only imagine what you must have been going through."

Antony used the momentary distraction to break his attacker's hold and force the vampire to the floor. Even as Antony struggled to rip out the vampire's heart, the other couldn't stop looking toward Randal. He tried to squirm out of Antony's grip, but could not break the hold. He fought just long enough to prevent Antony from plunging a fist through his chest, before once again reaching out to the boy. When he felt Antony's bite, he yelped and turned his focus back to the fight.

Antony opened a six-inch gash in the opponent's neck. The other yowled like an injured wolf and tried to bite Antony back. Antony easily dodged all the attacks against him. He took another big bite out of his adversary's neck. He spat out the glob of flesh, and even as it left his mouth, the chunk turned to ash.

The ancient vampire pushed Antony away with fantastic speed and strength. Antony flew up and tumbled over backward. He instantly pounced back onto his feet. The attacker flew at Randal. The boy's arms came up to block his face as he was lifted off the floor.

Antony saw that the vampire was trying to run with Randal, and he flew at him, driving his adversary onto his hands and knees. Randal broke out of the vampire's grip and tumbled away.

Antony wrapped an arm around his opponent's neck and squeezed, attempting to remove the head from the body. They twisted and squirmed in each other's grip, but neither seemed able to get the upper hand.

"Enough." The ancient vampire rose up and slammed Antony on his back. He stood over Antony victoriously. He picked up his staff and raised it over his head. Antony moved just as the skull crushing blow came and bounced up behind his adversary. He used his fists to pound the other back down to the floor. The ferocity of the blows kept the vampire pinned, and once again the staff skittered away from him, this time out of reach. Antony continued to hammer his back keeping him down.

As the pinned vampire struggled to turn over, Antony continued to hammer the monster against the floor. The squeal of breaks announced that the Zephyr had arrived.

David entered the house. "How can I help?"

Maggie entered and pulled Randal away.

"David, go. I have this." Antony averted his eyes, just for a second.

The ancient vampire flipped onto his back, shoved Antony into the far wall, and leaped to his feet. Weakened, but still stronger and faster than any human, he moved with super speed and grabbed David by the neck and yanked.

Something snapped.

The killer tossed David like a ragdoll, retrieved his staff, and flew from the house in a crackling gust of wind.

Antony moved to chase the killer but stopped when he saw the heap on the floor that was David's body.

In the distance, sirens blared.

Antony stared down at David. His preternatural hearing could detect a faint heartbeat coming from David, but the slightest move of David's head could stop it.

Maggie touched Antony's arm. "Go," she said. "It's over. You can't be seen here. I will take care of this."

Antony looked up. His eyes were red. He needed to feed.

But David was dying.

Antony howled and flew from the back of the house as the EMTs entered through the d front door.

Chapter Sixteen

As David lay under a pristine white sheet, the smells of Lysol disinfectant and other antiseptic cleansers permeating the hospital room., Maggie held his hand. Tubes and wires drooped and hung all around David's still frame. A hose running into his mouth helped a machine breathe for him. Another device monitored his heart rate and blood pressure. He sported a neck brace. David had gone into cardiac arrest twice before the doctors were able to bring him back to normal sinus rhythm.

The family Maggie saved didn't know how she did what she did, but they showed their gratitude and brought David flowers. The family didn't see what had taken place inside the house after they left but understood David had risked his life trying to bring the Houseguest Killer to justice.

Now, as David lay fighting for his life. Maggie could only sit and cry and pray. She had something important to discuss with David, and now she didn't know if she would ever get the chance.

Sobs overtook her.

Maggie stayed by his side the whole first night. After having fed, Antony and Randal visited. As Antony stood at the foot of David's bed and studied the still frame lying there, Maggie turned to him with a stoic look of helplessness.

"His spinal cord was severed at the C2 Axis, the doctors say. He cannot breathe on his own. He never will. He cannot eat on his own." Her voice broke with emotion, and she needed a second before continuing. "Of course, this is all academic since the doctors don't expect him to ever come out of the coma, or for that matter, live out the week."

Antony looked at her but said nothing.

"Would turning him fix all these conditions?"

"Yes," Antony said.

"Then you have to do it. Turn him and bring him back to us."

"I will not curse him to this hellish existence. You know about my failure with Bane. I will not be forced to kill another progeny."

"You must know David is nothing like Bane. If you don't do this, he will die. You're willing to let that happen?"

"Yes." Antony hissed. "This existence is worse than death, and I will not put this curse on him. I will let him die."

Maggie gaped, horrified by his admission.

Antony had taken an aggressive stance when voicing his cruel decree but softened as Maggie sank back in her chair, defeated.

"If I turn him, his love for you will be gone. He will never feel human affection for you again. His only desire will be for the blood. You think you will be okay with that but do not see it for the curse that it is. I will not give you that burden."

"Don't dare put this on me. If you let David die, that's on you."

Antony turned and disappeared in a gust of antiseptic wind. Maggie gaped at the spot where he'd been standing. She was going to lose David. Tears streaked her cheeks as she cried soundlessly.

Randal moved into Maggie's arms, releasing her from her shock. As she hugged him, Randal looked up into her glistening eyes. "If I could I would," he said.

She hugged him and cried harder.

They stayed with David for the rest of the night, but as morning approached Maggie walked Randal back to the Zephyr. She found Antony preparing the stainless-steel compartment for their daytime slumber.

As Maggie helped Randal into the sleeping chamber, it occurred to her that this compartment fit Antony and Randal comfortably, but there was absolutely no possible way it could hold another adult male. There was no place for David to sleep like a vampire. This caused more tears to flow. Antony climbed in beside Randal without acknowledging Maggie and closed the lid. A click of the lock and Antony was down for the morning. The possibility that David would be dead when he rose again was very probable.

Maggie returned to David's side.

He received many visitors on the last day of his life. The family he had saved brought more flowers and well-wishes. The police stopped by to check on his condition, and to ask Maggie a few final questions to wrap up the loose ends. Maggie told them what she could, made up some stuff to fill in the gaps for whatever she couldn't tell them, and managed to placate their curiosity enough to send them away without raising any red flags or further inquiries.

Maggie believed the taller of the two investigators seemed to suspect she wasn't entirely truthful, but he didn't linger. He left, satisfied that they had learned all the facts that pertained to the investigation.

What Maggie was hiding: that Randal, the survivor of a previous attack by the Houseguest Killer along with the group traveling in the Zephyr, was actually hunting the killer, and they needed to stay out of their investigation.

Maggie slept.

Night came.

Antony and Randal did not come to visit as she had hoped. Maggie held David's cold hand and tried to warm it. His lips were pale and dry. The machine monitoring his vitals blinked and beeped indifferently as it breathed for its patient. Seconds before it began to happen, Maggie had the vision of David's heart monitor flat-lining, and the nurses and technicians entering the room, disconnecting the wires and starting their resuscitation attempt. Her vision ended before she could see the outcome of their latest effort. Maggie closed her eyes and tears streamed down. A code blue alarm brought a swarm of nurses and doctors in to flutter and scurry around his bed. Maggie stood and turned to leave. She couldn't watch him die. They would not be successful; she knew this even if she hadn't seen it in the vision.

"We lost him," said one of the nurses.

Another voice said, "Okay, I'm going to call it."

Maggie looked at the time. It was ten minutes till sunrise.

Feeling suddenly sick, she looked for something in which to throw up. The vomit caught in her throat and she slapped a hand over her mouth.

She turned, confused when she felt a hot breeze brush by her and the crackling sound of air being parted with supersonic speed. When she looked back, the doctors, nurses, and technicians were standing around an empty bed.

She swallowed the acidy burn in her throat and laughed through her tears.

Chapter Seventeen

Maggie left the panicked hospital personnel standing around the empty bed without offering any explanation. She raced through the hospital to the parking lot where the Zephyr waited. She stormed inside and found Antony straddling David. Antony had finished draining David, then turned his head to look at Maggie. She saw tears gleaming in his red eyes, making it seem as though he were crying tears of blood.

"Pray we do not regret this."

"We won't." Her firm voice reverberated in the small space.

"We have built a new compartment."

Randal opened the space beneath the sink and showed her the smaller compartment. "I wanted my own room anyway."

Maggie laughed.

"David will take the larger compartment with me." Antony lifted his limp friend off the sofa and carried him to the space.

"I knew you didn't want him to die just as much as I did. Damn you for putting me through that."

Antony climbed into the compartment with David, and before closing the lid, Maggie stopped him.

"Thank you," she said.

"I will see you tonight." Antony closed the lid.

Maggie drove the Zephyr away from the hospital and spent the day finding a campground where the RV could be stored in relative seclusion. She was the last human in the group, and the realization of that was not lost on her. The thought bore down on her as loneliness hit her. She napped, then woke and worked out a viable list of prey. There was now a need for seven targets. She hadn't realized how daunting this task was when David shared the responsibility. But by nightfall, she had the unlucky prey planned out.

###

David woke to darkness with a start. He reached out and touched the cold steel box in which he lay and moved his hand along the cold steel wall until his fingers found a face lying nearby. His fingers continued to grope in the dark until he found a mouth with sharp teeth. David froze.

"Good morning," Antony said and expelled David's fingers from his mouth.

Antony reached across David's chest to unbolt the lock. The lid opened and light flooded into the compartment. David adjusted to the glare, and with his new heightened senses detected the heartbeat from a source of food nearby. The rustle of clothing on skin was as loud as sandpaper on wood. The scent of skin caused his nostrils to flair, and then the new smell of blood hit his olfactory nerves.

The drive to feed took over and David flew from the compartment, landing on the source of the heartbeat. He worried at the neck near the carotid, which was where the smell of blood was the strongest, but his flat teeth were not sufficient. The form beneath David thrashed and screamed. He bit into the flesh with the jaw strength of a jaguar and tore a gaping hole in the throat. The soothing, rapturous flow of blood filled his mouth, and he gulped down the delicious food. When the flow of blood slowed, and the heart stopped, David sat up and looked at what he had done.

Blood covered the man David had just drained. It dripped onto the floor and puddled around the body. The man was bare to the waist, and his hands were zip-tied behind his back.

Maggie entered the Zephyr just as David stood. He wiped at the blood on his chin with the back of his hand and watched her with red, bleary eyes. She ran to him and hugged him without fear, ignoring the blood-soaked hospital gown he still wore from the night before.

"Thank you," she closed her eyes and whispered to no one in particular.

David hugged her for several minutes then pulled away and looked into her face. The red haze was gone, and he could see her clearly now. She did not smell like food.

"I'm sorry," he said to her.

"Sorry for what?" she asked.

"I don't know." David looked around, confused. He glanced at the blood he had gotten on her blouse when they had hugged. "For making such an awful mess, I guess."

She laughed. "As long as you clean it up, what do I care?" She examined her bloody clothes. "I guess we can't expect much from a fledgling vampire."

"That was not a graceful display," Antony said.

David turned and hugged him.

"You gave me the gift." He barked a laugh. "I knew you would." His voice grew thick with emotion. "I know you didn't make that choice lightly." He held Antony's gaze for a long time.

"I have told you," Antony said at last. "What we are is hardly a gift."

David laughed and patted him on the back. "I'll have to see that for myself, I guess; because I'm just happy to be alive."

"Don't waste your breath," Maggie said. "He'll make the best of any situation." She turned to David. "I'm happy you're alive, too."

Randal entered the Zephyr holding a knife. "It's about time you lazy vamps woke up. I've been up for ten minutes. I'm all set for the night—fed on a pedophile." He pointed to the corpse slumped over the sofa. As he walked to the corpse, he glanced down at the mess on the floor. Then he turned his gaze to David. He shook his head. "Just what this place needed, another mouth to feed."

"I'm happy to see you, too." David raised an eyebrow at him.

"What can I say?" Randal shrugged. He pulled the body off the sofa and decapitated it "I found an ideal place to dump our prey." He tossed the knife to David.

David decapitated his own corpse that was sprawled out on the kitchen floor. The bodies were wrapped in plastic and carried out to the ravine Randal found. They were weighted and dumped over the edge.

"Do you know the depth of the water down there?" David asked Randal.

"About eighty feet."

David and Randal returned to the RV.

As Antony glanced over Maggie's notes, David joined him. "I want this one and this one."

"Okay, I will take the last three." Antony turned to David. "Let me see you use your vampire speed."

"Easy enough." In a rush of wind, David moved to the door...

...and bounced off.

Maggie laughed but covered her mouth. "Sorry, but that was so funny I almost peed."

"What did I do wrong?" he asked Antony.

It was Randal who answered. "You forgot that you can move your hands as fast as your legs. Use speed to also open the door."

"Very well stated," Antony said. "He is absolutely correct. Your entire body is capable of moving at the speed of sound. It is this that causes the crackling noise as you move. It is a telltale sign that someone near you is moving with a vampire's ability."

'But what—" David started to ask a question, But Antony stopped him.

"There will be time enough for learning," Antony said. "I will show you more another time. We will be driving back to the house in Philadelphia after finishing up with our hunt. We must leave here and think about how to proceed with the destruction of our adversary. We will return when we have a plan of action. We are too well known here at the present time and can return when the events of the past few days are not so fresh in the minds of the people here."

David improved significantly on his second and third targets that night, spilling very little blood. He used a razor instead of his teeth to open the artery and learned to time his throat muscles to spasm with the pulse of the prey's heartbeat. Blood poured down his gullet as if the victim and the vampire were one being.

He also learned to control the flood of memories that pounded through his mind as he drank. Confusing at first, David remembered Antony explaining how drinking the blood produced memory transference from prey to vampire. It was all very exhilarating.

As David drove the Zephyr back to Philadelphia, Maggie rode in the passenger seat. He caught her smiling at him several times.

"You're looking again," David said, catching her out of the corner of his eye.

"Can I help it if I'm ecstatic that you're back and better than ever? I agonized over your broken body for days before Antony finally came to his senses and fixed you. I watched you die again and again until I was sure that the next time you died, you would not come back."

She turned away, she kept her gaze fixed on the road in front of them.

David glanced over at her. "Maggie, what's wrong?"

She didn't look back at him. "I've got something to tell you, David. I didn't think I would get a chance to tell you, but— "

"What is it?"

Maggie's fingernail suddenly became very interesting. She couldn't stop looking at it. Her bottom lip quivered. Her eyes sparkled with the threat of fresh tears.

"Tell me what's going on. You're stressing me out."

"I just feel so lonely. I miss your presence during the day. We used to have such great times. As I plan the nightly events, I think about you and how we used to work so well together. I'm the only human in the group now. I'm the odd girl out."

"Do you want me to change you? I probably could, you know—"

"No." Maggie clutched her stomach protectively.

"I was just kidding. I'd never do anything against your will." David was devastated by her reaction. He never wanted her to worry that he would hurt her in any way.

"I know."

"Are you afraid of me?"

"No."

"I would never hurt you. You know that right?"

"Yes."

"God, Maggie if you think I would do anything to hurt you—"

"I'm pregnant. I'm having your baby."

The Zephyr screeched to a shuttering halt and listed to the right edge of the road. Outside a cloud of dust swirled past the windows. David stared at Maggie with his eyes glazed over and a smile forming on his lips. Shaking from the excitement, David reached out and took Maggie's hands in his. He pulled her into a hug.

"A baby?" David whispered into her ear. "We're going to have a baby. What amazing shit is that?"

Maggie pulled away. "Is this the right thing to do? I mean, a baby? In our lives? What kind of wacky family dynamic is that going to make?"

"An awesome one. We'll work this out. I'll take care of you, I promise."

David pulled back onto the road and continued toward home.

Chapter Eighteen

As the Dark One ran from the house, he raged at what he saw as nothing less than a betrayal. Why would another vampire care who he chose as prey? How pretentious was this other vampire? His rage only intensified as he reached his home and saw the corpse boy wandering aimlessly around the grounds. Not only was his favorite pet stolen, but he would now have to settle for hobos and schizophrenics. Useless trash that barely even knew what was happening to them.

At least he had killed the pathetic human male that had been in his path during his escape; and if there had been time, he would have drained the troublesome fool as well. For that matter, why would a human travel with a vampire? How did the other vamp control the urge to feed on his human pet? And the worst betrayal of all: the human knew what they were. No human should ever know vampires exist. The human had even meant to help fight against him. It was all so preposterous.

That other vampire had his pet, he had a witch woman, and they seemed to know everything about him. How was that possible? They had never crossed paths, and to his knowledge, he had never stolen prey from that other vampire. The other should have left well enough alone. How often had he, the father of the roped boy, inadvertently stumbled upon another vampire's domain? Too often to count, he surmised. He had moved carefully through the hunting grounds of other vampires during the centuries of roaming the land. Never had he dared to come between another vampire and their prey. The one who had taken his pet had crossed that line and would have to be taught the error of his ways.

He knew of the tabloids calling him the Houseguest Killer, but that was not a name he approved of. He would need a new name. He would need to tell his proposed army what to call him. He decided the "Master" would suffice. And so that same night, having lost his opportunity with that last family he had chosen, the Master picked his first disciple. He found a murderous-looking soul wandering the streets and offered to make him immortal.

Although the man first took this as some kind of joke, the Master soon showed him it was not. He took the man, drained him, and then carried his corpse back to the mansion. The Master then returned to the streets and found two more victims on which to feed. These two were not worthy of the gift and so were destroyed. The following night, when the new disciple rose, the two went out into the poor neighborhoods to feed.

The Master had learned his lesson and chose only the bums, the destitute and the infirm for his meals. No one would be missed. There would be no more high-profile attacks from the very heavily publicized Houseguest Killer. When the Master found a potential disciple, he brought them back to the mansion and offered him—or her—the gift. It was important that his minions want to join him. He would not risk another runaway.

Within a month of this recruitment strategy, The Master had three loyal disciples. After two months, his ranks had swelled to seven.

However, after six months and ten disciples, something unusual began to happen. His minion horde began to dwindle. Upon awakening, some nights, one or two of his newest minions would be turned to dust. Although the crowd slumbered in the basement where no daylight could touch them, there would be a drop in their numbers the following night.

To rectify this, The Master purchased more coffins. All his disciples would need their own coffins in which to slumber during the death sleep. He focused on twelve. Twelve coffins for twelve disciples, how fitting.

But this, he learned, would not be the solution to his problem. Even inside the coffins, his minions were not safe. For several nights, The Master continued to wake to empty coffins. Perhaps his minions were fighting amongst themselves, trying to develop a hierarchy. Maybe there needed to be a pecking order.

His very first vampire disciple was still with him. This one, he deemed his second in command. He judged the rest to be fledglings. They were to obey the Master above all else, and they would abide by the next in line of succession when the Master was out.

This seemed to work. The number of missing slowed to only one or two a month, which the Master promptly replaced.

After a year, the number of missing disciples tapered off, and The Master finally had his twelve disciples.

Of the twelve, The Master had eight males and four females. He taught them to fight. He showed them the basics of the hunt and the more delicate points on how to kill other vampires. His followers obeyed his every command. There was only one incident of dissension in the ranks. It was time for the vampires to prove their skills.

The vampires were labeled one through twelve. Number Six was a hairy beast of a thing who did not want a number. "My name is Sam, and I expect to be called Sam," he said to the group.

"You are Number Six," said Number Four, a female. "Live with it."

Six laughed. "I don't have to live with anything anymore. I already died, remember? We all did, you stupid bitch."

The Master overheard the conversation and instructed the group to attack with only a look.

The group fell on Number Six with the ferocity of a pack of hungry wolves. There were screams of rage and pain. When the attack was finished, and there was nothing left of Number Six but body parts crumbling to dust from one side of the room to the other, The Master renumbered his troops. Seven was the new Six; Eight was the new Seven, and so on.

The Master instructed his corpse boy to clean up the mess. Corpse boy worked diligently, disposing of the remains thoroughly. Afterward, there was hardly a speck of proof that the slaughter had occurred.

That night The Master created a new Number Twelve: a male.

His new Number Twelve accepted his rank without question.

Weeks after the disposal of the dissenter, The Master deemed it was time to tell his horde why they had been assembled.

"We must go to war," he said. "There is an enemy out there that must be destroyed. It has been determined, by me, that this vampire is a nuisance to all vampires and his punishment for this indiscretion is death."

"We've already shown what one vampire will face when we work together as a team," said Number Four. Others in the group mumbled their agreement.

"Do not be overconfident. This is not a mere infant. This vampire could possibly have been around as long as I, longer even for all I know. I have no way of knowing. We cannot overestimate him. He has proven himself very resourceful in a fight, and he is not alone."

"How many vampires does he travel with?" a male voice asked.

"Only one," the Master said.

Laughter erupted in the group.

"It's a vampire child."

The laughter grew.

The Master growled, and the laughter stopped abruptly.

"Do not be fooled by this. A child vampire can be just as strong and dangerous as any vampire. In some ways, they can be more dangerous. They tend to be faster, and more resilient: harder to kill, in other words. But that is not all that we must face."

The horde grew silent and listened intently to The Master's every word.

"He travels with a woman; she is a human, yes, but she has amazing power. This woman is—she is a witch, I guess. She has the power of sight. She will see us coming and will be able to warn her vampire counterpart. She must be made a priority target. We will eliminate her first, then the main target."

"What about the child?" asked a female designated as Number Four. He was impressed by her question. Maybe he should have made her the dominant force.

"The child vampire belongs to me. He is to be brought to me unharmed. I will have my roped boy back. If he will not be swayed to stay by my side as my personal pet, well... then, I will be the one to destroy him. Do I make myself clear?"

Everyone agreed.

When the group disbursed, The Master hunted in the poor section of Allentown. The bodies were buried in the surrounding mountains. The Master hated the taste of bums and outcasts. He dreamed of the day when he could return to feeding on the upper-middle class families that had been his favorite meal for so long. He was proud of his disciples and would reward them with lavish gifts upon completion of their task.

Of course, he would also have to destroy them. There was no way he could allow so many of his own creations to walk the earth. There was too significant a risk that their presence would be unfavorable for him in the future. But there would be plenty of time to figure out that mess later. As soon as the more pressing thorn in his side was destroyed, clean up on the horde could begin.

He watched his creations when they were not aware of his presence. They were following his rules well. He had forbidden them to take any minions of their own. Their prey was to be the dregs of society. Prostitutes, bums, and criminals were going to be declining in numbers in the hillside towns and valleys of the Pocono Mountains.

Upon watching the final few of his minions returning to the mansion, The Master ordered the corpse boy to ready the coffins. Corpse boy was expected to open the lids and see to it that all the coffins were sealed tightly upon closure after each vampire was put to rest. Unfortunately, the corpse boy did not communicate. Otherwise, The Master would ask him to watch over the coffins and report to him if he saw any vampires that were waking early and killing others while they slept. He suspected the culprit to be his second in command. If he caught his second in the act of doing this heinous deed, he would deal with it. Until the perpetrator was found, however, The Master's hands were tied.

Soon the horde would be on the move. The Master would have to prepare some mode of travel for himself and his twelve. Corpse boy was a big help, but he could hardly be expected to drive whatever form of transportation he chose for the trip. Corpse boy would have to stay behind and look after the mansion. The lump of rotten flesh would only be in the way on this mission.

The Master saw to it that everyone was laid to rest then he climbed into the only empty coffin and allowed the corpse boy to close the lid. Once inside, he bolted the lid, locking himself in place.

###

All vampires were reposed. The mansion took on the silence of a monastery. The only sound was the shuffling gait as the corpse boy moved through the house. He staggered up the steps to the basement and into the attached garage. He grabbed something off the workbench then returned to the basement. The boy placed a hand on first one coffin, then another. The boy moved through the maze of coffins until he found the one he wanted.

The corpse boy lifted the lid.

Inside the coffin, Number Four lay in the pink silk lining of her coffin, resting peacefully. Then, with both hands, the corpse boy lifted the machete he had retrieved from the workbench and cut off her head. The body turned into a husk of dried leather and the head crumbled into a pile of gray ash.

The corpse boy closed the lid and returned the machete to the garage.

He then retired to a corner of the basement, curled up into a fetal position, and waited for night to fall.

Chapter Nineteen

After leaving the hospital behind, and not ready to deal with their opponent for the moment, Maggie decided to begin working on the baby's room immediately.

There was still some night left to plan. Maggie went room to room looking for the ideal location for the baby's bedroom.

"This room has plenty of windows. I want to put him in here. The crib can go here, under the eaves. I want him to have lots of sunlight." David said.

Maggie laughed. "You keep saying 'him.' So sure are you?"

"Yeah, a boy." David grinned.

"Perhaps you should leave it to the mother's intuition to figure that out. And not just any mother, a witch. I think I would know better than you what the sex of the baby will be."

"What say you, Mother?"

"It's…a…"

David groaned.

"It's a girl." She knew it wouldn't be, but she loved messing with him. She was hoping for a girl she could name Anna-Molly, but she had had a vision of a boy. David would get his boy, but it didn't mean he could spend the next nine months gloating about it.

David shrugged. "I'll love her, too."

First Trimester

Maggie and the crew prepared for the arrival of her new baby. She found a doctor that didn't ask too many questions about her home life. She took her prescribed prenatal vitamins and whiled away the daylight hours alone. She had given up chasing murderers and rapists and left the heavy lifting to the men. She still had visions and used them to help track prey for David and Antony, but she no longer took part in the captures. Strangely, watching them feed made her hungry as well. She couldn't be around them when they fed, or she would end up weighing five hundred pounds.

Antony, strangely, turned very paternal. He doted on her whenever he could, refused to let her do any lifting, or exert herself in any way, and he saw to her every need. David seemed jealous—to the point that he even accused Antony of fathering the child, as absurd as that was.

Maggie just took comfort in the fact that the baby would have two diligent fathers looking after her/him. Maggie had convinced herself it was a girl growing inside her. Or so she hoped. David hoped for a boy, of course.

And then there was the uncle, as Randal referred to himself when he mentioned the baby. What more could a baby want than to have three vicious vampires looking after her?

Maggie laughed at the thought.

She napped a lot during the day. Being alone made her feel lonely. And the loneliness led to depression. Depression made her sleepy. She dreamed a lot. One dream in particular disturbed her more than any others. In the dream, she saw a man. He was a handsome man with unruly auburn hair. The man liked to strip naked and run around on all fours.

He was a murderer, this man. He ripped people apart with his teeth and ate their flesh. She had found that the dream seemed to come in twenty-eight-day cycles for some reason. She wanted to tell David and Antony to go after this man and bring him back to face their distinctive form of justice, but she could not pinpoint his exact location. She didn't want to bring David and Antony into a discussion about this vision until she could determine the specifics of it.

There was another aspect of the dream that confused her. She was aroused by the naked killer with the mop of reddish-brown hair.

On several occasions, she woke from the dream soaked in sweat after having made love to this stranger in her dream. Some days she awoke with a scream on her lips because the stranger had been eating her flesh. On these days, she would place her hand on her stomach and just to feel the baby in her baby kicking. That kicking life inside her always could calm her racing heart, no matter the reason it was racing; be it from fear, or from ecstasy.

The visions from the Dark Father's victims had tapered off until she no longer sensed his activities. She didn't know the reason for the inactivity, but she suspected he had might have moved out of her range of power. He had always only been on the cusp of her visions, perhaps now he was finally off her radar.

Or perhaps the baby had something to do with that as well. Sensing the Dark Father's victims had always taken a toll on her emotions. Maybe her body was protecting the baby by blocking those visions? The only downfall was that it left them vulnerable if the monster decided to attack.

Second Trimester

Randal stood in the doorway of the baby's room. Maggie stood beside him and placed a hand on his back. He looked up at her.

"You seem deep in thought. What's on your mind?" Maggie asked.

"Did you tell David it's a boy yet?" Randal asked.

She sighed. "Yes, unfortunately, he knows. But that's not what's on your mind."

He shook his head. He glanced down both directions of the hall. Maggie did, too. They were alone. He stepped into the room and motioned for her to join him. She entered and closed the door, sensing that privacy was required. She didn't speak but waited for him to tell her what he had on his mind in his own time.

Several moments of silence passed, then he asked, "Have you ever had dreams of me? Or visions, whatever you call them."

She motioned for him to sit in the plush, navy Modway, and she sat in the nearby rocking chair. "I don't typically have visions of the people I see day to day. I think it has to do with proximity—meaning in location to, and in emotional attachments. So, no I don't have visions of you. May I ask what these visions would be if I did have them?"

He shrugged. "I supposed nothing. But I'm having…thoughts."

"You're trapped in an adolescent's body. Of course, you'd have thoughts of—"

"Thoughts of killing innocent people." Randal stared at the floor.

"Oh." She was at a loss for words.

"Am I bad? Am I doomed to be like my father?" He looked up at her. "My vampire maker, I mean."

His eyes dropped back to the floor.

"I know what you mean. And I can assure you it's not the case. You are not like that beast in any way. Have you acted on these urges?"

His head came up, and he looked at her again. "No."

"That's good. That's a start. You'll just have to stay vigilant to these feelings. Don't act on them, and if they get too strong, promise me you'll talk to me before doing something rash."

"I promise." He moved to rise.

Maggie placed a hand on his leg, and Randal stayed seated. She forced him to look into her eyes. "You were right to come to me. I will keep your secret. You cannot tell Antony. I can't imagine how he would react, but I don't want to take the chance he wouldn't understand. Also, if—God forbid—you act on these urges, come to first, and we'll decide together how to handle the situation. If Antony must know, I want to be there when he finds out. Can you promise me this?"

He nodded, stood and hugged her.

Third Trimester

Antony took Maggie to his New Jersey house. They acquainted themselves with the caretakers there, and then Maggie started interviewing nannies. Antony explained that if the danger got too close, she and the baby would need somewhere to take refuge. He didn't want to leave her on her own so a nanny would need to be hired. In the end, Maggie chose an English woman whose aura and personality was ideally suited. Antony peered into her soul, looking for any sign of evil intent. There was none, so he gave his seal of approval, and they had a nanny.

The nanny was given room and board at the mansion on the beach of the Jersey shore. Her one hundred thousand dollars a year salary would start immediately, even if she didn't. The nanny understood that she, like all of Antony's employees, needed to be available at any time in any given situation. She agreed.

Not long after visiting New Jersey, Maggie received a visit from the local law enforcement.

"I'm Detective Smith, and this is my partner, Detective Jones. Do you mind, Ms. Owens, if we ask you a few questions?"

Being called Ms. Owens brought back memories of being on trial. She did not want to revisit that part of her life. "Ask," she said gruffly.

"We'd like to ask you about Grover Dixon. Have you seen him lately?" asked Detective Smith.

"No." She hoped the lie didn't show on her face.

"Are you sure?" Detected Jones asked.

"I'm sure." She knew she was overly hostile with the detectives, but after everything she'd been through, she didn't feel like being helpful to them.

"If you see him, please contact us, ma'am. We have a warrant out for his arrest."

"Why?" Maggie asked.

"We're not at liberty to discuss—"

"Bullshit. If you want to know where he is, you'll tell me why you want him," Maggie said. "You bastards tried to pin my daughter's murder on me. You owe me."

"With all due respect ma'am, we don't owe you—" Detective Jones started to say, but his partner stopped him.

Detective Smith cleared his throat. "There has been a review of the evidence. Apparently, the coroner missed it the first time, but the bruises on Baby...on Molly's body were too large to have been done by... a woman. You have been exonerated of any wrongdoing in this case. We are now looking at Grover as the prime suspect."

"Do I hear you correctly?" Maggie felt her face getting redder by the minute. "You ignored exculpatory evidence that could have cleared me to get a conviction, and now you want my help putting the real perpetrator of this crime behind bars? Is this correct?"

"Ma'am," Detective Jones started to say.

"Call me ma'am one more time you little shit and I'll..." She was going to say, I'll sic my vampire friends on you. She took a deep breath and calmed herself instead.

"If you've seen Mr. Dixon..."

She noticed the cop to the left kept looking at her belly, and she could practically read his mind, though that wasn't one of her...skills.

"No, I haven't seen him. And before you get any ideas, this isn't his baby. But at least you're starting to see this from my point of view, now that it's too late." She flushed.

"Too late? Why do you say that?"

Maggie scrambled for a cover. "I have nothing to do with that monster anymore. He's your problem now, and you'll probably never find him. He should have been arrested when I first told you what he did. It makes me sick that he got away with this. So you should really get out there and start doing your job."

The Birth

Gardner Thomas Jervis was born at 1:18 a.m. on a Wednesday. Maggie fell in love with his doughy flesh, round face; his red button nose and rosy cheeks the minute the nurse placed him in her arms. She was so happy that both David and Antony could be there for the birth. Randal did not come to the hospital but chose to stay home and wait there for word on Maggie's and the baby's status.

That would change, however, as Randal proved he could not only be trusted around the baby but actually a kind and attentive uncle. Sometimes Randal looked at Gardner—or Gar, as Randal would affectionately refer to him—with a look of stern determination and unconditional love that led Maggie to believe Randal would die to protect the baby. Eventually, Antony learned this, too, and relaxed his attitude toward the child vampire. When Antony realized Randal was not the vicious monster he'd expected him to be, Randal officially became part of the group.

Maggie spent many days alone with Gardner, and her mind turned to new ways in which she could help others. She wanted to be a voice against domestic abuse and began research into opening up her own women's shelter. She enlisted David and Antony's help. The three worked out the details, and construction started on Molly Owens' Shelter for Abused Women and Children, or MOSAWC. This turned out to be a doubly good idea since David and Antony could target some of the more aggressive and dangerous men out there abusing women and children.

There were some men not chosen as prey: men who were not overly aggressive, and who had at least some redeeming qualities; but the men who beat their women and children mercilessly, and showed a tendency to escalate their violence, soon became part of the missing just like all the other violent offenders in town.

Maggie liked to make her presence known to the women at the shelter whenever she could. She returned home from the woman's shelter and climbed the stairs to her room where she met up with two of her favorite men.

David sat on the edge of the bed and watched his seven-month-old Gardner swinging and shaking the colorful plastic key ring he held in one plump pink fist. When Maggie entered the room to feed Gar, David stood. "Goodnight baby bunting, daddy's goin' a hunting."

"Okay, that's just creepy, considering what you're hunting," Maggie said and laughed.

David admired his newly formed fangs in the mirror over the dresser. The fangs had started to grow in two months ago. Since then, they'd doubled in size.

They were finally sharp enough to use tonight. His second weapon was a katana, which he bought it a couple of months ago to use when disposing of the corpses. It was a genuine Japanese katana and was as sharp as Maggie's tongue.

"We're going after a group of thugs that kill the elderly for their pension checks. We are performing a very noble act if you ask me." He sounded offended.

"They are still people was my point. Anyway, I was just kidding."

David turned to her and flashed his fangs.

"Impressive," she agreed. "Is Randal going with you tonight?"

"Yes. Will you be okay on your own?"

She scowled at him.

David offered his most charming smile, kissed Gar on the forehead, and then headed out to meet up with Antony.

###

David found Antony in the Livingroom waiting not so patiently, with a glare that said, *why are you not ready yet?*

David shrugged. "I had to give my son a good night kiss."

Randal, standing to the left of Antony, perked up at the mention of his little buddy. Randal smiled, and David could see that his fangs were coming in nicely.

The three took off into the night. Within minutes, they reached their destination and surrounded the five men they had targeted. The muggers had finished trolling in a dark alley and were divvying up the night's riches. The youngest looked to be about seventeen. Randal claimed him. The others were in their twenties. The group seemed unconcerned by the trio's arrival. To the muggers—who outnumbered the newcomers—they were just three new victims. And one of them was only a kid. The muggers surrounded their prey.

Randal was the first to strike. He was hungry and could wait no longer. He leaped and brought his prey to the ground, his fangs piercing the boy's neck. Instantly, the blood flowed.

Two men converged on Randal, intending to protect their young member, but Antony intervened. Antony grabbed one by the throat, holding him in place as he pulled the second into his deadly bite. Antony drank the first then tossed the body aside and drank from the prey he had been holding out at an arm's length.

David waited for one of his two attackers to move. As the man swung his leg up waist high with a powerful roundhouse, David easily ducked under the attack and moved to stand behind the kicker. Wrapping his arm around the man's neck, immobilizing him, David grabbed the final man as he approached. David pulled him into his embrace and drained him. As that victim crumpled to the ground, David turned to the man struggling against his iron headlock. David delighted at the ease of his fangs sinking into the man's neck, sending the delicious flood down his throat.

The three vampires stared at the five corpses littering the ground around them. David unsheathed the katana on his hip and went to work decapitating the bodies. The bodies were collected and disposed of in the sewers. Randal was finished for the night, so he returned home while the others continued to hunt.

Antony's third victim that night was a rapist he had read about in the Philadelphia Enquirer. This rapist was accused of killing his latest victim. The police had no leads, but Antony had Maggie. Antony paid his prey a visit as he lay sleeping in his bed, and just like that, there was one less rapist in the world.

David visited a rather nasty child molester in another part of town. He returned to find Maggie asleep in the recliner, Gardner nestled on her chest. He covered them and headed to his room to retire for the night. Once again, his skill at walking through the house without making a sound came into play.

Maggie woke as Gardner began to stir. She peered out the window at the bright morning light. The vampires had returned and, like silent phantoms, had let her sleep. What thoughtful monsters they are.

She fixed Gardner a bottle and fed him, played with him, and napped when she could. The day passed quickly, and the vampires woke to find her walking the floor with a crying baby in her arms. David leaned over and whispered something in the baby's ear so low all Maggie could hear, even at such close range, was a light breeze. But whatever David had said quieted Gardner. He kissed her cheek and followed Antony into the den.

The den was the computer room Maggie, and the vampires used to oversee the acquisition of prey. Randal took note of a child killer that he decided would never see the inside of a courtroom. He headed out with the information he needed to track down his prey. Antony scanned the clutter of notes and scrap paper, where Maggie had jotted down the different dreams and visions she'd had. He didn't see anything that spoke to him.

Maggie entered the room, bouncing Gardner in her arms.

"Not much to choose from," Antony said.

David picked out who he would track down and disappeared in a crackling puff of wind.

Maggie stepped closer to the desk and looked into Antony's eyes. "I have been having a dream lately that has been disturbing me. I've avoided telling you because I was having trouble pinning down exactly what—or who—I was seeing. I have what I need now, and I think it's time to track him down. His name is Dylan Moyer, and he lives in Delaware. Exactly where, I'm not sure, because he moves around a lot. He's a nomad, homeless. He is a cannibal, stripping naked and eating his prey alive. He's an exceptionally horrendous individual, and my dreams would indicate that I might be one of his victims one day."

Antony set his jaw. "I will find him. And you will have nothing to fear from him."

Maggie sighed, relieved to hear this. She handed Gardner to Antony and jotted down the information Antony would need to find the cannibal killer. Antony rarely made to hold Gardner, now held the baby out at arm's length, unsure what he was doing. The baby dangled there, staring at Antony with a dull expression of curiosity. A line of drool dripped from the child's bottom lip to his onesie. Antony scooped up the notes and was gone as soon as Maggie took the baby out of his hands.

Maggie's notes were surprisingly detailed. Antony used vampire speed to travel to Delaware and learned that there was a Dylan Moyer at the homeless shelter. He captured Dylan easily, and after looking into the auburn-haired man's hazel eyes, he could not determine if there was evil in this man. Dylan definitely had murder on his soul, but there was something else there, too; something that looked like… innocence. How could someone be guilty and innocent? Antony finally decided that Dylan would have to go back with him to Philadelphia. With Maggie's help, perhaps they could get to the truth. He drugged the man and carried him over his shoulder, running at the speed of sound.

Antony had spent the entire night hunting Dylan, and then had not even taken him as food. David saw the desperation in Antony and brought back three pedophiles for Antony. Pedophiles were the fastest prey to catch. David enjoyed taking them off the street, as did the majority of the public.

Having fed, Antony woke Dylan. The drowsy man sat up on the sofa and looked around. He was definitely not at home. He looked over the trio of individuals standing in front of him. He lingered a little longer on Maggie. He smiled at her. She did not offer one back.

"You have murdered, but you are not evil; you must explain this inconsistency." Antony drew Dylan's attention away from Maggie.

"Who are you?" Dylan asked. He showed no fear of them. Instead, he seemed to pity his captors. His eyes were almost sad.

"It would seem to me that the abducted person should answer the abductor's question, not the other way around; is that not a clear assessment of this situation?" Antony moved closer to him as he spoke. He recalled Maggie's fear of being eaten by the cannibal, and he didn't want to take any chances.

Dylan considered this and concluded his abductor was correct.

"I have murdered, but it was out of my control."

"How is that possible?"

"You're better off not knowing. Why have you brought me here? Who are you people?"

Maggie couldn't stay quiet any longer. "You have eaten your victims. I have seen you do it. Do you deny that?"

Dylan turned and looked at Maggie once again. However, this time he did not flirt. He looked at her with fear, but not for himself. This man feared *for* her. When Maggie saw him giving her this look, as if he could kill her and yet still feel remorse about it, she grew annoyed. She needed pity from no one. She squared her jaw and crossed her arms defiantly over her chest.

Then suddenly the man's expression changed. Now he looked at her as if he had forgotten to turn the oven off before leaving home. He tried to stand, but Antony knocked him back down.

"You saw me kill?" he asked, looking at Maggie. "You said that. You saw it?"

"It was in a vision." Maggie dropped her hands.

"What did I look like… in this vision?" He said this last word as though he were only humoring her and did not believe her.

Maggie was confused. She turned to Antony for guidance. He urged her to continue with a glance.

"You looked like you do now, only you were..." She thought about what she should say. "You were nude."

Dylan nodded, fascinated by this revelation. Finally, he turned to Antony and spoke. "I have a personality disorder," he said. "I have a dual personality that I have no memory of when it is in control of my body. This other personality is very violent. I have tried to keep this personality in check, but sometimes I mess up."

"How do you keep this personality in check if you do not know when you might relinquish your power over to it?"

Dylan laughed. "Oh, trust me I know when this personality takes over. It's like clockwork. I lose control to my murderous side every twenty-eight days. Like I said, I am aware of when I lose control; I just have no memory of anything that happens during that time. I can lock myself up before the time comes and let myself out when I regain control.

"You say you have a pretty regular cycle then," Maggie said.

"Pretty much, yes," Dylan gave her a knowing smile.

"When do you expect this cycle to occur next?" David asked.

Dylan seemed to consider whether or not to answer him, and then sighed and continued. "In about forty-eight hours. Trust me, guys. You don't want to be near me when this happens."

"We're in no danger from you, David Banner," Maggie said.

"You are our guest for the next forty-eight hours; I insist," Antony said.

"You're kidnapping me?" Dylan asked.

"Look on the bright side," Maggie said.

"Yea? And what's that?"

Antony finished for Maggie. He spoke in a whisper, and with a demonic grin stretched across his face.

"We were just going to kill you."

Dylan tried not to show a response, but he shivered at the words anyway.

Chapter Twenty

Maggie stood in the doorway of the bedroom where they had stowed their mysterious guest and watched him sitting on the edge of the bed studying the chains that bound him to the bedpost. She tried to discern why his aura was an oily brown color. There was something preternatural about him, but she didn't know what. Determined to figure out his secret, she visited him several times throughout the day, coming up with questions to ask and other reasons to be there.

"Back again?" he said, though he hadn't turned to look at her.

Maggie entered the room with Gardner in her arms and sat in a chair out of reach of the chains.

"I'm impressed," he said.

Maggie kept a firm grip on Gardner as she took a seat in the recliner at the foot of the bed. "Impressed by what?"

With his hands bound, Dylan bowed to the young master of the house. "That you would bring the young master to visit me."

He was a very well-mannered prisoner, but a prisoner just the same, she reminded herself. "He's safe with me."

"Is this handsome man your son?" he asked, and Gardner laughed at him. He reached out to Dylan, but Maggie turned him away.

"His name is Gardner."

"Who's the Daddy?"

"Not your concern." Maggie's face heated. "And I'll ask the questions if you don't mind."

"It's the tall blond guy, right?"

She didn't react to this, but she knew he had somehow read this truth in her face.

"He has his daddy's eyes and chin. Are you married? Or, should I say: are you a couple?"

"I'd like you to tell me more about what I saw in these visions of you."

"They're your visions. I'd have thought you knew everything there was to know about them. I'm just fascinated by the fact that you had a vision of me at all. Are you psychic?"

"I can't help but notice you try to answer all my questions with a question of your own. Do you think I'm stupid enough to fall for that?"

Dylan shrugged. "Hey, I tried."

"Let's try this again. If you answer my questions, and I approve of your response, I'll let you ask me a question."

"A game. Let's play."

"Now, in my vision you are nude, running on all fours, killing people with your teeth. You seem to know why I would have this vision. What do you know about the source of this vision?"

Dylan inhaled deeply then released his breath slowly. "Here it is: I have periods of blackouts. It must be during these periods of my life that you are having visions of me. I'm not aware of what I do. I can't stop it. I wish it weren't true, but it's just a part of me. That's all I have."

"Was that so hard? Now ask me one question."

"When you have these visions, do you send the men out to kill the perpetrators of your visions?"

"It's not like that. There are checks and balances. Antony and David can see the truth when they look into the eyes of the prey—or, uh predator.

Dylan's questioning gaze caused her to look away.

"You said 'prey.' That's an odd word to use."

Maggie's head whipped around to him again.

"I didn't ask a question. I'm waiting for you to ask me one."

Maggie's chest heaved. She took a few seconds to slow her breathing. "How long are you in this blackout state?"

"They last about twelve hours. Basically, we're talking sundown to sunup. I'd like to ask another question."

She gave a single quick nod.

"Antony and David are here in the house right now I'm taking it. But they are very quiet. And I notice only you go to Gardner when he fusses."

"You haven't asked a question."

"That's simple: what are they doing during the day?"

Maggie suddenly regretted her visit to their prisoner.

"The game is over." Maggie stood to leave.

"Please don't go yet. I have one more thing I wanted to ask you."

Maggie returned to her seat.

"In your vision of me, was I human?"

She bounced Gar in her arms as if she were trying to calm him from crying even though he wasn't. "Human?" She found that to be an odd expression.

"Yes. You were in the nude, but you were definitely human. Why would you ask that?"

"Let's just say that I was under the impression that my alternate personality was... less than human." Dylan shrugged. "Anyway, the important thing is my alternate personality is strong. These handcuffs and chains will not hold him. Do you have an iron cage? I need to be well confined and far from you and Gardner when I... switch personalities. Do you have something like that here?"

"We do, actually."

"The best thing to do is to move me there before it's too late."

"Are you a Dr. Jekyll and Mr. Hyde?"

"Sort of, but much more dangerous. I would have expected you to see some changes in my appearance. That's why I'm shocked you see me as a human in your vision."

"Well, that's not impossible. My vision is just an interpretation of the moment. It's not like I see the actual event as it happened. My vision might be stripping away the unnecessary details for me to recognize you."

"An interesting analysis," Dylan said.

"Anyway, why do you think you would look differently? What do you turn into?"

Dylan laughed. "You'll find out first hand if I stay here much longer."

As Dylan sat on the edge of the bed, Maggie shifted Gardner's weight. The baby slipped out of her arms. As she reached out to catch him, Gar sprinted away from his mother in a surprising show of speed and ran into Dylan's arms.

Maggie jumped up but didn't move beyond that. She drew her hands up as if surrendering. "Give him to me."

Dylan held Gar up at eye level and looked into the boy's eyes, then he looked at Maggie. Her scowling eyes filled with tears and her hands clenched into fists at her sides.

Dylan continued to hold the boy at arm's length but kept his eyes turned to Maggie.

He looked at Gar. The boy was laughing. Dylan smiled, pulled the boy closer, kissed him on the cheek, then put him on the floor. Gar ran back into his mother's eagerly waiting arms.

"He wasn't afraid of me," Dylan said. "He has no reason to be. Neither do you. For now, anyway."

"I don't care. You don't go near him, or I'll kill you myself."

"I would never intentionally hurt your son or anyone else for that matter. Not until the night following tonight. Just remember to move me to the cage you said will hold me."

Maggie wasn't really listening to Dylan anymore. She was scurrying out of the room with a death grip on Gardner. The boy turned, pointed at the man chained to the bed and uttered what was very likely his first word.

Gar said, "Doggie."

Chapter Twenty-One

Maggie paced until the vampires woke. Then she avoided them until they left for their hunt. She didn't want to deal with their "Hangry" judgment of her actions during the day. When they returned, she told them that Dylan had agreed to be locked in the panic room.

"He's not sure if it will hold, though."

"Hold… him?" David laughed. "That wimp couldn't break a bendy straw." When Maggie didn't laugh at his joke, he relented. "Sure, moving him might be a good idea. Better safe than sorry."

Maggie didn't tell him she had taken Gardner into the room and then lost control of the situation. If David didn't kill her, he would surely have killed Dylan. She also didn't tell David about Gar's first word, mostly because she wasn't sure what Gar had said. It sounded as though Gar had called Dylan "daddy," and she didn't want David's feelings hurt knowing his son had named another man—a stranger, in fact—daddy.

David fixed Maggie with a questioning glance, and she knew that he was aware that there was something not being said. When she didn't elaborate, he didn't pursue the issue. She sighed, visibly relieved to let the matter go.

"I agree he should be moved," Antony said.

The threesome climbed the stairs to the room. Maggie cringed when she realized Dylan could give away her secret.

Dylan stood and faced his visitors. Maggie saw the fright on his face.

"Relax," she said. "We aren't here to kill you."

David gave her a confused squint. He turned back to Dylan and smiled. "We're moving you to the panic room."

It took a long time, but Dylan eventually took his eyes off Maggie and turned to David. "Panic room?"

"Yeah, but it's not what you think. You'll be locked into a room made of six inches of solid steel."

"Okay. If you think it will hold, lead the way."

"You're a very cooperative captive, I must say," David said as he removed the chain but kept him in the handcuffs.

"I know you're doing the right thing, that's all. By controlling me, you're doing me a big favor. Why wouldn't I cooperate?" Dylan's broad smile seemed genuine.

David walked beside Dylan, and Maggie laughed silently to herself when she realized he was puffing out his chest and exaggerating his height in an attempt to impress the stranger.

"You're homeless?" David asked.

Maggie gave him a shove.

He turned back to look at her. "What? Well, isn't he?"

"Rude," she said.

Dylan laughed. "I don't mind the question. Yes, I was living at a homeless shelter when you found me. I'm a traveler by nature, but I stopped for a soft place to sleep and a hot meal. I would have been leaving there anyway if you hadn't caught me. I try to get away from populated areas when my… personality changes."

"Personality changes." David scoffed.

Dylan stopped to look at David. "You joke, but it won't be a laughing matter if this tin room of yours doesn't hold."

"It will hold," Antony said. The group continued walking.

David nodded. "Right, I wouldn't allow you to stay if I thought you would put my defenseless child and his mother in danger."

"Defenseless?" Maggie shoved David's shoulder again.

"Gar is." David shrugged. "Hey, I'm trying to make a point. Relax."

"I'm looking forward to seeing this room. I'd like to inspect it before I get locked in. If I don't think it's going to work, I'll have to insist—for your own sakes—you let me go so I can get as far away from civilization as possible."

David said, "You aren't going anywhere, but you don't need to be locked up yet. Let's head to the living room and talk."

Antony glowered as David removed the handcuffs on Dylan's wrists.

He rubbed his sore wrists and thanked David quietly. "You won't be disappointed."

As the group started walking again, Maggie pulled David behind so she could talk to him privately.

"Do you really think it's a good idea to let him run around free? I don't trust him."

David hugged her and held her hands after he stepped back. "Do you think he can overpower—not one, but two—vampires? Not to mention Randal will tear off his head if he went near Gardner. He can't run away, either. Well, he can run all he wants, but he's no match for our vampire speed."

Maggie stared at her hands after David released them.

"But I'll tell you what I think. I think he's safe. I want us to trust him, and him to trust us. I want him to join us."

Maggie dropped her hands, and her eyes flicked up to David's face. "What?"

"Think about it. If he's trustworthy—and I really think he is—he can be here to help protect you and Gar during the day."

Maggie scowled. "I'm not defenseless, David—"

"I'm not saying you are. But face it, wouldn't it be nice to talk to a grown up during the day?"

"Are you two planning to murder me back there?" Dylan didn't stop walking or look back.

Maggie started walking again. "Why does it have to be him, though."

They led Dylan to the panic room where in a few hours, he would be kept safe from harming others. He pounded on it. He measured the door and tested its lock.

"How do you open it?" Dylan asked.

"Like this." David hit the big red button about chest high on the adjacent wall, and the door opened slowly.

"And you can't open it from the inside? What if one of you got locked in there by accident?"

"I guess we'd have to wait until one of the others came along and let us out." Under his breath, so only Maggie could hear him, he added, "In the case of us immortals that could be a really long time."

She giggled.

When Dylan glanced over at her with a knowing smirk, she stopped. He turned back to the room and clapped his hands together. "This just might work."

The four exited the basement and entered the living room where Randal sat on the floor playing with Gar. He pulled the baby closer to him when he saw the stranger in their midst.

"Don't worry," David said. "He will be confined again at dawn."

"There is really no danger from me until tomorrow night."

Randal walked around Dylan, leaning into him and sniffing the air. "His blood smells funny," Randal declared and walked away.

Dylan just stared at the boy.

Dylan proved to be as good as his word. He was helpful and courteous. He showed no signs of making any attempt to escape. Maggie prickled at the thought of everyone getting along with this imposter.

There was some anticipation about the following night, although no one was willing to admit they were thinking about it. The main topic filling the room was Dylan and his violent alter ego. When dawn approached, Dylan was escorted to the basement.

David said, "We're doing this is to keep Maggie and Gardner safe. You get that, right? Maggie and Gar's safety is of utmost importance to us. We will see how tomorrow night transpires, and if all goes well you will be free to go, or you can stay with us if you want."

"Or to go." Antony and Maggie said it at the same time.

Dylan smiled, nodded and watched the others duck out of the steel room then close the door.

###

Dylan listened to the whoosh as the doors were hermetically sealed. He sat down on the futon they had provided for him and waited out the seclusion in semi-darkness. There was some light shining down on him from above, where several LED lights, no bigger than pencil erasers, dotted the ceiling. Also embedded in the ceiling were small, round vents pouring fresh, HEPA-filtered air into the room. He was not cold, he was not warm. In fact, the atmospheric conditions were so ideal he felt himself getting drowsy and had no trouble falling asleep.

Dylan bolted out of a sound sleep. He had no idea of the time, but he was sure it was close to nighttime. He looked toward the door. It was still sealed. He walked over and inspected the seal. He suspected that the door was magnetically sealed. Depending on the tons of pressure it could withstand this door should be able to hold him in. If not, nothing could help this family from the horrors that would befall them when his alter ego escaped.

If there were cameras on him, he couldn't see them. There was no change in the steel walls, not even welding creases, so he doubted there were cameras. And if there were no cameras, it could also be determined that there were no microphones either. The family outside was blind and deaf to the activities occurring in their panic room.

Dylan's stomach cramped, and he knew that he had slept through the day, and it was the night of his transformation. The alter ego was struggling to be set free. If he fought against it, the process would be excruciatingly painful. He had learned not to fight. The cramps dropped Dylan to his hands and knees. Recovering from the first set of pains, Dylan stood. He stripped off his shirt and then stepped out of his jeans. He had become a commando kind of guy since all this had begun happening to him. When you needed to undress quickly, it was best to have as few clothes on as possible. He folded his clothes neatly on the futon. He had no sooner finished this when a new series of cramps wracked his body. He screamed and collapsed to the cold steel floor of the panic room, rolling and crying out as the pain took him into a new consciousness. Apparently, some part of him still wished to fight the alteration. In the soundproof room, however, no one could hear his screams.

Chapter Twenty-Two

David hit the light switch at the top of the stairs, illuminating the rickety wooden steps leading down to the basement. It was a basement like any other: cement walls, cement floor, wood beams in the ceiling marked the rafters of the floor above. There were cobwebs covering everything, hanging down like gray gossamer drapes. The basement was a well-lit, open space below the house. There was a partition cutting the basement in half. In the first half of the basement, where the stairs were located, the incinerator sat like a giant steel oven in the corner. In the other side of the cellar, beyond the partition, was the panic room.

This room was airtight and soundproof. There were six inches of steel locking Dylan in. He could not escape the room, no matter what this other person thought it could do.

David stood near the door to the panic room as Maggie stayed in the doorway of the partition, ready to bolt at the first sign of trouble. Randal, having already hunted for the night, stayed upstairs with Gardner.

Antony stood on the side of the panic room. He placed a hand on the steel outer wall to the right of the door.

David stood halfway between the door to the panic room and the entrance to the stairs. He stared intently at the door, wondering what was happening inside the room. From where he stood, it seemed as if nothing was going to happen.

Then…

He heard nothing, but he saw a dent form in the steel door. David jumped back, forgetting that he was the monster. He laughed nervously when he saw Antony's disapproving glare.

David moved back even further when he saw another dent form in the door.

"What the hell could dent seven inches of solid steel?" He looked to Antony for an answer, but there was no answer to be given.

Maggie, seeing the dents forming in the door now, moved closer to the panic room, concerned for David.

David moved closer to Maggie, motioning for her to get back.

Maggie didn't move.

Another dent hit the door, only this time it was accompanied by… sound?

It was true. The panic room was no longer soundproof. When another thump on the door resounded, everyone flinched, including Antony.

Boom—and the door dented again.

Boom—

Boom—

Antony studied the door, checking the magnetic seal.

David, thinking the door was about to breach, shoved Maggie back toward the doorway. He used a little too much vampire force, and Maggie flew against the wall. Her shoulder bumped the lever to activate the sealed door.

Even faster than Antony could move, the door opened with a whoosh as the vacuum seal broke. Something large, heavy, and hairy burst out of the panic room, jumping over Antony's head. The brown furred beast landed on the floor between David and Maggie. It growled at David, and he had less than a second to study the wolf before it turned on Maggie.

The wolf was too large and misshapen to be an ordinary wolf. It snarled and attacked her, going for the neck. She had just enough time to lift her hands and ward off the bite that would have ripped out her throat. The snarling, foaming fangs made another attempt at her, but David was there; he ripped the beast off Maggie by its hind legs and threw it back into the panic room. As it struggled to gain its footing, David hit the lever and closed the door. Antony was there at the entrance to push it back when it tried to leap out of the room before the doors closed again.

But then the doors did close, and the wolf thing was once again locked inside. It pounded on the door for a while longer, and then seemed to settle down for the night.

David helped Maggie to her feet. "Are you okay?"

She nodded, shaken but apparently unharmed.

"I saw its eyes," she said and shivered. "It had human eyes. It had Dylan's eyes."

This was what Dylan had been reluctant to tell them. Dylan wasn't a killer, but his werewolf was.

"I need to hunt," Antony said to David. "Will you be okay here alone?"

David nodded. He turned to Maggie. "You should go upstairs. I doubt he will get out again, but if he does, I'll have a better chance at capturing him if I'm alone."

Maggie understood and headed up the stairs.

Antony hunted first, and then David headed out when he returned.

###

Maggie entered her room and stripped out of the slobber-stained and torn blouse. There was blood. Panicked, she ran to the bathroom and washed her arm so she could see why she was bleeding. There was a row of puncture wounds across her lower arm, near her wrist. There were four teeth marks in the skin, and the two outer holes still bled where the teeth had penetrated.

"Oh no." Her voice was a hoarse whisper. Her hands trembled with the realization that she had been bitten by a werewolf. Her mind raced with the possibilities. As she stared at the wound, she could see the skin repairing itself. Within minutes, she saw pink scar tissue where the bite had been. After another few minutes, the scar cleared, and perfect skin once again covered her arm.

She ran downstairs where Randal and Gar were playing a round of peek-a-boo that had the baby in hysterics.

"There's been a complication downstairs," she said.

"I heard the commotion. What happened?"

"Apparently, we've been harboring a werewolf. He escaped, but we managed to put him back in the panic room."

"I kind of figured. Is everyone okay?"

"We're golden," Maggie said and rubbed the arm that still itched from the healing. "But I'm wondering if Gar wouldn't be safer somewhere else."

Randal said, "Ah-boo." And then was met with hysterical baby giggles.

"Would you be willing to take him to the Jersey safe house if things start to go wonky around here?"

"Of course," Randal said. "Gar's safety is the most important thing to me."

Downstairs, Antony and David traded off. Maggie returned to the basement. Antony glanced at her. He read something in her eyes.

"What is wrong. You look scared. You never look scared."

She recovered quickly. "I'm concerned about Gardner. I asked Randal to take him away if things go bad down here."

"Good idea." Antony turned back toward the door. "Should be fine, though. He has been quiet for hours. I think he is finally settling down."

"When are you going to release him?"

Antony glanced at the door. "I think we should wait until tomorrow night."

"I want to be here when you open them."

"You should go back upstairs. I can handle this. You are vulnerable to an attack."

"I'll be okay. I have questions, and he has to provide them. Or at least help me figure out how to get them..."

As Antony stood to watch over the door, o more attacks came from inside. David returned a short time later.

"What's she doing here?"

"She insists on being here when we opened the doors." Antony glanced at her and returned his watchful gaze to the panic room door.

David stood over Maggie. He has to stay there until tomorrow night. You should—"

"Let him out."

He sighed. "Fine. We might as well see what's happening in there."

"David, stand by the controls. Maggie take a position around the corner where the wolf will not see you when it emerges if it is still in there. I will stand in its way if it tries to escape."

He nodded for David to open the latch when everyone was in place. David slapped the button that Maggie had hit while backing up earlier that night, and once again the panic room door popped open with a hiss of the vacuum seal breaking.

Antony inched closer to the opening, ready if something jumped out at him. David stayed by the button in case they needed to seal it again in a hurry. Maggie tried to see around the corner of the panic room, but Antony motioned her back.

Antony stiffened as he passed the threshold. He peered in, but what he saw there did not cause him alarm. He stepped away from the door.

Maggie came around and peered in.

The human Dylan lay curled in a fetal ball on the floor, naked and asleep. When David came over and saw this, he slapped roughly on the steel wall.

"Wake up sleepyhead and get dressed."

Maggie scowled at him.

Dylan lifted his head and looked at them. He stood. Maggie was amazed at his lack of modesty.

"Aren't you the confident one?" she said.

"Huh?" He realized he was naked and reached for the clothes he had folded and laid neatly aside. "Oh. Sorry. When you wake up naked, as often as I do, you start to forget it's not normal."

Maggie entered the room and looked around. She gaped at the deep grooves in the steel. "You tore this place up. You're going to have to pay for this." She backed out of the doorway to give him a modicum of privacy. When he had finished dressing, he joined them near the basement steps.

"It's actually quite comfortable in there," he said.

"I'm sure the people we normally stash in there wouldn't feel that way." David grinned.

Dylan looked back into the brightly lit room. The lights glistened off the steel, making it even brighter. "So that's where you stash your murderers before you execute them."

"Something like that," Maggie said.

Dylan turned toward the stairs and headed up.

"Not so fast, Rex," Maggie said. "We have a baby upstairs, and we need to know he's not in any danger from you."

"Oh, okay."

"You got out while you were in your hairy state. We know what you are now, lycanthrope." Maggie watched his reaction.

Antony stepped forward to clarify the matter. "By accident. You were released for a few seconds, but we managed to get you back inside before you were able to do any serious damage."

Dylan looked concerned. "Was anyone bitten?"

"No," David said. "You went after Maggie, but we forced you back into the panic room in time."

"Were you bitten?" Dylan turned to Maggie.

"No, she said she was okay," David responded for Maggie. Typically, she wouldn't have allowed him to do, but at the moment, she stayed quiet.

"Was anyone else bitten? And how were you able to contain me?"

David said nothing for quite a while. Now it was time to tell Dylan the truth about Antony and himself.

"Biting Antony or me wouldn't have mattered," David finally said. "You aren't the only monster in the room. We're vampires." David smiled and flashed his fangs.

"I knew it." Dylan slapped his leg. "I mean, I didn't, but I suspected."

"Our blood doesn't pump through our bodies. You can't infect us. And we are immortal. We cannot be changed or altered in any way."

Dylan studied David, fascinated. He turned to Antony, and he, too, showed his fangs.

"What about Randal... and the baby?"

"I only just turned to vampire within the last year, so I'm a noob." David laughed. "Gardner was conceived when I was still human. When Maggie was pregnant, I was attacked and almost died. To save me, Antony had to turn me. Randal is a vampire. We—you might say we adopted Randal. He was created by a vampire with no respect for human life. It was that same vampire who almost killed me. You could say the evil being that created Randal also created me."

"Don't all vampires lack respect for human life? I mean, you all kill to continue to exist."

Antony spoke up now. "We must drink human blood, yes: at least eighteen pints every night. If we do not obtain this by night's end, our killer instincts take over, and we are not able to control our own actions. We would kill without discretion. We would kill anyone within our reach. For that reason, Randal,

David, and I only hunt murderers and pedophiles and rapists. We hunt the corrupt, depraved, and immoral. Killers that get away with their crimes, or just cannot seem to stop their vile acts are our preferred prey. We do not attack the innocent or the repentant. We would never have killed you after knowing you were not responsible for your actions."

"Could you drain me? I don't know… would that kill me?"

"We do not drink animal blood, so we could not drain you as a wolf. But I see no reason why I could not drain you in your human form. But I have never known a werewolf, so I do not have an answer for you. I do not know if you would die from lack of blood as you can regenerate quickly, correct? Therefore, I would believe you could regenerate blood faster than I could drink it," Antony said.

Dylan nodded. "Interesting hypothesis, but I'm not curious enough to find out."

"You are in no danger from us, and you are welcome to stay with us if you wish. We can help keep the public safe from you," said Antony.

"I would be happy to stay. It's been a while since I've been around someone who knows what I am."

David said, "We will gladly let you join our ranks, but there is one more thing I must tell you before you really make this decision. You heard me mention the vampire that tried to kill me, and who made Randal an orphan vampire, but you should know that we are at war with this vampire. Our goal is to destroy him. Being with us will put you in danger."

"I'm not afraid," Dylan puffed out his chest. "You can count me in."

David smiled and shook Dylan's hand. "Welcome to the group."

Part Four: Dylan

Chapter Twenty-Three

Dylan ate half the contents of the refrigerator once he was allowed upstairs. When he was finished chomping on a ham and cheese on wheat, a quart container of rocky road ice cream and a half a dozen cold chicken wings, he was ready to answer the rest of Maggie's questions. Maggie sat to the left of Dylan and David sat to his right. Maggie opened her mouth, but David was so anxious to question Dylan himself he didn't allow her to form the words.

"Why didn't you tell us you were a werewolf? Just how powerful are you in that state? How could you turn into a werewolf when the full moon isn't for another six days?"

After washing down a mouthful of chicken flesh with a root beer, Dylan interrupted the stream of questions to begin his answers.

"I didn't tell you exactly what I was because I didn't know how—or if—you could handle knowing the truth. Would you have taken me seriously if I had spouted off about being a werewolf from the start? I wasn't sure, so I didn't take the chance. I'm sorry for not giving you the benefit of the doubt. And honestly, I don't know how powerful I am. I believe I'm stronger than an ordinary wolf, but by how much, I don't know. Never tested the theory. And if you've never seen a werewolf, I didn't think you would know the difference between a wolf and a werewolf. They are quite similar in appearance."

"I know you're uglier than an ordinary wolf," David said.

Dylan ignored him.

"My transformation cycle isn't in synchronization with the moon. Some werewolves probably do, and maybe that's where the myth was born, but not mine. It's been over twenty years, but there is still so much about the ability that I don't understand."

"Maybe Maggie could help you," David said.

Maggie flushed with guilt and shame for the lie she was carrying. Did David know of her new power to heal rapidly? She thought she had been so careful. But then it dawned on her that he was speaking of her visions, and she regained her composure.

She shrugged. "I'm clairvoyant, but that won't help me to understand what he is. In fact, in my visions, I never see a wolf. The best I can do is to tell you that werewolves have a brown aura. That's not much help here, though."

"Let me see if I have this straight," Dylan said. "I'm in a house occupied by a witch, three vampires, and a human baby?"

"And now we can add a werewolf to the mix," David said.

Maggie cleared her throat. "Let's not forget the witch is human, too."

Dylan shrugged. "Okay."

David whispered to Dylan. "She likes to be included on everything."

Maggie reached across the table and punched David in the arm. "I can hear you."

David laughed.

"Is there time for me to tell you how I became a werewolf? I mean, I know vampires have to hide from the sun, right?"

"We do," said Antony. "But there is still time. Tell us your story."

The group retired to the living room where they could all get comfortable. Randal took Gardner to another part of the house, apparently disinterested in hearing what the werewolf had to say.

David and Maggie sat on the couch side by side. Dylan took the recliner, and Antony stood near the window.

Dylan looked around the room at the eager faces and smiled. "I'm elated to tell my grim story. What does that say about me?" He laughed. "But then I've never had anyone to tell it to."

Maggie said, "Until now."

Dylan's Story

It started twenty-two years ago on a two-week camping trip with my friends to the Bridge Bay Campgrounds in Yellowstone Park. It was the trip of the century, and we'd been looking forward to it all year: Alan, Jacob—or Jack as we affectionately referred to him, Maria who was Alan's girlfriend, and Julie. Our campsite was ideal just off Yellowstone Lake. It was secluded enough so that we didn't run into a lot of other campers until we left for the various sights. We were really looking forward to seeing Old Faithful and the different hotspots; at least I know I was. Julie was our serious nature lover and animal spotter. She could pretty much tell you the name of every species of bird, fox, rabbit, and deer we ran into. She was also our plant specialist, and thanks to her I managed to avoid spending the last five days of the trip afflicted with poison ivy.

Alan was our resident firebug. He was a hulk of a man and a firefighter, so he knew how to build them and knock them down, so to speak. He could have a blazing campfire stoked and flickering high into the sky in just a matter of minutes. Jack was the worrywart. "That fire's too high" or "We're going to get sick if we eat that," or "Don't touch that, you don't know where it's been," were just a few of his favorite catechisms. Maria and Alan were the only official couple in the group, but I think Julie had her eye on Jack. Maybe it was the other way around. I'm not sure, but it doesn't really matter now anyway.

Alan and Maria shared a large tent with three separate rooms. One room was a fully equipped kitchen, and the other two rooms were a living room and the couples' bedroom. Jack, Julie and I had our own tents for sleeping stationed around that big one, but we spent the rest of the time in the living quarters of Al and Maria's tent.

Day one was spent setting up tents and getting to know the surroundings. We had a quarter mile hike to the bathroom, which the girls both seemed to have to hit at the same time. Mostly we guys did it like the bear does it if you know what I mean—even though it was against the rules.

Day two was designated as our sight-seeing day. We got to see old faithful and a few other spots we wanted to see. Day three we rested, mostly. We nursed our aching muscles and soothed our sunburns.

Day four was a disaster. It rained so bad that we had to wait it out in our cars. After the rains swept through we had some cleaning up to do. Night four Julie thought she saw a bear at the campsite. We tried to convince her that the bears didn't come into the campgrounds, but the next night we all saw it. Turns out, Alan wasn't throwing his trash away with the rest. Julie had stressed the importance of all foodstuffs and trash needing to be bagged and taken to the primary disposal site to prevent the animals from coming into the camp.

"'What's the big deal?" he said. "I have a few candy wrappers in my knapsack."

Julie said, "It will be a big deal when the bear rips your face off while looking for the source of the food."

After that, we remembered to burn any trash we could that didn't make it to the disposal site.

Over the weekend, so many things seemed to change. Suddenly, Alan and Maria were at each other's throats—although, in hindsight, their whole relationship seemed strained from the very first day of the trip. It just seemed that whatever beef they had been having had come to a head on that day. Then there was Julie and Jack, who had become inseparable. They went off in search of adventure and would be gone for hours. Alan took off, no doubt looking for a bar, which left Maria and me alone to chat and hang out by the fire Alan had started before he went. We cooked s'mores. Maria ate the marshmallows uncooked, because she didn't like graham crackers, and I gobbled up the chocolate. We let the fire die down, neither of us knowing what to do to keep it going.

“Alan’s going to be angry with us for letting his darling little fire die,” she said as she crammed another fluffy white cube into her mouth.

“Then I guess he should have stuck around to keep it going,” I said.

She seemed to be on the verge of wanting to say something else but didn’t. I got the impression she wanted to tell me why she and Alan had been fighting.

“Besides,” I said, continuing when she didn’t speak. “He’s the firefighter. If I try to build a fire, the forest will burn down without him here to prevent it.”

“‘You’re not that bad,” she said, tapping my shoulder playfully.

Of course, I acted like she just broke my arm. I wailed and moaned. She leaned in, worried that she had actually hurt me. I stopped the act and smiled at her. She snarled at me in fake anger and tapped me again, harder this time. I reached over and tickled her. She cried out for me to stop, laughing hysterically.

When I did, our mouths were only inches apart. I bravely leaned in even closer until our lips were nearly touching. She did not pull away. I went for it and kissed her, a quick peck on the lips, testing her resolve. When I pulled away, she followed me and initiated the next kiss. This one was deeper and more prolonged. When the kiss ended, we both fell apart from each other and turned back to the fire as though it was the most fascinating thing we’d ever seen.

“I’m sorry—” I started to say, but she cut me off.

“‘There’s nothing to be sorry about. What happened—happened. It didn’t mean anything, and no one needs to know.”

I agreed, and we left it at that. Not long after the kiss, Jack and Julie returned. I wondered what they were up to, but they weren't saying. And I couldn't very well ask him what he had been doing if I didn't want him asking the same thing from me.

Alan returned late that night. He didn't seem like the angry drunk I expected, and he started a new fire. We all sat around it for a while. Julie retired to her tent first, then Jack. Maria left soon after that and when it was just Alan and me.

He asked, "Want to come canoeing with me tomorrow?"

I said sure, tossed a few sticks into the fire then went to bed. I'm not sure how much longer Alan stayed up that night, but when I woke, the light was out, and Julie was the only one up before me.

Alan and I left for the lake after lunch. We rented a two-man canoe, and he paddled us out onto the lake. Somewhere near the middle of the lake, he stopped paddling, and we just floated for a while. A few speedboats were rushing by, and somewhere far off there were jet skiers, but for the most part, we were alone. I mentioned we should have brought fishing gear and he mumbled something I couldn't make out. He wasn't much for fishing, and I knew it. I was just talking to break up the quiet.

Then out of the blue, he said, "Did you make out with my girlfriend?"

I hesitated then said, "Who told you?"

He laughed without any humor and said, "You just did."

He hit me with the oldest trick in the book. I walked right into it, and he was probably going to kill me, right there on the lake where he could dispose of the body.

"It was nothing," I said. "We kissed; that was all. It was an innocent kiss, no tongue or anything."

"'Who initiated it?"

I couldn't believe I was telling him this. I must have really wanted to die. "We were just sort of screwing around, tickling each other, and then I kissed her," I said.

He just sat there waiting for me to continue. I did.

"Then she kissed me." I couldn't believe I had admitted to it.

Alan stood up in the canoe. It rocked a little, but he steadied it okay. He was a 230-pound guy, which is a good fifty pounds on me, and this guy had muscles on his muscles. If he hit me, there was little I could do about it except take the blow. But he didn't hit me. Instead, he heaved the paddle into the water about twenty-five yards away, then sat back down. I was about to ask him why he did that, but when I looked back at him, he was crying.

I'd never seen him cry—didn't know he could—but he was sitting there with his head in his hands, and he was crying. I wanted to console him but didn't know how. I never had to reassure another guy before, so I just sat there and did nothing. It was the right thing to do.

When he stopped crying, he said, "I messed up."

"What do you mean?"

He said, "I slept with Tracy."

Tracy was his ex, and to say she and Maria did not get along was an understatement. I knew what an immense betrayal this must have been in Maria's eyes.

I said, "Does Maria know?"

"Yes," he said.

"Shit," I said. "You royally messed up."

We were quiet for a while.

Then I said, "When did it happen?"

"Couple of weeks ago, I was with Tracy at her place, you know, being defiant. There was no way Maria was going to say who I could and couldn't be friends with. Then Tracy came out into the living room wearing a nightie. My eyes popped out of my head. I couldn't believe she would do that. Her nipples poked out of the see-through teddy, and I couldn't help it. We did it right there on her sofa. I felt terrible about it, I gathered up my clothes, and I left and haven't looked back since. I told Maria. She cried, and I cried. I promised her I would never see Tracy again as a friend or any other way. I meant it, too. I was stupid to think I could have that kind of control."

"What did Maria say? I mean, does she believe you?" I asked. I think I asked that because I didn't believe it. If he could cheat once, he could do it again. I wanted to make sure he didn't plan to do something like this to Maria in the future. She was, after all, also my friend.

"She said she believes me," he said. "But she doesn't trust me." He sounded so sad as he said that last part like he knew deep down, she had a reason not to trust him. I thought he was going to cry again, but he didn't, though. Thank God. I never wanted to see another grown man cry for as long as I live.

I said, "So, you knew she would probably retaliate, and you thought it would most likely be with me." I was flattered, I think.

"You and I have been friends ever since the third grade. If she wanted to hurt me, she knows that sleeping with you was the worst thing she could do to me."

I said, "Well, you can give me credit for holding your friendship to a higher standard than sleeping with your hot girlfriend, and you can give her credit because she never went through with it. The kiss was as far as she was willing to take it. She must still love you. And as much as she is hurting over this, she seems willing to forgive you. She won't do anything in retaliation, I'm sure of it because she had the opportunity and didn't take it."

Alan shrugged.

After a moment of quiet, I said, "So… what are we going to do about a paddle?"

"I threw it so you would have to go get it," he said.

"And do I have to, you know, go get it?"

"I have something else to show you," he said, ignoring my question.

I waited as he flattened himself backward on his seat and pulled something out of the pocket of the jean shorts he was wearing. He flipped the small box open and held it out to me.

It was an engagement ring. And I can't speak for a woman, but I thought that was, like, the most beautiful thing I had ever seen.

I said, "What? Because I saw you cry I have to marry you now?"

He snarled at me, "If you ever tell anyone what you saw out here on this boat, I swear, they won't know where to find the pieces of your body."

I remember laughing at that. In a few hours, what he said wouldn't seem so funny, but at the time I laughed.

"She's going to love it," I said to him. "She's going to say yes. And if she doesn't, I'll marry you."

"If she says yes, I want you to be my best man."

"I'd be offended if you didn't offer the role to me. And I'll be honored to be your best man."

"'Great," he said. "Now that the easy part is over go get the paddle."

He ended up getting the paddle himself, and we returned to camp. Later that night, during the campfire, he got down on one knee in front of the three of us and proposed. Tearfully, she accepted. Julie and Maria went off to examine the ring without the prying eyes of the men looking over their shoulders.

To my knowledge, she died wearing the ring.

Jack asked Alan who he wanted for his best man. It was a dumb question, really, since Jack had only been in the group for a couple of years. Alan and I were practically brothers. He wasn't upset when he found out, and I agreed that he could help me plan the bachelor party.

That night, the main tent was rocking so hard, small animals fled, as if from an earthquake or something. They were loud about it, too. How rude.

The following day was our last full one, and we would be picking up stakes and heading home the next morning. Maria and Alan were inseparable, which left Julie, Jack, and me to fend for ourselves. We went for a hike. It was around dusk when we started heading back. By the time we came within spitting distance of our camp, it had turned dark as hell and fog was beginning to settle in. The flashlights we brought were useless in the fog, but Julie was confident she could get us back to camp by following landmarks.

We came to a clearing that allowed the moon to help light our way, and we continued toward camp. The mist curled around the trees, moving with a purpose, it seemed. Goosebumps broke out on my skin. In the distance, I noticed a pack of wolves that had emerged from the haze like wraiths. There were four of them.

"Something's wrong," Julie said.

"I know," I said. "Those wolves look hungry." I wasn't too worried, because I had heard wolves were afraid of people.

"No," she said. "There's something wrong with the wolves."

"What do you mean?" Jack asked.

"Look at them... They're all wrong. Their heads are almost—"

"Human looking," I finished for her. I studied the small pack blocking our way. They weren't quite all wolf. Their eyes were strange, hungry.

We started to back away.

Julie said, "Don't turn your back on them and don't run. Doing so will only invoke their hunting instinct."

I said, being the wise-ass that I am in all ways and at all times, "Their hunting instinct is already invoked."

We continued to inch our way back and to the left. I studied the wolves very intently and was interested in their different coats. All four animals were a different color. There was a light brown one, a black one, a silver-colored one, and a blond one. As we started to hit the trees again, two more wolves stepped into the clearing, light brown, and a red one. Now there were six in all, and the two newest wolves were much closer to us.

"We're being surrounded," I heard Jack mutter under his breath.

"We have to run," I said.

Julie agreed. I grabbed her and pushed her into the darkness of the forest. We ran.

Jack was the first to go down. When I heard him scream I looked back just in time to see two of the wolves, the red one and the black one, tearing off body parts and eating him—even as he continued to struggle.

I ran with Julie in front of me. We zigzagged through the trees and could hear the panting and footfalls of several animals as they rushed through the underbrush. My adrenaline kicked in, and I got Julie to the second clearing where our camp could be seen. I saw Alan building his massive fire. Julie found her second wind and pulled ahead of me. Maria came out of the tent to see what was going on.

"Get to the cars," I managed to puff out of my weak lungs.

"Why," Alan looked confused, doubtful. "Where is Jack?"

"Dead." Julie burst into tears.

That was when the animals started breaking from the trees and gathering behind us. I knew by the look on Alan's face just what he was seeing.

"They killed Jack," I confirmed. "They ate him, and he was still alive."

Alan needed no further convincing. We ran for the cars. Julie saw that the wolves had broken formation and were already anticipating our escape plan. She dodged to the right and ran for the car closest to her. Maria, Alan, and I made it to his SUV. As we got in and Alan started it up, we knew instinctively something was wrong… terribly wrong.

Julie was in Jack's car. She had no keys, and the wolves were surrounding her. The blond one jumped up onto the roof of the vehicle, and Julie screamed so loud we could hear her in the SUV. Two other wolves buffeted the side of the car as if in an attempt to knock it over.

"We have to do something to get her out of there," I said desperately.

"No shit, Captain Obvious," Alan said. "How?"

Maria said, "Maybe we could run them over, or at least run them off. Use the car to chase them away."

Alan said, "These animals took too smart—or too hungry—for that. It'll never work."

As the night marched on, we started to think we were okay as long as we stayed in the cars. Shit, maybe they would get bored and leave. No such luck. Alan shut off his engine to prevent the waste of gas. Once we were all safely in the SUV and could go, we would need that precious gas. We watched as the wolves seemed to get bored and took to tearing our campsite down. Alan's fire burned bright, keeping the area visible even after the moon was gone behind the clouds. In the car, Julie seemed to be resting since the wolves had stopped attacking.

As dawn steadily approached, the wolves as a group decided to attack the cars again, focusing mainly on Julie. All six wolves started pummeling her car as if she, above all, could not be allowed to see the coming day. A window in the car cracked and Julie screamed so loud our SUV vibrated with the sound. Alan had had enough. He climbed out of the SUV and ran for the fire pit.

He picked up a burning length of wood and held it out at the wolves. The light brown wolf took up the challenge and raced after him. Alan swung the burning log at the animal's head. The weapon connected and the wolf yelped, falling onto its side. The black wolf raced to the scene and leaped at Alan. Alan fended the wolf off, but a third wolf joined in the fight.

I don't know if she thought she had a plan, or if she was just hoping to buy Alan some time, but this was when Maria climbed out of the SUV.

Julie took the opportunity to get out of her car while it seemed all the animals were looking at Maria and Alan.

I opened the back seat of the SUV to allow Julie access, but neither of us saw the silver wolf as it came around the front of the car until it was too late. The silver wolf knocked Julie onto her back and then proceeded to tear her stomach open with its teeth. She screamed and struggled, but I knew it was too late for her when I saw the wolf pulling her intestines out of her like gory Christmas decorations. I closed the door to the SUV, drowning out her screams as they faded and then stopped altogether.

Maria and Alan were in the middle of a crowd of wolves now. The silver wolf, having finished eating the choicest parts of Julie, entered the ring around them. I noted, as did Alan and Maria I'm sure, that the ring was slowly getting smaller.

I thought. Damn, this can't happen. I can't lose all my friends in a single night. I looked in the glove compartment for some kind of weapon: nothing. I looked under the seat. I looked in the console between the driver's and passenger's seat, and there I found the knife. It was a red-hilted switchblade with the emblem for the fire department on it. The blade was only about four inches long, but it was better than nothing.

I got out of the car. Alan said, "Get back in there, Dylan. I got this."

"You have the keys, dumbass," I said. I rushed the closest wolf with the knife: it was the blond one. I drove the knife into its back with all the force I could muster.

The wolf howled.

Now all the wolves were focusing on me. Or so we thought. Maria used her only chance to get away and broke for the car. From my angle, this is what I saw: Maria running toward me, toward the car behind me. The red wolf giving chase. Then Maria just stopped running, her eyes were so immense they looked like boiled eggs wedged into the sockets. Then she just crumpled. The red wolf had bitten her spine in half. The wolf continued chewing until Maria was separated into two halves. Maria never screamed. The red wolf dragged her legs away.

Alan, now lost in grief, attacked the two wolves that were eating at the top half of Maria. I helped him, stabbing with the knife, but it had little effect.

Then a wolf had me. It bit down on my leg, and I screamed. Blood poured from the wound. It was the silver one. Alan jumped onto its back and twisted its head violently to the side. There was an audible crack as the wolf's neck snapped. It collapsed in a heap on my legs, dead. Alan helped me to my feet. I limped, holding onto his shoulder as we inched our way back to the SUV.

Just as we reached the driver's side door, Alan stopped moving. Behind him, I could see the hulking shape of a brown wolf rising up on its back legs. Alan took my hand in his and laid his keys into my palm. Just as I opened the door to the SUV, Alan's head fell from his shoulders and rolled, thumping against my chest, leaving a red splotch on my shirt. For a split second, I had the absurd vision of Alan's body with a wolf's head on it. Then the body collapsed, and the wolf behind it was all I could see. I climbed into the SUV and locked the door. I turned the ignition, and the vehicle started up on the first try. I looked back and saw a naked old man with white hair lying dead where, just a moment ago, I had seen a silver wolf.

"On the passenger side, Blondie was bashing at the window trying to break the glass. I put the car into gear and sped away, spitting stones out the back as I went. As I drove down the long dirt path, I looked back to see the blonde wolf chasing me. As I eased the SUV into a steady forty miles per hour, the sun finally started to tickle the tops of the trees with its light. I looked back only once more, and what I saw was a naked blonde man running after me. He gave up the chase and slowed his run to a jog then stopped. He turned and headed back toward the camp.

When I got back to civilization, I told the authorities of what I had witnessed. I left nothing out.

There was an investigation, and body parts were found, but no proof of anything I had seen. It was determined that bears—not wolves—had attacked our camp. They concluded that the events I related to them were delusions caused by shock.

I lost every friend I ever had that night. I have no family. Ever since that trip I've been a loner. I've met people in the years since, but I couldn't risk endangering them, so I always moved on.

###

"You have friends now," David said and placed a hand on Dylan's shoulder.

"You have a family now," Maggie said, correcting him.

"What about your first change, Dylan?" Antony asked. "When did that take place?"

"The following night I started my cycle and killed some people. I had no clue what would happen to me, and only dimly realized what I was when I woke up in the bushes outside my house wearing no clothes. I watched the news and discovered that a couple walking their dog the previous night had been killed by a bear or some other large wild animal. I'm sure that was me. The dog was found several blocks away, exhausted. It had run from the attack and hadn't stopped running until it collapsed. The dog lived. Its owners were my first two victims, and hopefully my last. Now that I knew what I was, I built a heavy-duty shed in my backyard and locked myself in whenever I felt the change coming on. I learned to trust my cycle, and it never let me down. Depression got to me, and I lost my job. I lost my home. I've been wandering ever since I was horrified at what I had become and struggled to control it. Years later, for a brief time, I met up with another werewolf, an old guy who had been a wolf for much longer than me."

"Whatever happened to him?" Maggie asked.

"He moved on. He had no interest in showing me how to control myself. He gave me what little information I have, but it's not much. The rest I've learned on my own. I've had a lot of odd jobs since becoming a werewolf, but I think my favorite was when I worked for a freak show. My preternatural ability to heal gave me the perfect performance."

"It has been a busy night," Antony said. "And the sun is coming up quickly. One last bit of business must be handled before the night ends. Vampires are extremely vulnerable during the day. I do not think it prudent to have a person who has not yet proven himself trustworthy running free while the vampires slumber. Indulge me a little while longer and spend the day inside the panic room."

"Is that completely necessary?" Maggie asked.

"I am afraid it is."

"It's fine," Dylan said. "I'll do whatever is necessary to prove I'm worthy."

"Good. It is settled."

Dylan entered the panic room without a fight, and they locked him in. The vampires settled in for the night and Maggie and Gardner spent the daylight hours doing what they did when the boys were asleep. She thought about Dylan, though. She remembered what it was like to have someone there with her during the day. She also thought how strange it would be. She was so used to being alone during the day. She would enjoy having adult company for a change.

The next night came, and the vampires emerged, one after another. They opened the panic room and let Dylan out.

Antony, Randal, and David went off in search of the hunt. Randal returned first, needing only one victim to satisfy his need. David returned soon after.

"Where is Antony?" Maggie asked.

David shrugged. "Said he had something planned. I think he still needed one more kill."

###

Antony had someone special in mind for his last victim, and it was thanks to Maggie's shelter. He raced to the house where this man lived and waited for the perfect time to strike. Peering into the window, Antony saw the object of his bloodlust: the abusive husband and father, and he was in rare form tonight. He saw the woman lying on the floor, the man Antony planned to feed on was on top of her, choking her. The boy was there, too. He was a young boy. Antony did not know his name, but the man was Howard Klein, and the woman was Hilary.

The child beat at the man's back trying to get him off his mother. The man swung out with his right hand and swatted the boy halfway across the room. Perhaps it was time for Antony to intervene on their behalf. Before he could make his move; however, the boy found a new way to protect them from their abuser. The boy picked up a high heeled shoe and threw it at the man. The pump tumbled through space in slow motion from Antony's point of view and then hit its mark. The man looked up to see where the boy had gone just as the shoe was thrown. Its steel tipped, six-inch stiletto caught the man just above the right eye.

Blood flowed immediately in that way head wounds had of looking worse than they were. The boy successfully saved his mother.

But now the focus of the man's anger was on the boy. If a human's eyes could turn red in the throes of a bloodlust, this man's eyes would have done so.

As the man stalked the boy, the woman got to her feet and picked up her cell phone. She dialed 911 and talked to dispatch. An ambulance was sent. Antony considered intervening, but when the man backed off from his aggressive stance, the vampire decided to stay hidden.

He followed them in the ambulance to the hospital and even walked inside the waiting room of the ER. He watched as the doctors stitched the man's forehead. The situation was defused for the moment, but there would be more abuse for mother and son when dad got them home. Antony was there to make sure it didn't happen.

Antony never lost sight of the man.

When Howard was out of earshot, Antony heard the doctors asking Hilary and the boy if there was anything they needed to know. In other words, did they need to call the police? The woman grew visibly paler at the thought of the police getting involved. They couldn't get the boy to talk, either.

Antony had an idea. He made a phone call.

Moments later, someone walked up to the reception desk, spoke to the receptionist, and then stepped back. The receptionist then spoke into the intercom for the entire ER to hear, "Hilary Klein, your taxi is here. Hilary Klein, your taxi is waiting. Thank you."

There was some confusion about who had called the taxi. She emphatically denied calling. Howard decided it was okay if she and the boy went home, but he assured her he would be back soon. She spoke to the taxi driver and explained she had no money, and that she hadn't made the call. The driver smiled at her and told her she need not worry about that. As it turned out, the fair was already paid, and with a sizable tip. The woman was suspicious, but she and the boy went with the taxi driver to the waiting cab.

When she and the boy were safely on their way home, Antony was able to focus all his attention on the man. He waited patiently for attendants to finish bandaging their patient. Howard demanded that the receptionist call him a taxi as well. She kindly refused and pointed to the pay phone for just such occasions. He called for his own cab. He complained about the service, and that the bill was too high, but left without making too big of a scene. He had other matters to attend to. It was in the parking lot that Antony finally found the chance to make his move.

As Howard dug through his pocket for taxi fare, Antony dropped down and stood silently behind him. He cupped a hand around the man's mouth and lifted him off the ground. Tucking him securely under his arm, Antony raced home with his prize.

Howard had passed out during the trip back to the house. Antony asked Maggie to confirm that he was indeed worthy to be chosen.

Maggie looked into the panic room at the man handcuffed inside. "Yes," she said. "I don't know what he's done, but his aura is red. He's guilty of something horrific."

Dylan was morbidly curious and asked if he could watch.

"If that is what you wish," Antony said.

The man sitting in the panic room didn't seem scared, only annoyed. He hissed at Dylan and Maggie but otherwise ignored them. "What the hell is this?" Howard asked. "Are you going to show me what will happen in a prison shower if I don't shape up?"

"No," Antony said, and his vision turned red. "I am going to prevent you from killing anyone ever again."

There was no time for further discussion as Antony stepped forward and bit down on Howard's neck. Dylan tried to watch but slapped a hand over his mouth and ran away to throw up. The smell of the corpse burning in the incinerator caused Dylan to pass out completely.

"Bizarre," Antony said upon Dylan's recovery. He studied the sick man as he wavered unsteadily on the sofa.

"What is?" Dylan's eyes couldn't seem to focus.

Antony responded: "A werewolf sickened by death."

Chapter Twenty-Four

Though Dylan had officially been brought into the fold and he didn't have to spend his days in the panic room anymore, Maggie kept her distance and didn't allow Gardner anywhere near him.

She also began to do something abnormal to her personality—she withdrew from the group. Slowly at first, and then to the point where she was nothing more than a recluse. The others asked questions, but she would not answer them. She continued to provide names and locations of killers and rapists and the like but showed very little interest in the group in any other way. She was waiting on a specific time of the month before she could confess to the others why she had become so secretive.

On the twenty-fourth day after her encounter with Dylan in the basement, Maggie had a dream. The dream helped her to understand what she had to do. When the vampires woke on the twenty-eighth night since being bitten, Maggie was ready to tell the reason for her anti-social behavior.

And true to her nature, she planned to be dramatic about it.

Randal and Gardner were to stay in the baby's room. Maggie led David and Antony into the basement. Dylan had been locked up in the panic room, but she needed him present. She unlocked the panic room door and Dylan, naked and confused, stood in the doorway staring dumbly out at them.

"You'll want to hear what I have to say," she said. "I've been hiding something from everyone that I am only now willing to share."

Dylan stepped forward, and she motioned him to come out.

"I had a vision, and it helped me to understand why Dylan can't remember his time as a werewolf."

Dylan, covering his groin with his hands, hopped from one bare foot to the other. "Can you hurry this story along? I'm on a time limit here."

"There is a key component to controlling the wolf, and it has to do with the pack mentality. Every wolf needs an alpha."

"Maggie, what are you saying? This is not safe. Dylan can't be out tonight. You know this." David paced.

"A sole wolf can't be his own alpha. If Dylan has a leader, he can keep his human memories, even when he is in his wolf form; because he now has an alpha."

"Who?" Dylan's hands moved from his groin to his stomach. He doubled over in pain.

Maggie began unbuttoning her blouse. "Me." Her voice was a growl.

Her shirt slid off her muscular arms to the floor. Next, she stepped out of her slacks; she pulled off her panties.

"Don't interfere," she said in that same growling voice to David. "I've had a vision and know what must be done."

David took Maggie by the arm. "You were bitten?"

"You are—" Her rumbling voice became nearly imperceptible. "Very perceptive." She doubled over and clutched her stomach; at the same time, Dylan did the same. As Antony and David watched, Dylan and Maggie changed. It was a fluid transformation; no bones were broken and reformed, this was more like putty being reshaped. Flesh and bone and blood became unsolidified and changed its shape. The animals emerged from the mound of flesh. Hair grew out and covered hide. Maggie's coat was a glossy black, and Dylan's beast was a reddish-brown hue.

The Maggie-creature turned to David and calmly lowered her head. The Dylan-beast stalked forward snarling and slavering, snapping its jaws as if it would eviscerate everything around. As the Dylan approached what the wolf considered prey, Maggie turned away from David and stepped in front of Dylan. She growled and snapped at the brown wolf with a ferocity that cowed the male werewolf and forced him down on his belly.

Maggie's snarl was relentless, and her muzzle pulled back to reveal her razor-sharp teeth. If Dylan tried to get up, she snapped at him and drove him back to the floor. She didn't relent until Dylan rolled over onto his back in a show of deference to the black she-wolf. As Maggie backed off, Dylan slowly regained his footing. Keeping his head lowered, he strode up to her and lay at her feet. She walked away from Dylan and lay down at David's feet.

Dylan took his place at Antony's feet.

David turned to Antony. "I think we just adopted some pets." He backed toward the stairway leading out of the basement, but Maggie followed. When Antony walked toward the stairs, Dylan followed. The group headed up the stairs and entered the parlor.

Randal stomped down the stairs and entered the parlor looking down at his feet. "Baby's asleep. He—"

Dylan snarled when he spotted Randal, but Maggie was there to snap and growl at the male wolf, forcing him to remember who was in charge. Dylan lowered his gaze and fell silent.

Randal stood, unmoving. "What the—"

Maggie used her power and influence to drive Dylan to the front door. She turned to David and glared at him with those eerie human eyes set into that wolf's face. She looked toward the door, then back at David. Reluctantly, David stepped over to the door and opened it. Maggie raced out into the night, Dylan on her heals.

After a moment, Randal said, "Was that a good idea? Letting them go out into the world like that, I mean."

"I don't know, but are you going to argue with a couple of werewolves?" David asked. Then as an afterthought said, "Especially if one of them is Maggie?"

"What happened?" Randal asked.

"Apparently, Maggie was bitten during that first encounter," Antony said.

"She seems to have better control over the transformation than Dylan. She definitely has control over him."

Randal used vampire speed and appeared directly in front of David. He peered up at him. "I'll ask it again; was it wise to let the werewolves out?"

###

The wolves raced through the night. Maggie used her ability to control the she-wolf, and in turn, controlled Dylan's wolf. They raced and frolicked together. After sniffing Maggie's behind, Dylan mounted her. She protested but didn't stop him. When the act was done, and Dylan had moved off, Maggie led Dylan farther into the forest. As they moved through the trees and underbrush, Dylan playfully snapped at the fireflies lighting up the dark forest. When they smelled another pack of wolves, Maggie gave the signal to follow them. They tracked the other wolves for several miles, but tired of the game and headed off in search of prey. Dylan craved human prey, but Maggie's she-wolf refused to allow him that option. She led him to an open field where a family of deer were grazing. Staying downwind, Maggie prowled forward. Dylan followed her example, staying low. The pair of wolves came within feet of the doe and pounced. Dylan held the deer to the ground as Maggie gripped the struggling, desperate doe by the throat with her fangs. Maggie's human eyes stared into the doe's wild-eyed gaze. Her soothing voice echoed inside the doe's frantic brain as it died.

Dylan bit at the deer's tender underbelly, but Maggie's she-wolf snapped and drove him off. She gripped the carcass by a leg and proceeded to drag the prize back to the house. Dylan's beast learned what his new mate was doing and helped to carry the food back to their lair.

###

Maggie and Dylan returned with the deer and sat in the yard eating it.

David, Antony, and Randal stood at the large picture window and watched the wolves tear the deer apart.

David said, "Look at that; Maggie's teaching Dylan to control the hunt. She's teaching him to hunt animals instead of people."

When the wolves had their fill of deer, they entered the house, Maggie in the lead.

The werewolves moved through the house, walking in circles around the vampires. Dylan seemed leery of the bipeds around him but showed no aggression. Maggie peered up at David.

"Am I crazy, or does she know who I am, even in her wolf form?"

Upstairs, Gar woke, crying. Maggie's ears perked up at the sound. Dylan made an irritated growl deep in his throat. He was on the move before anyone knew his intentions. Maggie gave chase.

David moved with vampire speed, but Maggie had already placed herself between the Dylan-wolf and the crib. She was crouched down; growling and matching Dylan move for move. Dylan flinched, testing Maggie's speed. It was a mistake. Maggie was on him at once, her teeth biting into his neck, pinning the male werewolf to the floor. David walked past the wolves, picked Gardner out of the crib and carried him downstairs, leaving the beasts to work out their dominance over one another.

Gar quieted down as he entered the living room and saw Antony and Randal. Randal began a game of Peek-A-Boo that got Gardner giggling hysterically.

As David watched Randal and Gardner playing together, he smiled. "You're a natural with him."

Randal glanced up briefly. "I feel like he makes me real. I don't know how to explain it. Playing with Gar helps me to forget I'm a monster."

David frowned. "Is that how you see yourself? As a monster?"

Randal Picked up Gardner and bounced him in the air. "Don't you?"

David shook his head. "I don't. I guess I am, but I don't feel like I am. To be honest, I haven't given my vampire existence much thought. I guess that's because of Gardner. I have no time to think about anything other than him. Even Maggie helps in that regard, I guess."

Randal set Gardner down, and the boy ran toward Antony.

"I know you have the baby to keep you grounded, and I get that, but I'll never know the joy and connection of being a father. I get to be this stunted child-thing for as long as I exist. I feel like a monster, plain and simple."

"Randal, I'm sorry." David reached out to touch Randal but thought better of it and pulled back. "I never gave your situation much thought. I can see how that could make you feel less than certain of what you are, but I assure you that it's not the case. You are a part of this family, and that makes you special. Your presence here means a lot to me, and I'm sure Antony feels the same way. I know you're important to Maggie, and Gardner just adores you. Whatever you think of yourself, at least know how important you are to us."

Randal nodded but said nothing.

"There is another issue that I haven't given much thought, but it's something Maggie and I have to come to terms with soon." David turned toward Gardner, who was begging for Antony to pick him up, but Uncle Antony—though thoroughly in love with the boy—did not hold babies.

"What is that?" Randal asked.

David turned back to Randal. "Gardner is human. And now that she has been turned into a werewolf, she's immortal like us. Gardner is going to grow up, grow old, and die. Do we let that happen, or do we do something to make him immortal?"

Randal collapsed into a chair. His face took on a stunned expression. "I never thought of that." He glanced up at David. "What are you going to do?"

David shrugged. "I want to turn him immortal, maybe when he's old enough to understand what we are. Maybe he will choose to become immortal. If he does, could I kill my son, just to watch him be born again into the immortal life? I don't know. What if he chooses not to become immortal? I guess I would have to live with the decision, but still; I can't bear the thought of living an eternity beyond his mortal years."

"You have to make the decision for him." Randal spoke with the confidence of someone who has made up their mind on a subject.

"Okay, but what if Gardner met a girl, fell in love and had a child of his own? Would I still be doing the right thing by making this decision for him? Then Gar would have to watch as his own family age and rot away right in front of his eyes."

"You can't worry about that tonight. He's still a baby, and there is still time to sort all this out." Randal yawned.

David glanced toward the window. He gaped. "The night got away from us." He pointed at the orange breaking through the trees in the distance. "The sun will be up soon."

Randal glanced out the window. He stood and walked up the stairs.

David rescued Antony from Gardner and took the baby upstairs with him. Antony followed. They walked past the nursery and the sleeping werewolves. As Antony entered his room, and David carried Gardner to his bed. He undressed and climbed into bed next to his son. Gardner yawned and fell asleep wrapped up in his father's arms.

David, deep into his death sleep, did not feel it when Maggie lifted the baby from his side.

Chapter Twenty-Five

Maggie called for a gathering the next evening when the vampires awoke. She sat down next to Dylan and took his hand. What she had to say was bound to upset him.

"I know I've been aloof lately, and now you know why. I wanted to wait until I was able to put all the pieces together, and I couldn't do that until I actually turned. I felt this was best." She turned her attention to Dylan. "I can now safely say I have complete control over both wolves."

"I remember our time together in the forest. I remember being a wolf. How did you do that?"

"Don't think of me as the wolf; instead think of me as a trainer for the wolf. As a witch with the ability to project my consciousness into the wolf, I can see what the wolf is doing. I can tell the wolf what I want from it, and it listens. I'm the Alpha."

"Why couldn't I control my own wolf before?"

"Your human self is dormant when you are the wolf. You are a man dreaming of a wolf. When you wake you lose the dream. You would have to train yourself to take control of the dream." She sighed. "As long as we are together, you won't have to worry about that."

Dylan's shoulders slumped.

"There's more. I believe I can even control the time and duration of the transformation."

"What do you mean?"

"I'm saying I think I can turn anytime I want, and even turn back anytime I want as well. I can show almost complete control over the wolf."

"Does that mean you can keep from turning into the wolf at all?" His eyes searched her face. "Like, indefinitely?"

"Right now, no. I don't think I can control it to that extent. If I do not force the transformation, I am still at the mercy of the twenty-eight-day cycle. I tried to stop it last night, but I couldn't."

Maggie could tell Dylan had many more questions he wasn't asking. She would get together with him later and explain what she knew in more detail, but right now there was so much the others wouldn't understand. If she continued, she would only confuse them. She resolved to finish the discussion with Dylan in private.

"I have one other question," Dylan said.

"What is it?" Maggie asked.

Dylan thought a moment then said in a small, halting voice, "Can you control my transformation?"

Maggie looked at the others standing around. Strangely, everyone seemed to be curious to know the answer to the question. Even Randal, the anti-werewolf vampire, leaned forward. She smiled at their eager faces.

"I think I can force your change when I am in your immediate proximity. If this is the case, you will no longer be at the mercy of your cycle, either. But this depends on how close you are to me. If you move out of range—and I haven't tested this range, so don't ask—I will not be able to affect your change."

"In that case," Dylan said. "I am never leaving your side."

Maggie laughed and hugged him.

As the discussion tapered off, and everyone disbursed, Maggie and Dylan entered into a more one-on-one conversation.

Randal headed out in search of his nightly meal.

David played with Gardner for a while, but when the hunger began to set in, he headed out with Antony.

After a couple of hours passed, the group slowly began to unite once again. Randal had been the first to return, and he played with Gardner, giving Maggie a break. But as the day approached, Maggie took Gardner back from Randal so he could hide from the sun.

When the vampires were all safe for the daylight hours, Dylan sought out Maggie. She was in the nursery with Gardner, cleaning up the toys Randal had left out.

"He is a deadly vampire, but he's still nothing but a kid." She could see there was something else on Dylan's mind. "You look troubled. What is it?"

"Will you go for a ride with me—you and Gardner?"

"Okay." She was intrigued.

Dylan wouldn't tell her what he had planned, but he drove the RAV4 out of Philadelphia. He took her to Delaware—back to the group home where he had been living when Antony had first found him. He led her to the room where he had been staying.

The people in the group home, residents, and worker alike showed their surprise at seeing him again.

The social worker in charge of his care, Mary Butler, actually cried with tears of happiness when she saw him.

"Dyl, you've come back to us."

"Only temporarily, I'm afraid." Dylan opened the door to his room. "I've found friends who are willing to take me in. I'm homeless no more."

Mary hugged him. She then turned to Maggie. She cooed at Gardner, making the baby laugh. Dylan introduced his new friends to Mary.

Mary returned her attention back to Dylan. "I'm so happy for you. I have paperwork you will need to fill out before you go."

"Sure," Dylan said.

Mary made one last face at Gardner to get him laughing and then walked away. Maggie followed Dylan into the room.

She glanced around at the mostly sparse room but stopped in front of. One wall of the room that was covered in newspaper clippings and sticky notes with messages scrawled on them. There were maps as well, with red pushpins stuck to them and red yarn that seemed to depict pathways. Maggie studied it carefully.

"What is all this?" she asked.

"It's everything I know about the movements and habits of the werewolves that killed my friends. The beasts that did this to me, to us. I've been hunting them for years, and I think I've finally tracked them back to their den."

"Where are they?" she asked.

"I think they're in New Mexico. I haven't quite pinpointed them down to an actual address, but I'm sure that's where they return when they aren't killing innocent campers."

Maggie turned away from the wall and looked at him. "We'll help you with all this. If that's what you want."

"It is. And I'll be eternally grateful for any help you can give, thank you."

She helped him collect all the material from the wall, careful not to disrupt the flow of the information. "I have no names yet, but I do have in-depth descriptions of all the werewolves in their human forms. I also learned that there was another werewolf that had not been at the sight of the attack on my friends. She could very well be the elusive alpha-wolf you mentioned every pack should have—she has a silver hair like the mate I think I killed. Well, Alan did."

Once the possessions were boxed up, he headed to the office to sign the paperwork Mary had requested of him. Maggie waited in the car. When he came out, they drove home.

Dylan took his boxes to his new room inside the house on Lansdowne Drive, and Maggie took Gardner to the nursery.

When he finished putting his things away, there was a knock on his door. He opened it and let Maggie into the room. She held a baby monitor in her hand.

"I just put Gar down for a nap, and now I'm bored," she said.

Dylan started to say, "I was thinking about what you said..." But he was forced to stop mid-sentence when Maggie kissed him. She led him to the bed.

"I said I was bored," Maggie said. "And talk is boring."

Dylan needed no convincing to get undressed, and he climbed into bed with her. He mounted her roughly, suddenly wanting to be inside her as quickly as possible. Maggie spoke softly into his ear, and she calmed him down. But quelling his eagerness was a losing battle, and she gave in to his harsh techniques, deciding that his painful nips and bites were quite arousing. She gasped as he bit into her shoulder. The sex was hot and frantic, and although it did not last long, the coupling was satisfying for both. They fell asleep entwined in each other's arms, sweating and panting.

Maggie woke when the baby monitor began to emit the sounds of Gardner stirring in his crib. She pulled herself from beside Dylan's sleeping form and found her clothes. Before dressing, she examined the teeth marks all over her body. They were healing quickly. She picked up the monitor from the bedside table and carried it with her to the nursery.

Gardner played happily in his crib. She lifted him and carried him downstairs.

Night came, and the vampires rose.

David sat next to her. "You look nervous. Is something wrong?"

"It's nothing," she said. "Drop it."

"If something happened you can tell me. I may not be here during the day, but I still feel protective over you. Don't shut me out." Maggie blushed, looked at Dylan, and then back at David. "Everything is fine David. Drop it."

David followed her gaze to Dylan. "He didn't… you know, hurt you, did he?"

"No, David. God, no. It's nothing like that. It's—" She couldn't finish.

"You mean, you and him… you… you're a couple now?"

Maggie took David's hand, not wanting him to feel threatened. "It's not like that. Not really."

"I'm not saying there's something wrong with the two of you getting friendly," David said, voice rising. "I'm actually glad to hear it. I think you know I have strong feelings for you, but we also know I can't give you what you need on a human level. If he makes you happy, then I'm happy for you both. That's all I'm trying to say."

"Thank you for that." Maggie kissed his cheek. She then stood and walked out of the room, carrying Gardner with her.

David stood and walked over to Dylan. He smiled down at him.

Dylan sputtered. "Listen, I—"

"Don't look so worried," David said, interrupting him. "I approve."

Dylan let out a long sigh as David walked away.

Chapter Twenty-Six

His name had been Milo Curtis once upon a time, but then the monster came along and drained him of blood, allowed him to rise again as another blood-drinker, and now he no longer carried the name, Milo. He was now known as the master's Number Seven. He didn't complain about losing his title and becoming a number; he had seen firsthand what happened if he had.

And Seven understood the dangers of his new life. The creature that had created him was a tricky and volatile fellow, to say the least. Actually, he was a complete nut case. Number Seven had to tread very lightly around him, or else end up like the last fool who dared to challenge the master's authority.

There had also been the mysterious deaths of those who would never wake again. A rash of unexplained deaths had rocketed through the Dark Master's numbers like wildfire. Those deaths seemed to have stopped after the end of the female known as Number Four, however, and with any luck, they would not start up again.

Number Seven stood in his designated place in line as the Master inspected the troops.

"The time to attack is drawing near. We have not yet located their lair; so tonight, and every night henceforth, we must go into the night and search for their whereabouts. We know who they feed on, and we know how they do it. We just don't know where. We must be diligent in our hunt. We must find out where they are hunting and how to track them. We will keep our vampire eyes and ears tuned to every bit of information we can wean from the townsfolk. Who is talking about killers and pedophiles going missing? Where are the stories most concentrated?"

The Master walked with his hands behind his back from one end of the line to the other, and then back again.

"Once we pin down their location," he said, picking up where he left off. "We will close in and strike. Before heading out for the night, I would like to see you all working on your formation. We must first dazzle them with our footwork, and then we will close in for the kill when they least expect. I must go out now and find a lowly hobo to feed on, thanks to those interlopers. I so despise hobos. I long to return to the families I love, so let's get this conflict resolved quickly."

The group broke up to do what had been demanded of them, and the master headed out in search of his own meal.

The minions dispersed. Number Seven, however, knew something the others didn't. He had been monitoring police reports for missing persons and unidentified murder victims that had been drained of blood and decapitated. He had initially looked for his own contribution to the list, but instead, what he had found was a distinct pattern that led him to the steps of the Philadelphia Police Department.

The FBI was investigating a rash of disappearances involving pedophiles. This made Number Seven curious. No one cared about the missing sex offenders and even the FBI's investigation stank of disinterest. These disappearances, though, were unquestionably due to the work of the group his dark master hunted.

The perpetrators of this serial crime were in no danger of being discovered, though. The FBI had placed this investigation at their lowest priority rating.

For Number Seven, however, this was priority one.

He used the information he had obtained to track the pedophile hunters right back to their front steps. He already knew they had been hunting heavily in the Allentown area. But the data suggested the group had moved on from there, heading south. He tracked the group to western Philadelphia.

Unfortunately, Philadelphia took him much too far from his own lair and put him in danger. This limited his tracking time drastically. But being the quick thinker he was, Number Seven devised a plan. He raced to Philadelphia, hunted quickly, and took three homeless men who had been living in the sewer. Having satisfied the hunger, he then scouted out an alternate lair. He located a hole in the ground that would do nicely, used a cement slab to cover the hole, and sealed himself in.

Upon waking, he removed the slab. With the extra time the makeshift lair provided, Number Seven located an internet café and searched the FBI database for the required information. Once he was sure he had what he needed, Seven headed out to track his prey and fed along the way. The master would possibly punish him for not returning as per regulations, but if Number Seven succeeded in locating the enemy, he was sure the master would forgive his momentary lapse of protocol.

Number Seven began hunting the very pedophiles his enemy seemed to cherish as a food source. He planned to pursue what they sought and thus bring himself into their orbit. This was decidedly dangerous, but it was worth the risk.

And the risk paid off.

Three vampires appeared like wraiths right in front of him. He concealed himself in the shadows and before they were able to detect him. He recalled the master telling the group about the small roped boy he had lost. And now the boy vampire was walking by with the two adults blood drinkers. But this boy was no wild child the master had described. This boy had apparently perfected the craft of killing. These vampires were very good at what they did, including the kid. Had the situation been different, he might have joined this group and learned a few things. He continued to stay well out of sight as he followed the trio back to their lair.

Seven smiled devilishly. He had them.

He returned to the makeshift lair and slept. When he woke, he fed quickly and raced back to the master, but was not greeted with the respect of a loyal—and successful—comrade.

The master gripped him by the throat as Seven entered the nest. The others watched with interest, enjoying a proper execution.

"Tell me why I shouldn't just bend your neck right here and end you for disobeying my direct order to always return to the nest at dawn?" the master seethed.

"Because if you do, you won't know what I know about those you seek," Number Seven replied.

The master released him unharmed.

"Tell me," he said.

"First promise me that you will allow me to be the first to attack."

"Done," he said. "Now tell me."

Number Seven relayed what he knew, then walked away to be questioned by the others. They were curious to know how he had done what they could not.

The master turned to his Number One. "Poor sap," he said and laughed.

"What do you know?" Number One asked.

"I know that the first one through that door is going to be the first to die."

Number One smiled and nodded agreement.

Chapter Twenty-Seven

Maggie lifted her glass of lemon water to her lips. Her hand wavered when the image hit. She dropped the glass and gripped the counter. The glass shattered on the floor at her feet.

"He's coming." Her lips moved, but there wasn't enough breath in her to make the sounds. Once she felt steady on her feet again, she rushed into the living room. "He's coming. And he's not alone. I count twelve with him."

"Okay, we are prepared for this," Antony said. "Randal, as much as you want to be here to confront him you must protect Gardner. Take him to the Jersey safe house."

Randal frowned but nodded his acceptance.

David said, "Do you know when they will get here? How much time we have?"

"Maybe half an hour. One hour at most," Maggie said.

Randal helped Maggie pack an overnight bag for Gardner. They packed extra food and toys into a backpack and Randal strapped it onto his back. Maggie secured a harness on his chest and slipped the baby into it. Gardner kicked happily, oblivious to the panicked and rushed manner in which those caring for him operated. Maggie kissed Gardner on the forehead, kissed Randal on the cheek, and then they were off.

Antony motioned for Maggie to join Dylan and David in front of him. "It will be best if you and Dylan stay out of sight when they arrive. You are confident you can transform at will?"

Dylan turned to Maggie. She nodded.

"Good. Stay in the basement until you have transformed. You will be our little surprise." Antony turned to leave but stopped and turned back. "I am setting out the bear traps around the house. Ideally, this will slow the attacks. Do not—and I cannot express this enough—get caught in these traps.

Within the hour everything was set. All the defenders could do then was wait.

###

The air was stale and dry. Dylan coughed, and everyone looked at him. He shrugged apologetically. The room grew quiet again. No one moved. The ticking clock on the wall was the only sound, and it was deafening.

Maggie closed her eyes and then opened them again. "They're here."

She and Dylan headed to the basement.

###

The solid oak door blew inward and shattered to pieces against the far wall. David had to duck as it flew past him. The creature that had kicked the door in stormed into the house, head swiveling in a frantic effort to avoid a sneak attack. Antony stepped up from behind the fool and tore the head from its neck. Antony then stood beside David as the house filled with vampires. Four creatures stood in a line facing David and Antony. David unsheathed his katana with a flourish. The vampire closest to David smiled, winked, and then motioned for him to bring it on.

Seven more vampires flooded into the house. Antony held a machete out in front of him. The creatures stepped forward, moving in unison, then to the side; and then stepped back again. Antony turned to his compatriot, but David only shrugged. They watched the well-choreographed formation.

"Nice country line dancing," David said. "But can you fight?" He swung his katana, forcing a vampire to dodge the blade. "I can cut you in half no matter where you're standing."

The vampires then broke into three groups: two groups of four, and one group of three. Apparently, the gap in the third group's formation was for the headless husk still resting in the broken doorframe. The defenders were clearly outnumbered, but again, the attackers did not make a move; they merely continued circling the front of the room in their macabre, synchronized dance.

The last vampire to enter the house was their leader, clad in a brown trench coat and cowboy boots. He carried his ivory capped staff as he weaved in and out of the undulating horde. David stepped forward brandishing his katana in front of him like a shield. He watched as the smug look on the tall vampire's face faltered.

"I know you," he sneered. "I killed you."

"I survived," David flashed his fangs.

"I should have decapitated you. Well, you won't be making that claim for much longer." The Master turned his back on David. He stepped into his group of vampires. "Kill them."

A wave of vampires rushed forward. David kept his attackers at bay by swinging his katana, chopping at the air, and driving the advancing horde back. Antony stood to his left, and any vampire trying to duck under David's blade would have him waiting for them. David twisted to the right, spun back to the left, rolled over Antony's back, and then popped up on Antony's other side. He decapitated the unsuspecting creature standing there.

The attacking horde fell back and blended into a single mass. Th group became an undulating wave, subverting David's katana, and effectively surrounding the two defenders. Antony and David stood back to back and spun around in an attempt to keep the attackers from blindsiding them. Antony managed to decapitate an attacker with his machete as she moved in to attack what she thought was their weak point. Another attacker moved in to take her place as she shriveled into dust at their feet. David decapitated the second attacker.

"They are closing in," he said.

Antony replied calmly. "I know."

Before David could recover from his momentary lapse in concentration, he was disarmed. He watched as the katana flew across the room and landed behind the recliner near the back window.

"Forget it," Antony said, seeing that David's attention had been dangerously diverted from the attacking horde. "Use your hands. You are stronger than they are."

David pushed off his first two attackers, keeping himself from being pinned down. He back-peddled and was able to prevent another vampire from getting behind him. He maneuvered through the advancing horde. Antony struggled with the two who were holding him, and a third attempted to take off Antony's head with his bare hands. Antony easily shook off the two holding him and wrapped an arm around the neck of the third. With an immense twist of his arm, Antony removed the vampire's head. He tossed the dried husk to the floor.

Still outnumbered three to one, Antony and David regrouped.

"When does the Calvary arrive?" David asked.

"We can handle them on our own," Antony said.

The remaining seven vampires attacked as one. The machete was knocked from Antony's hands, and the two defenders were separated. Six vampires immobilized Antony's arms, and a single adversary held his legs. When David tried to intervene, the leader came forward and knocked him down using the stave. David retrieved his katana, but the staff had a better reach. Though Antony struggled against their hold, couldn't shake his captors. David attempted to use speed to assist, but the older vampire thwarted his every attempt. David had been outmatched for speed, strength, and endurance. David flicked his katana from one hand to the other. He charged, but the ancient vampire caught him in the wrist with the ivory head of his staff, and the blade skittered away once again. The leader gripped him around the throat and lifted him off the floor.

"I could snap your neck…" The tall vampire turned and glanced at Antony struggling against his captors. "While I make him watch."

"Then why don't you?" David kept his eyes on his adversary.

"Or I could just say the word, and my loyal subjects will tear your master into so many spare parts."

David growled defiantly.

"But I have questions, first." He lifted David higher. "Bring out your witch. Make her appear here—and not like she was before. I want her here in the flesh so I can kill her." He turned to Antony. "Do it, if you don't want to see your beautiful blond-haired boy vampire shrivel into a useless pile of dust."

"She's safe from you, and you won't get her," David said with a sneer. "Go on and kill me."

"We'll see," said ancient one. "My next question is where is my roped boy?" The last word was a snarl, and David felt the vampire's grip on his neck tighten. With just a little more force, David was sure his head would just pop off.

"He, too, is out of your reach," Antony said triumphantly.

"Bring him to me." The leader bellowed and lifted David up over his head as if he weighed no more than a feather pillow.

He slammed David to the floor on his back; the wood beneath him cracked. The vampire lifted his ivory capped staff over his head, intending to bring it down and crush David's skull.

The black wolf crashed into him, knocking him off David and onto his back. As the wolf leaped into the crowd of vampires holding Antony down, she caught one by the throat with her massive jaws and bit down, severing the creature's neck. The head rolled to the floor and burst into a cloud of ash. She whipped her head to the side and tossed the husk of its body across the room.

Once freed, David jumped to his feet and raced to his katana. Feeling the reassurance of its sturdy hilt in his grip once again, David returned to the fight. Behind him the rust-colored werewolf rushed into the crowd of vampires, severing a hand and then managing to bring down a second by pouncing onto his back. He bit down into the neck and tore the head from the body.

The vampire leader watched as the two wolves tore through his horde. He gaped at his dwindling numbers and then gave an anguished cry of disappointment. He commanded the survivors to flee. He disappeared in a crackling whoosh of air just as the black wolf leaped for him. Maggie landed on all four legs and skidded across the hardwood floor, having missed her target.

Antony killed the handless, lingering vampire who was apparently too stupid to realize his comrades were abandoning him.

In all, five vampires escaped, including the leader. Antony rushed into the night, but his quarry had scattered in too many different directions. Antony returned to the house where David stood in the middle of the living room with dry, crumbling body parts cluttered around him. Dylan sat in the corner worrying at his prize: a withered leg. Maggie stood behind David, ready if the vampires were to return. Antony inspected the empty door frame. "Perhaps a steel door is in order."

David examined the frame. He turned to Antony. "We had the element of surprise this time, but that will not be the case if they return. If they have enough time to prepare, we will be in serious danger."

"If they have time to regroup…"

"We won't let them," David said.

"How do you propose we stop them?" Antony asked.

"We go to them before they have time to recuperate."

"We still do not know where they are hiding," Antony said.

"We found him once before, we can do it again."

Antony looked down at the black wolf. The wolf looked back at him with those eerily human eyes and growled. The growl spoke volumes. The wolf was saying she would find him, and when she did, she would rip out his vile throat.

Chapter Twenty-Eight

Randal moved through the night with a speed that caused the air around him to crackle and pop. Gardner rested peacefully on Randal's chest, tucked safely into a cloth baby carrier strapped over his shoulders and around his waist. He reached the house in a half hour. By car, the trip would have taken two hours.

Upon arriving at the house, the au pair Maggie had hired met him at the door. She looked past him to the empty Driveway. She glanced at him questioningly.

"Where is the car that brought you here?" she asked.

"I ran," Randal said.

She huffed. "Lies will not be tolerated, young man. Go wash up for bed. Do you wish a snack? There are baked goods in the kitchen." She took the baby and scurried away.

"You could be my snack." Randal chuckled at the thought.

There were housekeepers and other workers running around, doing what they must to keep the empty house in working order, and several offered their assistance to Randal, but he sent them away. He wondered if they knew what he was. Apparently, at least one of them didn't. She continually brushed at his hair, tried to feed him cookies and straightened his clothes. When she finally moved off to perform other duties, Randal felt a great relief that she was gone. Just a few minutes more and he might have fed on her just to be rid of her.

Once he was finally alone, Randal reached into his pocket and pulled out the ruffled piece of paper. He unfolded it. This was the picture of his family he had thought to shove into his pocket when the vampire had killed them and turned him into the roped boy. He looked at the image of his mother, his father and his pain in the ass older sister. He missed them immensely, and although he led the others to believe he had no memory his human life, he actually remembered it in excruciating detail.

He recalled how his father used to putter in the garage to avoid visits from his mother-in-law; and how his sister used to pass her dessert to him under the table (hooray for anorexia), and how his mother used to insist on saying grace every Thanksgiving, even though no one in the family ever attended church.

His father always provided the same prayer for grace: "Good food; good meat; good God, let's eat." His mother hated this particular dad joke, but it always seemed to serve the purpose. And besides, she wasn't going to get anything better from either him or his sister.

At the time, it had seemed his life was one big dramatic mess; but now, as he stared down at the picture of his lost family, all he remembered were good times.

Randal refolded the paper and shoved it back into his pocket. He felt the rush of emotions washing over him and didn't want to let it surface. He walked the house, watching the staff busy themselves with their menial tasks. Some of the help seemed leery of him, some outright feared him as if they sensed what he really was. Antony had assured him, however, that no humans knew of their true nature. These people were nothing more than human servants getting well paid to care for a house no one lived in. Still, Randal couldn't help but wonder what they thought.

The au pair was not afraid. She stared at Randal suspiciously whenever he entered the room. She wasn't thrilled about him being close to Gardner, but she didn't prevent him from spending time with the baby, either.

When she decided Gardner had had enough attention from the wild-eyed boy, she spirited the baby away, telling Randal it was time for a feeding. He knew she was really just keeping Gardner away from him.

He sometimes had impure thoughts about ripping the au pair's throat open and drinking her blood. He doubted he would ever act on such a thing, but if she showed even a hint of being the type of au pair that was less than trustworthy, he wouldn't hesitate to drain her.

Randal paced, and grumbled whenever a servant tried to assist him. He didn't want to be pampered—he wanted to be fighting the Dark Father with the others. He hated that they could be winning the fight and ridding the world of the foul monster without his help.

He also thought of the other possibility; they could be losing the fight, and in effect leaving Randal and Gardner alone. It would be hell if he were forced to live at the Jersey house with these servants taking care of Gardner for the rest of his life. Randal couldn't take it anymore. He had to go see what was happening in Philadelphia. He had to help them if the Dark Father and his new minions were more than his family could handle.

Randal was just about to rush at sonic speed to Philadelphia when the phone rang. He waited for the servant to answer it. When the servant motioned for him to take it, Randal did.

"Yes," he said.

Maggie's voice came through on the line. "It's over. You can bring Gardner home."

Randal placed the receiver in the cradle and went off to collect Gardner. He secretly hoped the au pair would refuse to give up the baby. He'd love to teach her that lesson.

Chapter Twenty-Nine

Randal removed the picture of his family from his pocket and stared at it for a moment. Still holding it, he walked into the living room and looked at every one in turn. "I have something to say." He spoke slowly, hesitantly.

David lifted an eyebrow. "Everything okay, buddy?"

Randal nodded.

Maggie encouraged him with her eyes, and he continued.

"I wanted to let you all know that I have remembered my past life, my human life, little by little for some time now. I remember everything that happened to me, and to my family. I mean my family before you; because I don't feel like an orphan at all. I feel like I have a new family that is just as caring and important to me as that past family had been. I never want to forget my human family, but that doesn't mean I care about all of you any less. I hope you understand what I'm saying. I don't think I'm explaining myself very clearly."

"You're doing just fine," Maggie said.

David hugged Randal then pulled him down into the sofa beside him. "What brought all this on?"

"I guess I wanted you all to know that I no longer have holes in my memory. I don't want to have secrets…"

Randal stopped and stared down at his hands. When he looked up, Maggie was there, smiling.

"I also wanted to explain… my inability to…"

Randal wanted to say, my inability to distinguish between innocent and guilty. But he didn't want to lose their trust. So instead, he finished with something else.

"...to fit in."

"With us?" Maggie asked. "Sweetie, you fit in just fine."

He stammered as he continued. He couldn't meet Maggie's gaze. "No, not just you. With all immortals. I feel lost. I feel trapped in this child's body—this child's mind."

Randal shook his head and turned away from them. Maggie reached for him, but he sped into the night and hunted.

Tonight, he would hunt for real, so he had ignored Maggie's notes and wandered the dark streets in search of someone who would think Randal was a scared, vulnerable child. Maybe he would just take the first person who tried to help him; he didn't see why they were limiting themselves to killers and other human waste. All humans were struggling to live a life that was only going to end in death anyway. He didn't see any point in prolonging their pain.

But for now, he would respect Antony's wishes and feed only on the scum of the Earth. Still, he wondered what an innocent would taste like.

In the end, Randal took the man who had attacked him with a knife, but only because he had presented himself first. Maybe there were no innocent people out there. Who was innocent? Was the business tycoon who crushed the little people under his shoe heel innocent? What about the corrupt cop that overlooked the drug deal just so he could pad his pocket with a bit of extra cash?

Or what about the schoolteacher who ignored the rich kids beating up on the younger, more defenseless children just because she had a better rapport with the wealthy students; and wanted to stay in their good graces? Was she innocent?

Randal was missing the point, and he knew it, but still, he couldn't shake the feeling that he needed to taste the blood of someone other than the scumbag with the switchblade at his throat. Of course, that was very satisfying, too—watching the would-be attacker's confusion when Randal turned from the scared young boy into the laughing, angry, red-eyed monster that was about to tear out his throat.

When Randal was finished with him, he took off the thug's head with his own switchblade and tossed the remains into a dumpster. He was supposed to bring the corpses back for the incinerator, but he wanted to read about this in the paper tomorrow.

Randal wiped the blood from the blade and pocketed the knife; it was a cool knife.

Back at the house, Randal saw that David had set up a map of the Poconos on a cork board and colored pushpins marked potential lairs. When Maggie saw him, she smiled and motioned for Randal to join her. He felt shame burn through him, remembering his desire to kill someone Maggie would never consider to be a fit victim. He knew that if he went down that path, there might never be an opportunity to turn back. Would Maggie forgive him? Would Antony or David?

He thought Maggie probably would, and David, too; but Antony would destroy him. And that destruction would probably be the end of the group. He believed Maggie would never forgive Antony for what he'd done, and David would be torn between the vampire who sired him and the mother of his child. Randal would be no better than the Dark Father if he were to destroy this family. He made up his mind that innocent blood would stay off his lips.

At least for now.

When he saw that Maggie was packing her bags, he gave her a questioning gaze.

"We're heading out to the Poconos with the Zephyr. We want to be as close to the lair as possible when we find it."

"What about Gardner?" Randal asked.

"Gardner will stay at the Jersey house while we're out."

With the Zephyr packed, they attached the RAV4 to the back of it in case a smaller vehicle was needed.

David struggled to change the baby's diaper, and Maggie and Randal laughed as they watched. She used cloth diapers, distrustful of the plastic ones, and David was having trouble manipulating the safety pin. "We do have Velcro diapers you know."

"No, no. I'll figure this out."

Once the comedy was over, they drove first to deliver Gardner to the au pair, and then it was off to the Poconos to catch a killer.

Chapter Thirty

The master's wild eyes flicked from one face to the other of what was left of his soldiers. "What a pathetic bunch you are," he said. He glared at the one female and three males standing at attention in front of him. He no longer knew or cared about numbering them. His second in command was gone, and the rest were just fodder. The male to the far right was balancing on one foot; a swipe of the blond man's katana had severed the other above the knee. This one had barely made it back. The Master walked up to him and examined the missing foot.

He tore off the head of the useless vampire.

The male who had been standing next to the one-legged vampire tried not to meet the Master's gaze when it fell upon him.

"Do you have any idea how to defeat these foul creatures?" he asked. The nervous mutterings he received in reply angered him. "I should destroy the lot of you and start over from scratch… But I won't. I don't have enough time. They're hot on our trail. If I don't attack again, and soon, they will be bringing the fight to me. I can't allow that."

He stepped up to the next male in line. He placed his fingers in the vampire's mouth and forced him to open wide. He pried the vampire's mouth open wider as if looking for cavities. He continued pulling the two jaws apart until the mouth ripped and the top half of the head broke away from the rest of the body. The vampire burst into dust.

He stepped in front of the blonde female in his group. "What did you do that for?" the female asked.

"Why did I do that?" He looked down at the dried-up mess at his feet. "Why did I do that?" he said again as if asking himself. Then he turned back to the female and shouted, "He irritated my dots, that's why."

He kicked at the dust pile until there was nothing left but the clothes he wore.

"And who said they could have werewolves?" He shouted into her face.

Her lip trembled as she waited for him to tear off her head, but she stood straight and tall, prepared to meet her fate. He let his features fade from a snarl into something sad and confused then turned away from her.

"I don't even know how to kill a werewolf—didn't even know they existed. It's not like there is a manual for this shit."

"Trial and error," the last male in the group said.

The Master turned to him.

"Trial and error," the Master repeated, agreeably.

"Yes, kill one and then you'll know how to kill them in the future."

"I agree. The only way to know how to do something is to do it. Step forward and be designated as my new number one."

The bearded male, dressed in motorcycle leathers, with steel chains on his pockets stepped forward. His broad shoulders were pushed back, proud and obedient.

The Master laughed. They didn't trust him. They feared him, and that was just fine. That was just how he liked his subordinates.

"I am sending you all out to hunt, to kill, and to recruit. I want only the strongest and meanest; no children, and no little old ladies. Find me an army. I want fifty, sixty… one hundred. We must have our army by the end of the month so that we can attack before the others can retaliate." He dismissed them then, and they moved quickly, ready to leave the master to his dark thoughts.

He went out into the night as well, to feed and to add to his numbers. He would soon have a grand army of blood drinkers, and no other vampire would dare stand in his way again.

Chapter Thirty-One

David parked the Zephyr at the Four Seasons Campsite near the small town of Scotrun in the Poconos. Maggie found a safe place in the woods for the wolves to run free and to hunt. The sleeping arrangements were more or less the same. Randal had the space under the sink, as David and Antony shared the larger steel compartment under the table. Maggie and Dylan would share the bed.

David and Antony used an app on their phones to find pedophiles and other sex offenders that lived in the area. There was no lack of prey. Randal had been growing bored of the typical victim and decided not to go with them. He would head farther north instead. But he didn't go out just yet. He wanted to push the hunger a little longer, to see just how much of the pain he could endure. He would stay with Maggie until the others returned.

She came out of the bedroom, bouncing with excitement. "I know you must be hungry," she said to Randal. "But if you can hold out just a little longer, I have good news to share with you."

When David and Antony returned, Maggie could barely contain herself.

"What's up?" David chuckled at her giddiness.

"I've picked up his scent."

David gaped. "You mean you know where to find him?"

"I said I picked up his scent, didn't I? And I mean it literally. My visions have morphed. I no longer just see the vision, I smell it, too."

"How is that possible?" Antony asked.

She shrugged. "It's something that happens with my visions. Think of it as evolution. As my power gets stronger, they tend to change to give me more help."

David said, "Upgrades."

"She giggled. "Yeah."

"So out with it," David said. "What do you know?"

"I had a vision of this house. It's a B&B—or at least it was. Now it's a hot mess. There was something foul—dead-smelling—in the house. When I heard the phrase 'Dark Father' spoken in the vision, I knew I had the right place." She paused and stared with a puzzled expression on her face. "I wonder if he's storing corpses in his lair."

"Creepy... and ultimately stupid," David said. "But we finally have something to go on."

Maggie marked the location on the map. David found the site on Google Maps. They now had an address. The noose was tightening.

Randal stared at the spot on the map marked with the blue pushpin. He focused all his rage and hatred into that spot until he thought he could burn a hole in the map with his eyes. He was vaguely aware of Maggie placing her soft hand on his back, comforting him. "It will all be over soon," he heard her say. Randal wondered if that was true. Would it be over? After the Dark Father is destroyed, will his rage go away? Will his desire to taste innocent blood be quenched when the Dark Father was no more? Randal wasn't so sure, and it scared him.

Randal wanted to share his secret cravings with Maggie, but would she understand, or would she cringe from him like he was some sick and rancid thing? He just couldn't risk losing her trust. He needed her approval right now.

After memorizing the spot on the map where his Dark Father resided, Randal excused himself. He didn't dare look into Maggie's eyes as he departed. He didn't want her to read something there that might tell her of his intentions. She already had that uncanny ability to know things no one else could. He left the Zephyr and moved with speed into town. He wandered the streets, not really hunting; he just wanted to be away from the others. He felt smothered. He walked at reasonable speeds for a while.

As he passed through the streets, not really thinking of anything, in particular, he heard the strange sound of machine guns going off, the wails of sirens, and the pinging of electronic equipment. He spotted the source of the sounds. Bright lights of all colors and varying brightness flashed at the place where his attention had been drawn. It was an all-night arcade.

Randal entered the building and looked around. There were mostly older teenagers and adults gathered in the building, but there were also a few kids his age there, too. Well, the age he had been when he died. It was the age he would probably feel for all of his eternal life. He approached one of the younger kids and watched him as he played a first-person shooter. The kid glanced at him briefly but didn't give him much attention beyond that.

Randal turned away and spotted another young boy playing something that had zombies and other scary pictures depicted on the side of the machine. Randal walked over to him and watched him. The boy's turn ended, and he dropped his hands away from the controllers. He turned to face Randal.

"My name's Bobby," said the boy.

"Randal."

"I like your fangs."

Randal slapped a hand over his mouth.

Bobby laughed. "It's no big deal. My little brother has fangs. My mother says he'll grow out of them. Maybe you will, too."

"I hope not," Randal said. "I need them."

"Do you have any money?" the boy asked.

Randal shook his head. He didn't.

"I have a whole pocket full of tokens. The machines only take tokens, from that dispenser over there, and I already turned my real money into tokens, so I have to use them up. I'll share them with you if you want. I have to go soon."

"Sure," Randal said.

The boy pulled a handful of tokens from his pocket and handed them over. Randal played the monster game for a while and then switched with the boy who had been playing the shooter game. He then found a game about vampire hunters, which made him laugh, and he played that one, too. When his tokens were all used up, he located the boy again.

"I'm all out," Randal said.

"Me too," said Bobby. "I'll be back tomorrow, but in the daytime. Will you be around?"

Randal shook his head.

"From out of town?" Bobby asked.

Randal nodded.

"Aw, darn. I was hoping to see you again."

"Me, too," Randal said.

"Oh, well. It was nice meeting you."

Randal grabbed Bobby's hand. "I know of a way we can hang out together, forever."

Bobby tried to pull away, but Randal's grip was firm. "Let me go."

"I wasn't strong enough before to pass on the gift, but I think I am now. I think I can change you."

"No." Bobby's eyes filled with tears. "Randal, you're scaring me. Let me go."

"It will be okay, Bobby. I promise."

Randal turned his head when he realized he had drawn the attention of several of the other people in the arcade. They pointed and whispered to one another. Randal's grip slackened, and Bobby pulled away. He ran from the arcade, crying.

Randal considered running after him. But, no. What was he doing? Had he really planned to do that? Randal ran from the arcade at supersonic speed. He stopped at a park and spied someone who looked familiar to him. He stepped up for a closer look.

It was his mother. He pulled out his picture and compared it to the woman in the park. He was sure it was his mother. She had survived. Was she a vampire, too, or had she only been wounded?

Randal stumbled up to this woman holding out his picture. The woman turned and glanced at him but did not seem to recognize him. He tried to press down his unruly black hair, but it was no use. He tried to straighten his clothes, to be presentable; but who was he kidding? He slept in a metal box. He wore dirty clothes and probably smelled bad, too. He was embarrassed to be reuniting with his mother in this condition. He gave up trying to impress her and approached. His smile faded she refused to recognize him.

"Mom, I've missed you." Randal's own voice sounded alien to him. She still didn't seem to recognize him.

Suddenly this woman didn't look as much like his mother as he had first thought. He looked down at the picture and then back at the woman. He held his picture up near her face to compare.

She slapped the picture out of his hand.

Randal dropped to the ground and snatched up his photo before it drifted away. He shoved it back in his pocket.

This woman wasn't his mother.

Randal's eyes went red.

Randal was on the woman before she could flee or even cry out. He was ripping his teeth into her throat and drinking from her, sucking at the gashes his teeth had made, lapping up the blood that spilled over his hungry lips. The woman was drained—dead—before he even realized what he had done.

Randal was devastated. He had taken innocent blood, and it tasted as good as he had dreamed it would. Looking down into the woman's dead, glassy eyes, he felt blame radiating from her like heat from a firepit. His guilt was all-consuming, blinding. He stumbled away from the deadly scene. He moved with vampire speed as far from the woman as he could get. He ran aimlessly, or so he thought; but when he stopped running, and scanned the surroundings, trying to orient himself, he realized where he was.

The large, looming mansion still carried the old sign that read Bed and Breakfast. Randal clenched his fists. He didn't hesitate. He didn't run away. Randal strode with determination toward the building. He hiked up the crumbling walkway to the steps. Four fluted pillars, as thick as tree trunks, lined the front porch. The whole place was in serious disrepair. Two double doors fifteen feet high served as the front entrance.

Randal headed to the doors, intending to bust them down if need be to gain entrance. He didn't even touch them. As he came within inches of the entrance, the left door swung inward, revealing the dark interior. Randal stepped tentatively into the darkness and came face to face with the skinny, rotten boy who had opened the door. The boy did not talk or move; he just stood there staring at Randal with glassy eyes. Maggots dropped from a hole in his cheek.

"Are you who Maggie was able to smell in her vision?"

The boy only stared at him.

After several seconds, the corpse boy tipped his head to the left as if listening, then motioned for Randal to follow. The boy walked with a staggering limp into the house. Randal followed, taking in the surroundings.

The house was furnished with large puffy pieces of furniture that were covered with dingy yellowed sheets, and layers of dust decades old. The oversized pictures in ornately designed frames on the walls were so dust covered, the images were hardly recognizable. This looked to be the reception area when the place was a B&B.

After passing through the archway, Randal then found himself in the main sitting room. This room had similarly designed furniture as the pieces in the reception area, as well as drapes on the windows: heavy crimson drapes that were mildewed and tearing. Magazine racks and bookshelves held the rotting remnants of their previous publications.

In this room, the corpse boy indicated that Randal should have a seat and wait.

Randal had no intention of waiting. He started a methodical search of the house. He stalked from room to room, but there was no one in the house except himself and the corpse boy. Randal found the door leading to the garage. He searched the various tools and debris for anything to use as a weapon. The only thing he saw was a dull and rusty ax, but it would have to do. He could use it to hack off the Dark Father's head. He returned to the house and continued his random search. Randal eventually located the door which led to the basement. In the basement, he found the coffins and smashed them into splinters.

Not long after that, he heard the sound of footsteps walking across the floor above his head: many pairs.

The Dark Father was home, and he wasn't alone.

Randal reconsidered his decision to confront the enemy.

Chapter Thirty-Two

When she first became aware of Randal's distress, it staggered her. She wasn't sure at first what she was sensing, and when David glanced at her, she smiled, reassuring him she was okay. The first sensation had been a mere ripple in a pond. The second was a surging wave. When the tsunami hit her, she screamed and fell to the floor. With Dylan's help, she managed to regain her composure. She was dazed and confused. Her ability had left her for a moment but soon returned little by little until she was once again able to pinpoint Randal's proximity. Her heart grew heavy with sorrow and fear. When Antony returned from hunting, she told them what she knew.

"He's gone to the lair," she said, in a rush of words. To aid in the confusion, she clarified, "Randal has done something rash. He killed an innocent woman. And then, went to the Dark Father's lair. Maybe he thinks if he destroys the Dark Father himself, he can come to terms with what he did. But he's too weak. Dylan and I will never get there in time. You have to go on ahead and stop Randal before it's too late. It may already be too late."

###

David rushed out at top speed, leaving behind a hot breeze in his wake. He arrived at the crumbling mansion quickly. Antony was not far behind. They stepped up to the double doors together. David was slightly disappointed the doors were already open. He had been looking forward to kicking them in. They glanced briefly at each other then entered the house. They listened and heard the shouts and curses issuing from below them. They followed the commotion until they found the door to the basement. The sound of struggles grew louder as they opened the door.

David and Antony descended the stairs and confronted the six vampires. Quickly glancing around, David located Randal, cornered and swinging an ax. He was only barely keeping his attackers at bay. They laughed as they toyed with him. His face had been disfigured by a multitude of slashes. Any one of the attackers could have disarmed him and killed him, but instead chose to draw out their fun.

The Dark One turned to confront his new arrivals.

"Have you come to take my pet from me again?" he said. "He found his way home all by himself. I don't plan on letting him go again."

"You do not have a choice," Antony said. "When we leave here, he is coming with us, and you will be dead."

"The two of you plan on taking on the six of us?" the leader said.

David snorted. "There were more of you as I recall," he said as he pulled his katana from its sheath. "Where are they? That's right; I already killed them."

"And I recall you had a few werewolves the last time we met."

"They are on the way."

The vampire scowled. "They aren't invited. This is a vampire's quarrel, no place for your pets."

"Noted," David said and held his katana out in front of him. He swiveled his wrist, and the blade made a figure-8 in the air, slashing at his opponent. The

Dark One staggered back, just out of reach of the sword's deadly edge. The other five vampire minions moved in to assist their leader. David slashed and cut the head off the first vampire to come into range. After that, it was all he could do to keep the vampires from swarming over him. Antony moved in to protect David, but the vampires were moving too fast. Their skills had improved since the last encounter.

As if the bell rang for the start of a cage match, bodies flailed, arms fluttered, and a flood of vampires swept over David. Antony struggled to pull vampires off and managed to tear the head off a female. David's katana flew from his grasp. He fought at the wave of bodies pressing in on him. He felt Antony's presence in there with him as both of them struggled to get the vampire attackers pushed back.

Teeth dug into David's neck. He desperately floundered in an attempt to pull the vampire off him. He regained his stability and pinned the attacking vampire in a headlock. Looking into the evil eyes, David slowly slid his arm down the vampire's neck, caressing his face one second before twisting the opponent's head to the side and taking it clean off.

David then watched as his katana rose in the hands of an enemy. He studied the glint of the blade as it slashed down at his head.

An instant before the katana found David's neck, Antony dived into the path of the blade. The weapon struck Antony in the back, nearly cutting him in two. Antony screamed and fell away from the blade. He could do nothing more to help.

###

Antony crawled toward Randal, struggling to keep his torso from coming apart. The katana-wielding vampire came back for Antony's neck. Antony had no more strength to defend himself. Looking up, Antony saw his looming fate mirrored in Randal's frightened, sorrowful eyes. Antony blinked and whispered, "Turn away."

The sword came down.

###

The sword began its downward arc, just as an ominous, snarling growl echoed through the dank basement. The Katana wielding vampire lost his head as Maggie bit through his spinal cord. The katana clattered to the cement floor in a cloud of vampire dust. Maggie and Dylan then tore into the remaining two minions without remorse. When the vampires were dispatched, save the Dark Father, the two wolves stood panting. Antony was down with a gaping wound in his back. David, as well, had been waylaid. Maggie padded over to Randal to protect him.

The auburn-haired wolf paced in front of the opponent. The vampire did not seem afraid. He stood motionless as the werewolf moved back and forth in front of him.

Abruptly, the wolf leaped into the air with a snarl, teeth in line to rip out the Dark Father's throat.

Dylan stopped in midair as the vampire punched a hole in his chest. The vampire withdrew his hand with Dylan's heart throbbing in his fist. Dylan dropped to the floor on his back. Within seconds, the wolf had transformed into the man. A hole, raw and glistening with blood, had been opened in Dylan's chest. His head listed to the left and his dead eyes stared at the wall.

Stunned, David retrieved his katana and staggered to his feet. Behind David, the black wolf howled, and tears spilled from her human eyes.

###

The Dark Father, fearing an attack from the remaining wolf, moved away from her. He kept the vampire with the sword at a distance as well; he knew when to retreat and that time was now. He walked back toward the stairs, not taking his eyes off the group. He smiled at David and gave a salute, then started up the stairs.

The fleeing vampire could not use his speed in reverse, but as long as he kept his enemies in front of him, nothing could surprise him. If the other vampire moved with deadly speed, he would see it coming and defend himself against the assault.

Once on the ground floor, he would move faster than any of them could comprehend. He sensed the open doorway approaching from behind. So far, the blond vampire and the wolf had not pressed an attack. What were they waiting for? Did they fear to have their hearts ripped out as well? The Dark father felt his foot touch the top of the stairway… at last.

As he stepped through the doorway at the top of the stairs, a thick, rusty blade burst through his chest. The shocked vampire looked down at the protruding steel that had sprouted from nowhere in the center of his chest. Then it was pulled free. Startled and confused, he managed to turn around in jerky movements, as if he had no understanding of how his body worked anymore. Once set, comprehension hit him. He stared at his precious Corpse Boy, holding a machete.

The boy spoke his first three words. The words were slurred and came from rotting vocal cords.

In a garbled, tortured—but distinct—voice, the boy said, "Goodbye, Dark Father."

Then he pushed the stunned vampire down the stairs.

###

As the Dark Father stumbled back, David stepped forward and swiped his katana, severing the vampire's head from his neck. The head flew against the side wall and burst into ash. The headless body continued sliding down the stairs past David to rest at the bottom in a dried, shriveled husk. The remains would continue to dissolve until there was nothing left to prove the vampire had ever existed. David stepped over the pile.

He stared up in stunned silence at the boy standing in the doorway. David had no words as he watched the expressionless face, stretched taut with mummified flesh, contort into a grimace. David realized suddenly that the creature was actually smiling. The corner of David's mouth turned up slightly, and he waved at the boy.

The moment passed, however; and the boy turned and disappeared into the rooms above. David continued to stare for a moment, shocked and confused, then headed back to the basement where Maggie was standing over Dylan's corpse. Randal brushed a hand across her fur, consoling her. Antony had already begun to heal and was leaning against the wall near the others. David walked over and helped him to the stairs.

In another section of the basement, to the left of the stairs, David saw with slight interest the collection of broken coffins. David, being a modern vampire who slept in a bed, found this ritual to be archaic and pointless. He turned to Randal. "Did you do that?"

Randal nodded. David ruffled the boy's hair, and then carried Dylan's body up the stairs and out of the mansion. He buried the body under the massive oak tree in the backyard.

Maggie and Dylan had driven to the mountain resort. It was why they had arrived so late. They had kept their clothes in the car before turning into wolves. Now, Maggie transformed into her human form, dressed, and made a marker out of wood to put on Dylan's grave. She stayed by the tomb after the others had gone. She stayed by the grave for days.

Chapter Thirty-Three

The woman came awake with a start. Her eyes were open but unseeing. Was she blind? No, she realized with some relief. She was just in the dark. She had no idea where she was. It was too dark to see, but she could feel. There was a sheet covering her naked form. She was hungry, so hungry. She reached out, and her hand hit the cold steel that was only a few inches away from her face. She pushed out at the iron over her head, felt it give under her mighty strength. She pushed until the bolts broke and the small door popped open.

She pulled herself toward the opening and the drawer on which she lay slid out of the hole and into the empty room. She climbed out of the drawer and realized she was in the morgue. She was having trouble piecing together the events of her last few hours. She remembered jogging in the park, getting ready to head home, and then the strange boy asked if she was his mother. After that, she could remember nothing. She pulled the tag off her toe and looked at her name: Sandra Pollack.

She pushed through the swinging doors and searched until she found a laundry basket with some clean hospital gowns. She slipped into one and continued down the hallway. In one room, she found a tray with utensils spread out on a blue quilted cloth. An operating room, she realized. She picked up one of the tools from the plate and held it protectively at her chest. She left the room and continued down the hallway. Florescent lights flickered overhead, confusing her, frightening her.

At a hallway intersection, the woman bumped into a maintenance worker. He apologized for his clumsiness.

"Should you be down here?" he asked grabbing her arm, intending to lead her to the elevators.

The woman lashed out with the scalpel in her hand and opened a two-inch gash in his neck, at the carotid. She covered the wound with her mouth and sucked. During her escape from the hospital, the woman came across two more hospital workers that met with similar fates. She left the hospital and pushed through the night in a blur of movement and crackling thunder.

She lived alone, and returned there., Heading into the basement, she instinctively began blocking out the windows. She needed a nest out of the sun.

She wondered what happened to that boy from the park. She decided she would look for him. Whatever had happened to her—whatever she was—it started with him. He would have to answer her questions. How hard could finding a boy be with fangs, who liked to attack people, and who would be the same age for the rest of his unnaturally long life?

Yes, she would find this boy and thank him.

Personally.

Chapter Thirty-Four

17 years later.

The blind woman watched as her dark companion finished his meal. When the vampire had drained all the blood from the prey, she used the knife at her side to decapitate the corpse. The body was then taken to a preferred dump site where it might never be found.

But then again, perhaps it would. It didn't matter to the pair. They took precautions, but they didn't live by any rules or standards. If the body were found, there would be no way to track it back to them; and even if it was traced to them, they were not afraid of Man's laws or his retaliation.

The woman and the vampire returned to the house on Lansdowne Drive. They watched from the darkness as the figures inside the house moved back and forth past the windows. There was a party. The vampire, known as Antony, and the child vampire were celebrating the graduation of the human offspring of the werewolf woman and the vampire known as David.

The man beside the blind woman ground his vampiric teeth. She had warned him against that—she couldn't guarantee they would grow back if he ground them down to nubs.

"They have no right to be happy," he said. "Listen to them laughing and carrying on. I could go in there and wipe them all out."

"Their time will come. As I've said before, we will know when the time is right to strike. And when that time comes, we will crush them. You will finally have your vengeance."

The vampire stopped grinding his teeth and opened his mouth wide to relieve the tension in his jaw.

"That time cannot come soon enough. Antony will pay for his past regressions, and I will have my day of vindication."

"Yes," the blind woman said. "That time will come sooner than you expect."

The cloaked vampire's shadowed face glared hatefully at the forms moving through the house. His vampire ears could pick up bits and pieces of their conversations, but he didn't care about anything they had to say. After a moment, the calmness of the woman standing next to him caused him to become still as well. He trusted what she had to say. He accepted her words.

She turned to him.

"A war is coming," she said and placed a hand on his arm. "Two sides. Yours and his. He will be making new friends, and new enemies, because even as his numbers will grow, so will yours. And when the time comes, you will get your revenge."

The hooded figure nodded slowly, and they walked away from the house, leaving those inside consigned to their fate.

Epilogue: Gardner

They all lived in the Victorian mansion together, although there had been some significant changes over the years. For starters, there was a distinctively feminine touch to the house. The bland, unadorned walls were now covered in family portraits and artwork. The living room had larger windows that allowed in more sunlight during the day, and more moon and starlight at night. The windows were covered in light, airy drapes that matched the furniture. Through the previous twelve years, the house had been adorned with the artwork and awards Gardner brought home from school.

Earlier that night, David watched as his son received his diploma and turned to Maggie at his right. She was crying. He hugged her. The night graduation ceremony ended and the group headed home. Gardner chatted quietly with Randal and Antony in the back seat. David could catch certain words spoken: college, tuition, major. Gardner was talking about his future. It was a future where he would grow up, marry; and he may even get a job, though he would never want for money. He would grow up, grow old, and die.

But not if David could help it.

When the others were all ensconced in their own business, David led Gardner to the back of the house, past the stairs leading up to their bedrooms and the stairs leading down to the panic room. He led him down the hall to the den, past the bathroom, under the pretense that he had something important to tell him in private.

"Yeah, Dad?" Gardner asked.

He was young and charismatic. It was the perfect time to turn him immortal.

"I'm very proud of you," David said.

"Thanks, Dad," Gardner said, and they hugged.

He wasn't sure if he should give Gardner the option to become immortal or make the choice for him. But he couldn't watch his son grow old. Soon, Gardner would look older than him. This just wasn't right. His son would grow old and die, and David couldn't sit back and watch that happen. It was a gruesome death, what David proposed for his son, but a glorious future.

But could David really do this? He planned on draining his son and killing him. He had debated this over the years, and he always came out with the same result. No matter the cost, he couldn't let Gardner grow old. How could a fifty-year-old Gardner introduce a twenty-something as his father? It was already becoming more difficult to convince people that David was old enough to be Gardner's father, and he was too proud of his son to ever have to lie about their relationship to each other.

But now the time had come, and David wasn't sure he could go through with it. His mind was spinning at the thought that this could destroy Gardner's trust in him.

David gripped Gardner by his shoulders and held the boy out at arm's length. He looked deeply into Gardner's eyes. Finally, he said, "Have you ever wondered why Uncle Antony, Uncle Randal and I sleep all day and only come out at night? Have you wondered why we three, and your mother as well, seem to be no older than when you were young? Or why your mother seems to know things before they happen?"

"Well..." Gardner paused. "You always told me Uncle Randal had a growth defect that made him look like a child even though he was really a grown man, and I know Mom has some uncanny abilities."

David squeezed his son's strong arms, still holding him out at a distance. "That may not be the complete truth," David said. He did not continue.

###

Gardner watched as his father's eyes turned red. Were they really red or was it a trick of the light? His dad pulled him into another embrace, stronger this time.

He felt his dad's head move, and hot breath touched his neck.

###

The time had come. His son was eighteen, young, handsome. If he waited much longer, Gardner would begin to grow old. He couldn't bear to see his son waste away and die. Gardner's skin twitched where David's fangs touched it.

The hug lasted a couple of minutes longer then ended. The moment passed. David couldn't do it. He couldn't kill his son no matter the reason. He smiled and held Gardner out at arm's length once again. David's red eyes had returned to a natural blue-green, and there were tears in them. Gardner used a finger to wipe them away.

"You will do well in college. I have every confidence in you." David kissed his son on the cheek and walked away.

###

Gardner stood there for a moment longer, confused. He was sure his father had been about to tell him something—some mysterious family secret. What had it been? Gardner sighed and turned back to the living room and the rest of the graduation party.

When it happened, Gardner barely even registered the event.

He walked down the hall, and as he passed one of the spare bedrooms, a black blur bolted out of the darkness. The mysterious animal bit him on the forearm and then shot away with preternatural speed. He barely had time to gasp.

He thought he knew the wolf, had seen it before when he was younger. Was it a family pet? There were a lot of oddities surrounding his family such as why Uncle Randal still looked like a boy after all these years. And what was up with that wolf?

It didn't matter. The bite wasn't bad, just a nip really. The skin was broken, but a single bandage would cover the wound. Instead of returning to the group, Gardner headed to the bathroom and rinsed the cut. He wasn't sure, but it looked like it was already starting to heal. The strangeness didn't end there.

Honey, your father couldn't do what he wanted to do because it would mean your death. What I have done is much less... fatal.

Gardner recognized his mother's voice but didn't see her. He looked out the doorway into the hall, but no one was standing there.

"Mom?" he asked aloud. "What's going on?"

Something wonderful. His mother's response did not pass through his ears but instead, seemed to echo inside his head. His mother wasn't talking to him. He was hearing her thoughts. He was confused at first but then began to understand a little.

This was not a new ability to him. He had known he could read thoughts of others from a very young age. But the talent had been hard to use, and harder to control. Now, something that his mother had done caused the ability to open up in him, blossom—like a flower whose petals had been closed, now spread wide. He could hear the thoughts with perfect clarity.

Gardner thought: *Am I going to learn all the family secrets now?*

His mother did not respond.

"Mom, where are you?" he said aloud.

Gardner looked back toward the bathroom door, and this time there was something there. The black wolf was standing in the doorway looking at him. Gardner saw his mother's eyes staring at him from the wolf.

Inside his mind, his mother said, *we have a dangerous mission ahead of us, and I had to give you my gift so you could protect yourself from what lies ahead. I hope you can forgive me for what I've done.*

What is this task? Gardner thought, but he received no answer.

Gardner concluded he was hearing his mother's thoughts, but she could not pick up his.

Please forgive me, baby. I have passed on my gift to you. Sometimes it will not seem so gift-like, but it is. It really is.

I've already forgiven you, Gardner thought but knew it was not being conveyed. What you don't realize is you've given me much more. Your gift has unleashed another power inside of me. Something I always suspected was there but didn't know how to use it. Now, whatever you did—whatever your gift is—it has unleashed my other power.

Moments later, his father moved to stand behind the wolf. Then Uncle Rand and Uncle Antony joined them. They were all looking at him. As he stood staring into the crowd of family members, he listened to their thoughts. Words and phrases and images all tumbled out of them and into his head. He could read their minds, but they could not pick up on his.

He now had a secret of his own.

Excerpt from Immortal Clash

It was dark and there was desert all around as she ran. The blood on her face wasn't hers. She had been running for a long time and was exhausted, but she couldn't rest. Not yet. She was hungry and cold. She was in the New Mexico desert, that much she remembered. She thought deserts were supposed to be hot? The light sheen of sweat on her skin was chilling her, causing her to shiver.

And she was thirsty. So thirsty.

In the distance a wolf howled and the girl stopped with a gasp. Were they close? How close? She had to know.

Remembering the carnage in the banquet hall caused her to cry but she stubbornly wiped away the tears. She had precious little moisture left in her body and crying was using up resources she couldn't afford to lose. She could grieve for her friends later, not now. Not while her own life was still in danger. There were so many horrible looking wolves. One minute the room was full of people, talking and laughing. Only moments later the wolves came, killing everyone. Just killing them. Why would wolves do that?

A sound nearby startled her from her memories of death: heavy breathing…

Emotionally and physically exhausted, she knew she should run. But she could go no further, didn't even want to. Instead, she dropped into the sand and waited to die.

Cringing in a fetal ball with her head cradled in her arms, she felt the hot breath on her neck…

Thank you for reading!

www.ingramcontent.com/pod-product-compliance
Lightning Source LLC
Chambersburg PA
CBHW030353310726
48979CB00001B/289

* 9 7 8 1 7 3 2 8 2 7 7 0 7 *